THE TUNNEL CUT ACROSS the corridor and into another room, and Jax's heart rate sped up. There was a bed, a sink, and a toilet. This was a cell.

Jax had no sense of an Emrys presence, but maybe the magic in the tunnel was blocking his vassal bond. When he patted along the wall, his fingers slipped into another hole.

No sooner had he stuck his head through the hole than a hand grabbed him by the hair and yanked him bodily out.

Jax looked up into a face he'd hoped he would never see again.

Also by Dianne K. Salerni

The Eighth Day

THE INQUISITOR'S MARK

Book 2 in the
EIGHTH DAY
series

DIANNE K. SALERNI

HARPER

An Imprint of HarperCollins *Publishers*

ISBN 978-0-06-227219-5

Typography by Ellice M. Lee
15 16 17 18 19 OPM 10 9 8 7 6 5 4 3 2 1
❖
First paperback edition, 2015

For my sister, Laurie,
who reads my first drafts
and actually likes them

1

JAX AUBREY'S PHONE RANG at least once a day, and it was always the same number. Only one person ever called him, wanting to know where he was, what had happened to him, and when he was coming back.

I'm not coming back.

Jax didn't know how to break that news to Billy Ramirez, although Billy should have figured it out for himself by now. Especially if he'd peeked through the windows of Jax and Riley's old house and discovered it'd been emptied of all their belongings.

It did feel good to know that somebody cared. The last time Billy had seen Jax, three weeks ago, Jax was being driven away in a hearse. When Jax got back the phone he'd lost that night, there'd been a long list of missed calls and worried texts on it.

But Riley had explicit instructions for him regarding the phone. "Don't contact that friend of yours.

What's-his-name. Billy."

"I have to let him know I'm okay," Jax protested. "After what he saw—"

"Sorry," Riley replied curtly. "Too many people are looking for Evangeline."

Jax sagged. It was his fault Evangeline Emrys had been captured by vassals of the crazy Kin lord Wylit. His stupidity had almost gotten them both killed, along with billions of Normal people who had no idea the residents of a secret eighth day had plotted to destroy the regular seven-day week.

So Jax didn't argue with Riley. But he did send one text. He owed his friend that much.

```
Jax: im ok don't worry
Billy: dude where r u
```

Jax didn't reply.

It was also Jax's fault that Melinda Farrow's house had burned down. Jax had almost broken into girly tears apologizing to his magic tutor when she delivered all his stuff from Riley's old house to their new hideout in the mountains of Pennsylvania. He felt even more guilty because the horror of almost losing her family had made Melinda decide she no longer wanted to be Riley's vassal. When Riley released her from her magical vow of service to the Pendragon family, Jax felt it in his own gut.

Jax had sworn his service to Evangeline, so he knew how strong the relationship was between liege lord and vassal. It may have been an emergency that caused Jax to take the oath, but now that the bond between him and Evangeline existed, he couldn't imagine severing it.

It made Jax sad to see Melinda leave Riley's clan. It was small enough already. Riley had no living family and only the three Crandalls as vassals—plus Jax, for whom he was legally responsible. In a way, the little clan was like a family in itself, and lacking any close family of his own, Jax was grateful to be a member.

Still, it was a tight fit in the house Mr. Crandall had found for them. A two-bedroom cabin on the back side of a ski area didn't provide much space for five people, not to mention the sixth person who was present one day out of eight.

In fact, they had to put Evangeline in a room that was meant to be a large closet under the stairs. "Just like Harry Potter," she remarked when she saw it.

Riley cringed. "Sorry. I suppose we could—"

"No, it's fine. I was joking," she said quickly, as if afraid he'd take offense. After years of living alone as the eighth-day "ghost" in the house of an old woman, it must've been alarming to discover she was expected to share a small space with a bunch of almost-strangers. In Evangeline's disjointed timeline, she'd been in a car driving through Mexico only a few minutes ago, even though it had been a week for everyone else. She looked dazed by the abrupt change in location. "I only need a place to sleep," she said. "It's not like I have anything but the clothes on my back." Clothes they'd swiped from a clothesline in Mexico— leaving payment, of course.

"I bought spare clothes for you," Mrs. Crandall assured her.

Evangeline kept close to Jax all that day. He didn't blame her. Mr. and Mrs. Crandall were big and intimidating— both of them built like tanks. Their son, A.J., was just big and goofy, but Evangeline wasn't used to the company of people at all. Jax was the first friend she'd had since she'd been forcibly separated from her family as a child. She still acted a little shy around Riley, too, even though it was obvious she had a crush on him and Riley had made it pretty clear he liked her back.

But there wasn't time to let her get used to socializing with a bunch of people. Evangeline would be with them only twenty-four hours before she vanished again for a week, and they had plans to make.

"The Dulac clansmen who showed up at the pyramid were told you were dead," Riley informed her. "But the eighth day is intact, so it's obvious an Emrys heir still exists, maintaining the spell. It's a fairly well-known fact that your father had three children—and the Dulacs also know one was lost years ago."

He said it as tactfully as he could, but Evangeline still

blinked back tears. Her younger brother had died at the hands of Wylit, the same Kin madman who'd captured her.

"With only one Emrys heir left—or so they think—the Dulacs are going to go looking for your sister, to prevent any more attempts by the Kin to alter the spell," Riley continued. "And what they call 'protective custody' will really be *servitude*. They'll use her. If she's anywhere near as strong as you were up there on the pyramid, they'll use her magic for their own selfish purposes."

Evangeline nodded solemnly. She was used to being sought by unscrupulous people—Transitioners and Kin alike. Jax thought it was a terrible burden she lived with: being a key to the Eighth-Day Spell that imprisoned dangerous Kin in an alternate timeline. In some ways, Evangeline and her sister were the two most important people on the planet, and Jax, as the sole vassal of the Emrys family, felt a little inadequate for the job of protecting them. Thankfully, he had Riley's help.

"We'll have to get to Adelina before they do," Evangeline said. "Do you know where she's hiding?"

"No, but I know who does and where to find *them*," Riley said.

"The Taliesins," Evangeline guessed, and Riley nodded.

"If you're in agreement," he went on, "we can act next week—well, your tomorrow. And after we find her, we'll come out of hiding. You and your sister. And me."

"What do you mean?" Mr. Crandall broke in.

"I'm done hiding," Riley repeated, looking Mr. Crandall in the eye. "From Ursula Dulac especially. Once we have Evangeline's sister, I'm claiming my seat at the Table."

Mr. Crandall and A.J. exchanged uncomfortable glances. Ursula Dulac was the head of the Dulac Transitioner clan, and was a powerful and corrupt leader who used her magic for personal gain. She had arranged for the assassination of Riley's family because the Pendragons wielded too much influence at the Table, the council of Transitioner lords descended from Knights of the Round Table. Riley's father had thwarted her attempts to influence Normal politicians and complete shady business deals. Consequently, Ursula had not only taken action to remove *him* as an obstacle to her plans; she'd tried to wipe out his entire family. She didn't know one of the Pendragons had survived, and it wasn't surprising that the Crandalls were uneasy about her finding out. But Jax did wonder why Mrs. Crandall was now looking with concern at *him* instead of at Riley.

"I agree with anything that reunites me with my sister," Evangeline said.

"You realize this puts you both in danger," Mr. Crandall pointed out gruffly. "You'll be targets for anyone who wants to eliminate you"—he looked at Riley—"or use you as a pawn." He turned to Evangeline.

"I'm accustomed to people trying to use me," Evangeline replied simply.

"And I don't intend to be an *easy* target," Riley said, decisively ending that discussion.

Evangeline offered to instruct the Crandalls on a way to protect this house from enemies who might be looking for them in the meantime. "I could do it myself," she said, "but I think your talent is better for this type of protection."

"At your service," Mr. Crandall replied. He and A.J. were both artisans with the talent of transferring magic into craftsmanship. A.J.'s specialty was tattoos, and Jax had heard that Mr. Crandall had a knack for making honor blades. From scratch. With a forge.

The eighth day passed with them making plans for the following Grunsday and working on protection for the cabin. Evangeline vanished at the stroke of midnight, as she always did. Jax grew bored in her absence. Melinda had brought his bike, and the June weather was cool and pleasant, but the nearest town was ten miles away, and its big attraction was a strip mall and a Denny's. In between, there was nothing but woods, bait shops, ski shops, bait *and* ski shops, and one dirty bus station run out of the back of a convenience store. The cabin's TV got only local channels, and although thanks to Melinda he now had his computer back, it wasn't connected to anything. Riley had ordered cable and internet, but it hadn't been installed yet.

Mr. Crandall approved of cable but complained about the internet. "Security risk."

"Let Jax have his computer," Riley said. "He learned his lesson."

Riley knew about that too, now—how Jax had contacted a Transitioner forum online, which turned out to be a trap, which led to him getting kidnapped by a bank robber, which led to his rescue by thieves, which led to revealing Evangeline's hiding spot . . .

Jax *had* learned his lesson. But the messages from Billy were getting more and more pathetic. Shortly after Jax ignored a call on Saturday, he got a follow-up text.

```
Billy: is it something i did
```

Jax sighed. He took the phone outside, away from the cabin, and sat against a tree. What was the worst that could happen? This was *Billy*.

```
Jax: u did nothing wrong
Billy: where r u
Jax: middle of nowhere
Billy: r u in trouble with the law?
```

Jax laughed out loud. What was he supposed to say? *No, I'm hiding from murderous Transitioners and evil Kin. Who are they? Well, the Kin are an ancient race of sorcerers, including some rotten ones who tried to take over the world back in King Arthur's time. To defeat them, King Arthur and his allies trapped all the Kin in a secret eighth day, and the descendants of the people casting the spell became Transitioners, who experience the regular seven days plus the extra one. No, I don't have a head injury, thanks for asking.* Of course, now that Jax thought about it, Billy would probably believe the whole thing. He loved everything related to science fiction and fantasy.

Standing up, Jax put his phone in his back pocket, leaving his friend's last question unanswered. Let Billy's imagination run wild. It would keep him entertained.

He was headed toward the front door of the cabin when he heard Mrs. Crandall's voice through an open window. "You should have talked him into accepting her offer," she was saying. "You should have *insisted* that Evangeline release him."

Jax quickly moved up against the side of the house, where he couldn't be seen.

"It's not my place to interfere between a vassal and his liege," Riley replied.

"But you're his guardian. You promised his father you'd send him back to that Naomi woman as soon as he knew enough to survive—not let him swear on as a vassal to the Emrys family. That's a dangerous position for any-one, let alone a thirteen-year-old boy!"

Jax held his breath, waiting for Riley to say, *But Jax is smart and brave and talented. He can do the job.*

Instead, Riley said, "Did you see how Evangeline stuck to Jax like glue? He's the only one of us she knows really well. We *need* him until she gets more comfortable with us. But you're right. By fall, he's got to go. He needs to be enrolled in school anyway."

"Sooner," Mrs. Crandall insisted. "Sooner is better."

Jax slid down and sat against the side of the house, feeling kicked in the gut. *Guess I'm not a member of Riley's clan after all.*

2

THE ELEVATOR ALWAYS STOPPED with a jerk, but whenever it went to the basement there was an additional bang that pretty much said: *You've reached absolute bottom.*

Dorian Ambrose thought the basement of his apartment building looked like the setting of every horror film ever made: moist cinderblock walls and yellow fluorescent lights. His father pushed open the elevator's metal gate, and Dorian peered down the corridor of closed doors. He knew what went on behind a few of them, thanks to some unauthorized snooping, but today he was getting an official introduction.

"Twelve is old enough," Dad had proclaimed that afternoon. "It's time Dorian observed a prisoner interrogation." Mom had hesitated but reluctantly agreed that it needed to be part of his training. Dorian was, after all, an inquisitor, just like his dad. When he asked questions, people were compelled to answer them. But being an inquisitor for Ursula

Dulac involved more than that.

Like cinderblock basements, locked rooms . . . and prisoners.

Dorian swallowed a little queasily.

Their footsteps thudded dully on the concrete floor. Dorian's father didn't look at him or make any effort to put him at ease. Dad was *preoccupied*—as Mom liked to say. Or in the words of Dorian's sister, Lesley, "Dad's got clan secrets."

His father had good reason to be preoccupied right now. Two and a half weeks ago, the night sky had cracked like an egg, and every Transitioner on the planet knew that someone, somewhere, was messing with the Eighth-Day Spell. The students at Bradley Prep had talked about little else since then, trying to bait Dorian and his fellow clan members into telling what they knew. Everyone assumed the Dulacs wouldn't just stand around wondering what happened. They'd act.

Dorian had nothing to tell them. He'd done a lot of spying and eavesdropping, trying to learn what had happened at the pyramid in Mexico, without much success. But now his clansmen had captured a witness, and Dorian, to his surprise, was invited to the interrogation.

The lights flickered as they reached the end of the corridor. If this had been a movie, there would've been an ax murderer in a leather mask waiting around the corner. Instead, there was just his cousin Sloane Dulac and a security man.

Sloane thumbed on her phone when they appeared,

making a point of checking the time so they'd know she'd been kept waiting.

Dad looked unconcerned by Sloane's displeasure. He motioned for the guard to unlock the door while Sloane returned the phone to the pocket of her school blazer. She must have come straight from Bradley without stopping to change. Ever since Sloane had turned eighteen, she'd been put in charge of more and more clan business. Not because Great-aunt Ursula was getting too old to do it herself. Nobody would make the mistake of thinking that. Ursula was just training her granddaughter to be the next clan leader.

The security man went in first as a precaution, followed by Sloane and then Dad. Dorian brought up the rear, close enough to step on his father's heels. Dad spared him an aggravated glance. "Don't be nervous, Dorian."

"I'm not," he protested, but it came out in a squeak, and Sloane smirked.

The prisoner was tied to a chair. He was big and burly with bristly blond hair, and when he spotted Dorian, he jerked as if making a lunge for him. Dorian flinched, but a moment later, the man's eyes narrowed in puzzlement and he turned his attention to Dorian's father.

"I'll give you the chance to answer my questions willingly," Dad said.

"Are you the Dulacs' inquisitor?" the prisoner sneered. "Do your worst. I have nothing to say to you."

Dorian's father nodded. "I'm aware of your resistance to magical influence." He removed a syringe from his suit coat pocket. "But even Normals find it necessary to question criminals, and they do it without any magic whatsoever."

Dorian looked away. This man was supposed to have a head like a rock, making him immune to the talents of both the Ambroses and the Dulacs. That was *his* talent: being impervious to magical manipulation. The syringe was necessary, but Dorian didn't want to watch.

While Dad injected the man's arm, Sloane murmured to Dorian, "He held off ten of our men single-handedly, until the women and children of his clan got away. And that's after eluding us in Mexico and over a week on the run across the country."

Her voice held a tone of both admiration and superiority, as if the man were a fierce wild animal they'd been lucky to capture. "Huh," Dorian remarked in false appreciation. He wondered what would've happened to the women and children if they'd been caught. Would they be in the basement too, tied to chairs and poked with syringes? Would Dorian be expected to watch?

This is what I'll have to do someday for Aunt Ursula—and then for Sloane. Dorian wouldn't take his oath as a vassal until he turned sixteen, but when he did, he'd belong to his Dulac relatives, body and soul. Lately, the thought had been making him squirm.

Now the prisoner looked confused and dizzy, his head swaying back and forth.

"What's your name?" Dorian's father asked.

"Angus."

"Angus Balin?" Dad prompted. "Vassal to the Kin lord Wylit?"

The prisoner's eyes grew wide. "My lord is dead!" He tried to stand up, forgetting he was tied to the chair.

Dad snapped his fingers in front of the prisoner's face. "Are you a vassal to the Kin family Wylit?" he repeated, testing for the truth. They already knew this part.

"Yes!" Balin was breathing heavily. "My lord's heirs are in Europe. I must go to them."

Dad shook his head in disgust. Dorian wasn't sure if it was at the thought of any self-respecting Transitioner swearing himself to a member of the Kin race or because the interrogation drug made the man so loopy. If they could've used their inquisition talent on him, this would've been easier.

Dad grabbed Balin's face to get his attention. "Tell me about the Emrys heir Wylit used to attack the Eighth-Day Spell. Who was it?"

"A girl, about sixteen years old."

"And she was allied with Wylit?"

"No, we captured her and her vassal." Balin glowered. "I was stuck babysitting that boy for almost a week. Waste of my time. I should've been on watch at the pyramids. I would've secured the site better. I could've prevented—"

Dad interrupted him. "Did the Emrys girl survive?"

For a moment, Balin blinked his eyes blearily, trying to think. "Must've," he grunted finally. "Somebody repaired the spell. Had to be her. Pendragon couldn't have done it alone."

Sloane frowned. "Finn, are you sure this drug works? The Pendragons are all dead."

Balin's wobbly head swiveled toward her. "You don't know everything then, do you?" He laughed wildly.

Dad smacked him across the face to get him to stop. Dorian flinched, but his father's voice was emotionless. "Was there a Pendragon at the pyramid?"

"Saw his mark myself." Balin bared his teeth in a grin.

"Describe him."

"Young—maybe eighteen. Tattoos all over his arms."

"Where'd he come from?"

"The same place the Emrys girl came from. And that boy." Balin's eyes swung back to Dorian, who sidestepped nervously behind the security guard.

Why does this guy keep looking at me?

Dad turned to Sloane. "If there's a surviving Pendragon, the Morgan clan must know about it. They coordinated the attack on the pyramid. And Deidre Morgan told me herself the Emrys girl was dead. I suspected she was lying at the time and couldn't do a thing about it." Now there was a hint of anger in his voice. No inquisitor liked letting someone get away with a lie.

"There's no use blaming yourself," Sloane said. "If you'd used your magic on Deidre, you would've broken Grandmother's truce with the Morgans."

Left undirected, Balin was rambling about the Emrys vassal. "Told my brother we should've killed the boy. Lousy inquisitor, like you. His magic didn't work on *me*, but—"

That caught Dad's interest. "The girl had an inquisitor as a vassal? A Transitioner?"

"Yes. *Aubrey.* I thought *you* were him when you came in." Balin thrust his chin at Dorian. "I was going to wring your neck. But you just *look* like him."

Dorian glanced at his father. "I've never heard of a Transitioner family named Aubrey."

"Not a family. Just the boy." The drug had the prisoner so far gone he was babbling. "There was a father, but he's dead. Rayne Aubrey was as worthless as his son."

"Rayne?" Dad repeated. "The boy's father was named Rayne? He was an inquisitor?"

"Rayne Aubrey. He cheated my lord Wylit, and he's dead because of it."

Dorian's stomach turned over. Dad ripped off his suit coat and yanked up his shirt sleeve so hard, a cufflink flew across the room. "Was this his mark?" He thrust his tattooed wrist into the prisoner's face.

Balin had trouble focusing on the Ambrose mark—the eye and the scroll, the flames and the bird of prey—but then his face hardened. "You're an Aubrey, too!"

"There's no such family." Dad grabbed the prisoner by the collar and yanked their faces together. "Rayne's my brother's name."

"Finn," Sloane said sharply. "Stick to the job."

"He's telling me they killed Rayne!"

Dorian stared at the floor, not wanting to watch his father come unglued. It was the first they'd heard of Dad's missing brother in over twenty years, and this man was bragging about killing him. Dorian felt sick himself.

"But it sounds like you have a nephew who's alive." Sloane's voice was calm. "Focus on that."

"Jax Aubrey," Balin agreed cheerfully.

Dad tightened his grip on the prisoner's shirt and spoke through clenched teeth. "Jax Aubrey, huh? Then let's see if you can earn the right to stay alive by helping us find him."

Help us find him? Dorian didn't dare raise his eyes to look at his father or the prisoner, but he was thinking that the last thing his runaway uncle probably would've wanted was for the Dulac clan to find his son.

3

JAX PRESSED HIS FACE against the window of Riley's Land Rover as they drove through a college campus shortly before midnight on Wednesday. Despite the late hour, two boys were playing basketball on a court in the dark. A girl with an oversized backpack pedaled furiously in the bike lane like the lady who took Dorothy's dog in *The Wizard of Oz*.

A second later, they all vanished.

The basketball whooshed through a hoop, fell to the ground, and bounced aimlessly around an empty court. The bicycle froze in place, caught in the moment between Wednesday and Thursday. Jax turned his head to stare. For the girl riding the bike and the players on the court, time wasn't passing. But it was for the ball. Why?

"Where are we?"

Jax whirled around. He'd been alone in the backseat for the past two hours. Now suddenly he wasn't. "Holy crap, Evangeline. I'll never get used to you appearing and disappearing like that!"

Evangeline gave him an apologetic smile. It probably felt normal for her—seven days passing in the blink of an eye. In order to be with them tonight, she'd climbed into the backseat of this car right before midnight on the eighth day last week. From Evangeline's point of view, that had been only seconds ago.

"We're almost there," Riley called from the driver's seat.

Mrs. Crandall pointed out a street sign. "Here's your turn."

"Is everything all right?" Evangeline asked Jax.

No, not really. Riley wants to get rid of me as soon as he doesn't need me anymore. But Jax couldn't tell her that right now, and besides, what she really wanted to know was if anything in their plans had changed while she was absent.

"No worries," he said instead.

They were on their way to visit the Taliesins, two Kin men who knew where Evangeline's sister had been hidden—because they'd been the ones to hide her. Like all Kin, they'd skipped over the last week and would just now be starting their twenty-four-hour secret day. Riley had timed this visit to coincide with the start of Grunsday so they could make every hour count.

If they had the chance to reach Adelina Emrys today, they were going to take it.

Riley turned the Land Rover in to a parking lot next to a building with glass walls. Bookshelves and study carrels could be seen inside. "These guys live in a library?" Jax asked. With a whole college to choose from, that's not what he would've picked.

"I'm sure it suits them," Evangeline said. "The Taliesin family has an eidetic memory. That's their talent—memorizing everything they've ever read or heard. A very long time ago, the Taliesins were known as bards and poets."

"Now they're cranky old men who look down on everyone else." Riley parked the car.

Evangeline smiled without any humor. "I see you've met them."

"But they're on our side, right?" Jax asked.

"The Taliesins want what we want—to preserve things the way they are, with the Llyrs and Arawens trapped in the eighth day and confined in prison," Riley said, opening the driver's door. "But they want to do it by keeping Evangeline and her sister hidden away forever. I don't think they're going to like me changing the plans."

"Are there any Taliesins left besides these two?" Jax asked as he and his liege lady got out of the vehicle. "Do they have *first* names?" He'd only ever heard them called *Taliesins*.

"I was eleven when I last saw them," Evangeline said coolly. "They shared no personal information with *me*."

Clearly, she wasn't fond of these guys. Jax supposed if someone had separated him from the people he cared about and dumped him someplace to wait indefinitely without telling him what was going on, he wouldn't like them, either.

Oh, wait, that's exactly what Riley did when he took me from Naomi—and what he's planning to do again when he sticks me back with her.

Jax glared daggers at Riley's back, following his guardian across the parking lot toward the library with Evangeline beside him and Mrs. Crandall bringing up the rear. A figure waited for them under the security lights near the entrance, someone with dark hair wearing a leather jacket, a matching miniskirt, and boots. Jax knew there'd be a pearl-handled pistol tucked in one of those boots and a gun holstered under the jacket. Deidre Morgan was always armed to the teeth. She probably slept with a gun under her pillow.

"Hello, Riley, Gloria." Deidre nodded to Riley and Mrs. Crandall and grinned at Jax. "Nice to see you again, cutie. How d'ya like my private college?"

"Sweet," Jax said. On the eighth day, Deidre had the campus entirely to herself, except for the men living in the library.

Then Deidre turned to Evangeline and looked her over from head to toe.

Riley managed a mumbling introduction between

Evangeline and his former fiancée. He and Deidre had briefly been engaged, but only because Riley had needed Deidre's mother's mercenary army to rescue Jax and Evangeline in Mexico, and there'd been only one thing Sheila Morgan had wanted in return: Riley Pendragon as a son-in-law and a vassal.

"The Morgans would have come to stop Wylit anyway," Riley had explained to Jax afterward, "but they wouldn't have cared who got killed in the process. I had to bargain for control over the mission."

Meaning he had to promise to marry Deidre and swear his future allegiance to her mother, or the Morgans would've made Swiss cheese out of Jax and Evangeline on top of that pyramid. The loss of Evangeline would have endangered the existence of the eighth day and the magical talents of all Transitioners, but if Evangeline had to die to prevent Normal civilization from being destroyed, the Morgans would have killed her.

Riley had traded himself for the right to direct the mission and rescue both his friends. Then Deidre had dumped him afterward because he'd kissed Evangeline.

Awkward, Jax thought. But Deidre was their liaison with the Taliesins, who were hiding themselves and their memorized knowledge from anyone—Transitioners or Kin—who might make evil use of it.

The campus library hadn't been open at midnight on Wednesday, so the front doors were locked now. Deidre led them around the side of the building to an emergency exit and squatted down to pick the lock. Jax watched her. Riley had promised to teach him this skill, an essential one for Transitioners who needed to enter without breaking. Now he wondered if it was a lesson he was supposed to receive before they ditched him, or if Riley had been just humoring him when he asked.

"Is your mother angry with me?" Riley asked Deidre while she worked.

"Since I'm the one who broke it off, she ought to be angry at *me*. But she thinks we cooked up the scheme together, so yes, your name is mud."

"Great," muttered Riley.

Evangeline looked back and forth between Deidre and Riley. Jax was pretty sure Evangeline had no idea about the bargain Riley had made to save her life.

Deidre kept her eyes on her lock picking. "But she's still got that ancient blade one of your ancestors gave mine hanging in her office. If she meant to break the old agreements between our families, she'd have taken it down and snapped it in half by now."

"Very reassuring," Riley said, not sounding reassured at all.

The lock opened, and Deidre stood up.

"Are the Taliesins expecting us?" Mrs. Crandall asked.

"I left a note for them in the spot we agreed upon for communication." Deidre paused and passed her gaze over all four of them. "Before we go in, I want to ask you about something pretty weird."

More weird than talking about her broken engagement in front of the girl Riley liked better? Jax leaned forward, all ears.

"Did any of you see anything strange in the ruins that night in Mexico?" Deidre asked.

"Bullets were flying and the world was ending," Riley said. "Other than that, you mean?"

"Someone who shouldn't have been there."

Jax shrugged. None of them should have been there.

Deidre sighed and explained. "It took a while for the story to get back to me from my squad. For obvious reasons, the men who saw her were reluctant to report it. But more than one of them saw a girl on the Avenue of the Dead during the action."

"Wylit had female vassals," Riley said. "Several of them."

"A young girl. Dressed in what may have been a short white dress, almost like a plain, old-fashioned shift." Riley shook his head, and so did Jax. Deidre huffed out her breath. "With crows," she added reluctantly. "Surrounded by crows."

Crows? Jax had never seen any animals on the eighth day. Evangeline had told him they were rare. But Riley burst out laughing.

"Combat fatigue," Mrs. Crandall said firmly, even

though she hadn't been there that day.

"My men don't suffer combat fatigue," Deidre said indignantly.

"What's the deal with crows?" Jax asked Evangeline, who didn't laugh at all. In fact, she looked worried.

"A legend," she murmured.

"A stupid legend," Riley stated. "No, Deidre." He held up fingers to count. "One crazy Kin lord, lots of people shooting at us, the sky broken into pieces—that's all I saw. No girl with crows."

Deidre turned to Evangeline. "What do *you* think?"

"A sighting of the Morrigan is a very bad sign," Evangeline said solemnly. "I hope your men were hallucinating."

"I doubt we'll be that lucky." Deidre shoved the door to the library open and led the way.

4

THE LIBRARY MIGHT HAVE been a pleasant place when it was open, but in the middle of the night, it was creepy. Jax reminded himself that this was also a secret day most people didn't know existed, so the likelihood of anybody lurking behind the towering shelves was pretty slim.

Deidre rapped sharply on a door labeled STAFF ONLY, pushed it open, and called into the hallway beyond: "Hello? It's Deidre Morgan with visitors to see you."

The staff area of the library included a break room with a refrigerator and a stove, two couches, and a private bathroom. Jax wondered if the Taliesins lived off people's leftover lunches and slept on those couches.

A man stepped out of the shadows, making Jax jump.

Jax had met only two people of the Kin race before, Evangeline and Wylit, but this man had the same pale blond hair and stunning blue eyes they did. He held a candle in an old-fashioned holder, and he was dressed in clothes that might have been in style in the 1800s—way worse than the 1980s clothes Evangeline had been stuck with when Jax met her.

Jax did some quick math. If this guy was about fifty years old, but lived only one day for every seven in the Normal world, he would've been born three hundred fifty years ago. Jax glanced at Evangeline, now dressed like a regular teen girl in shorts and a plain T-shirt. He'd once figured out that she must've been born back around 1900, before cars and airplanes and maybe even electricity.

Jax was a little fuzzy on history.

"Come this way," the Kin man said before vanishing into a room at the end of the hallway.

The Taliesin men had taken over the office of the head librarian. There was no electricity in the building on Grunsday, so they'd set candles on the librarian's desk and on the shelves. The man who'd met them in the hallway went to stand behind another Kin man, who was seated at the desk, leafing through a large book.

This man kept them waiting while he finished the page, being rude on purpose, Jax assumed. Finally, he looked up. His coloring was the same as the other guy's, but while the first one had a weak, twitchy face like a squirrel, this one had sharp cheekbones and a large, beak-shaped nose. "Pendragon," he said, greeting Riley without much pleasure. His eyes passed over the group, taking in each of their marks as they raised their hands to show the tattoos on their wrists—which was the 　　　　　 eighth-day world. "The voice of 　　　　 and a truth teller. Overkill, don't y　　

"It doesn't have to be," Riley r　　　 this pleasant."

Based on the man's expression, 　　　 assume this visit has something to do 　　　 the Eighth-Day Spell," the hook-nosed 　　 said, closing his book. He stood up and looked at Evangeline with slightly less affection than most people looked at a spider. "If *she* was the culprit, and you've delivered her to us for justice, I must remind you that is not our function."

"Hey!" Jax protested. "She risked her life defending the eighth day!"

"I was not *delivered* here," Evangeline said stiffly. "We came to find out where you've hidden my sister."

Taliesin paused a moment and then addressed Riley as if Evangeline weren't there. "It would be a very bad idea for those two girls to be together. They were separated on purpose for the safety of every member of my race. Our existence depends on theirs. Having them together would enable someone to wipe out the Emrys line at one blow, destroying the eighth-day world."

Jax could see the guy's point, even if he didn't agree with it. Evangeline and her sister were descendants of Merlin Emrys, the legendary wizard who had cast the Eighth-Day Spell fifteen hundred years ago. The spell was

...loodline of Merlin's family, and Evangeline ...ster were the only ones left.

"It's a very bad idea to have them *apart* any longer, to be picked off one by one," Riley argued. "Wylit found her brother, and then he found her. *Hiding* was not good enough. The Emrys line needs to reestablish itself, connect with old allies, and make new ones. They need to be strong enough so that no one dares act against them. My people benefit from the eighth day too; our magic is bound to that day. Without the eighth day, we lose our talents. I have to believe there are Transitioner clans who, for that reason alone, would make it their business to ally themselves with an Emrys."

"As you did?" the hook-nosed Taliesin replied, his gaze dropping pointedly to the honor blade Evangeline wore at her side. It was Riley's personal dagger, the one he'd used since childhood, which he'd offered to Evangeline as a symbol of their alliance after he had gained King Arthur's blade, Excalibur.

"He treats me like an ally and an equal," Evangeline said testily, "instead of a . . . a pawn." She repeated Mr. Crandall's assessment of her worth to others. "Someone whose personal interests don't matter as long as I'm serving yours."

Meanwhile, the squirrelly guy muttered and *tsk-tsk*ed to himself like an old woman. "This won't do at all," he said to his brother.

"I agree," the other one said. "We cannot support an Emrys clan led by this girl. She was educated in unsavory ideas by her treacherous father and allied with Kin who wanted to wreak havoc on the world. She can't be trusted to preserve the eighth day."

Evangeline flinched at that statement, and it ticked Jax off. It was true that Evangeline's father had plotted with that lunatic Wylit to break the Eighth-Day Spell. But it was unfair to suggest she'd been a conspirator in his plans. She'd been just a kid at the time. Jax opened his mouth to defend her, but someone else beat him to it.

"I can vouch for her actions at the pyramid," Deidre said. "She was *not* allied with Wylit, and she helped repair the spell."

Riley flashed Deidre a grateful smile, but Beak Nose didn't seem impressed. "Nevertheless, a female Emrys cannot wield the family talent well enough to lead her clan, and she'll be susceptible to those who would use and manipulate her." Here his cold eyes wandered to Riley in silent accusation. "I prefer that the girls remain separated. When they are old enough to marry, we'll choose appropriate matches for them and hope for a male heir who can someday lead the Emrys family with both magical strength *and* honor."

Choose matches for them? Wait for a male heir? These guys really were out of the Dark Ages! Jax had heard enough. He yanked out his honor blade and stabbed the tip into the wooden desk. A moment later he remembered this wasn't really a Taliesin's desk he was damaging, but it was too late to take back the dramatic gesture, so he went with it. "You! Chinless Wonder!" He pointed at the squirrelly Taliesin with his other hand. "Where is Adelina Emrys?"

The man stammered, fighting the compulsion to answer. Jax had picked him as the weaker target, but for a moment it looked as if he might still resist. Then Riley joined in, his talent causing goose bumps to rise on Jax's skin.

"Answer the question."

Jax's inquisitor talent and Riley's voice of command together defeated the guy. "Vermont," he whispered.

"What's the address?" Jax demanded.

Chinless Wonder shivered all over, but Beak Nose grabbed his arm, lending him strength. Jax gathered his talent to try again, and Riley moved forward, no doubt meaning to get a grip on the man, which would increase his power of compulsion. It also meant this was going to get ugly, and the Taliesins would never trust the good intentions of any of them again.

"Wait!" said Evangeline. Jax paused and Riley took a step back, although he put his hand on Excalibur. Evangeline lifted her chin and spoke coldly to the Taliesin leader. "My vassal and my ally can coerce the information out of you, but it would be better if you cooperated voluntarily."

"Why is that?" he snapped, addressing her directly for the first time.

"Because I *am* the Emrys clan leader whether you like it or not," Evangeline said. "Not some future male heir, and sadly, not my poor brother—who died because you couldn't protect him. *I'm* the leader of my bloodline, and I *am* committed to preserving the eighth day. You need to accept that. We shouldn't be fighting among ourselves. We're facing a crisis. The Morrigan was seen presiding over Wylit's attempt to destroy the world."

Deidre sucked in her breath but did not deny what Evangeline said.

"Chaos is upon us then!" gasped the Chinless Wonder.

"Not if I can help it," Evangeline said calmly. "The Morrigan may be guiding events toward some great conflict, but the outcome isn't preordained. The Emrys talent is supposed to run stronger in males, but I was strong enough to repair the Eighth-Day Spell. So *choose*, Taliesin. Are you really on our side, or not?" She closed her hand around one of the candles on the librarian's desk and whispered a string of words in an incomprehensible language.

Every candle flame in the room swelled to three times its size. Even the electric lights bloomed. The one in the ceiling flared impossibly bright and then shattered. Broken glass rained down, and everyone except Evangeline threw their arms over their heads to protect themselves from the shards.

She stood perfectly still and glared at Taliesin. "Where is my sister, you horrible man?"

"Impressive," Deidre said as they walked back through the empty library.

"Thank you," Evangeline replied. She held a paper with a name and address written on it.

"If you're coming out of hiding at last, Riley," Deidre said, "I approve. But watch your back. There are plenty of people who won't want to see you gain any influence."

"Noted," Riley grunted.

"That goes for you too, cutie." She looked at Jax. "Be careful."

Jax lifted his head in surprise. Who would be after him?

Mrs. Crandall narrowed her eyes at Deidre, then looked at Jax as if she wanted to stick a stamp on his forehead and mail him back to Delaware.

Deidre escorted them as far as the door, where she wished them good-bye and good luck. "Let me know when you've got the girl and you're ready to do business with the Table." She hooked a thumb over her shoulder. "I'm going to help Rufus and Enoch clean up the glass. As much as I enjoy a good explosion, I don't want this library getting a reputation for poltergeists. It'll draw unwanted attention here."

Rufus and Enoch? Really? Jax snorted. They were better off with the names he'd given them!

Back at the Land Rover, Riley spread a map across the hood and plotted a route. "It's about an eight-hour trip," he concluded. "We can get there by midmorning if we drive all night."

Mrs. Crandall cleared her throat. "She's living with Transitioners? Not being watched from a distance, but in their house? That's unusual."

"Why?" Jax asked.

"Because it's better not to get emotionally invested," Mrs. Crandall said vaguely.

"Mrs. Crandall means you don't want to get personal with someone who's supposed to be just a job," Evangeline explained. Jax remembered that she and Riley hadn't known each other's first names until Jax had stuck his nose into their business, even though they lived next door to one another and Riley had been guarding her.

"Addie's thirteen now, but she was eight when we were separated," Evangeline went on. "I'm glad they didn't make her live by herself, like they did me. I worried about that quite a bit. And Elliot was only six . . ." She bit her lip.

That was too sad to think about—how little her brother was when Wylit stole him away from his Taliesin-appointed protectors and forced him to try and break the Eighth-Day Spell. "What are we waiting for?" Jax said, to change the subject. "Let's go get Addie!"

Riley opened the car door for Evangeline. When she passed him getting in, he leaned over and said something to her. Jax probably wasn't supposed to hear what was said, but he did.

"You were never just a job for me."

Evangeline turned bright pink, but at least she didn't look quite so sad.

5

PINK TENDRILS ILLUMINATED THE purple Grunsday sky at dawn, when they made a rest stop at McDonald's. Jax shook Evangeline awake, then stumbled out of the car, rubbing his hands over his face. He hoped he hadn't been drooling in his sleep. He was looking forward to bacon and eggs until he realized McDonald's wouldn't be serving breakfast. He'd only have a choice of what was cooked and available at midnight on Wednesday.

"Get whatever you want," Riley said, leaving cash on the counter.

They helped themselves to wrapped burgers from the bins, and Riley pulled a tray of fries out of the hot oil. Evangeline took one of everything, as if she didn't want to miss a single thing in her first fast-food experience.

Jax couldn't blame her. She'd never eaten from a drive-thru or at a sit-down restaurant. She'd never seen a ball game or a play. She'd never been to the movies or even watched a television show. Jax grabbed a large paper cup and tackled the milk shake machine. Dang it, if there was anything left in the pipes, Evangeline was at least going to have a milk shake.

They sat down in a booth next to a table occupied by a single tray of half-eaten food and an open issue of *People* magazine.

"So, which one of you is going to tell me about this Morrigan person?" Jax asked, chomping on a french fry. "Is she a Transitioner or Kin?"

"Neither." Evangeline peeled back the bun on her burger to see what was in it. "She's not a person at all. She's a force of nature—the embodiment of destruction and chaos. The Morrigan takes the body of a girl or a grown woman or sometimes an old crone, and she's usually accompanied by carrion animals, like crows." Riley shook his head, disagreeing, but Evangeline put her burger back together and went on, ignoring him. "She hand selects combatants for conflicts that will change the world, and she supposedly decides who lives and dies. There are reports of her appearing at Normandy, the Somme, Waterloo, and the Norman conquest of England." She glanced across the table at Riley. "And the fall of King Arthur."

"It's just a scary story to tell in the dark," said Riley.

"Your friend Deidre believes it," Evangeline replied. "She's more superstitious than you might think."

"Most soldiers are," commented Mrs. Crandall.

Jax polished off his double cheeseburger and licked ketchup off his fingers, grateful for the hot meal. Then he realized something. "Hey! How can these burgers be warm? They've been sitting under a heat lamp throwing leftover light since midnight. Why aren't they cold?"

"Nothing will stay warm now that we've been here." Riley pointed a french fry at the neighboring table. "That food will be stone cold by the time the Normals get back."

"What do you mean, *now that we've been here*?"

"I keep telling you, Jax, it depends on the point of view of the observer. Don't you remember what I said about Einstein's theory of relativity?"

Well, he remembered Riley yammering in the car on their way back from Mexico, but as for what he'd said. . . . Jax's science wasn't any better than his history.

Riley saw the look on his face and sighed. "Time doesn't pass for inanimate objects on the eighth day unless someone observes it passing. No observer, no effect on the object."

"Back at the college there were some basketball players," Jax said. "Their ball kept bouncing after midnight."

"Because you were watching it."

"But I was watching a girl on a bike, too, and her bike froze in place."

"She's observing that bike a lot more personally than you were. But if the ball was already in the air . . . and if the velocity wasn't too great . . . " Riley paused to consider it. "Well, it's complicated. There are a lot of factors."

Evangeline slurped noisily at her milk shake. "Magic can't be explained with science. You might as well not try."

Riley grinned at her. "You believe in the Morrigan but not science?"

"Why didn't you go to college?" Jax blurted out. Riley was smarter than he looked. A moment later, Jax realized the answer to his question was sitting right next to him. Riley wouldn't have gone to college and left Evangeline unguarded.

But Riley gave a different answer. "Bad grades. Take that as a warning."

Jax slumped in his seat. Yeah, this wasn't a good time to remind Riley about sending him to school.

They finished eating, and Jax packed Evangeline's leftovers into a paper bag. They were waiting for her to come back from the restroom when they heard her scream. Riley reacted first, running down the aisle toward the ladies' room. Before he reached it, the door flew open and something the size of a large rat bolted out. It swerved around Riley, leaped onto a table, ran across the tops of several more, and came to a stop on a railing inches from Jax's face.

He yelped. The thing rose up on its hind legs and stared at him with black, glittery eyes. It was almost a foot tall when standing, with thick brown fur and sharp-looking incisors. "What is that?" he yelled. It wasn't a rat; it had no tail. And its face was flat, like a pug dog—or an ugly old man.

"It's just a brownie," Mrs. Crandall said with exasperation.

"What d'ya mean, *brownie*?" Brownies were chocolate desserts cut into squares, not dog-faced, tailless rats.

Evangeline came out of the restroom looking embarrassed. "Sorry. It climbed out of the trash can and startled me."

Riley waved a hand at the creature. "Shoo," he said gently. "Leave us alone."

The so-called brownie turned and scampered toward the kitchen, where Jax assumed it would chew on the food and leave poop everywhere.

"Did you *command* it?" Evangeline asked Riley in surprise.

"Nah, I just have a knack with 'em." He shrugged. "Not a skill I normally brag about."

Jax stared after the brownie. "That's the first animal I've ever seen on the eighth day."

"I told you there were vermin here," Evangeline reminded him.

"I thought you meant *mice*."

"No, not mice." She shuddered. "I used to have a

terrible problem with brownies at Mrs. Unger's—they got into the garbage and ransacked the kitchen—and then they stopped coming." She looked up at Riley. "Did *you* do something?"

Riley held the glass exit door open for her. "I saw you chasing a brownie out of the house with a broom one day, cursing and squealing and carrying on. And I asked them to stay away from our houses after that."

Jax thought that over. *Wait. What?* Even if Riley ordered one—or two or three—brownies to stay away, how would that make them *all* stay away? Were they intelligent animals? Did they communicate with each other? Or did Riley have some special talent he wasn't sharing?

He hurried after Riley, wanting to ask more questions. But Evangeline was protesting that she did not *curse and squeal and carry on*, while Riley was teasing her, saying yes, she did—quite impressively, in fact—and Jax missed his opportunity.

Around eleven o'clock in the morning, Mrs. Crandall parked the Land Rover three blocks over from their destination in a little Vermont town while they plotted how to approach the Transitioners hiding Adelina Emrys.

"Their talent is obscurity, according to the Taliesins," Riley said. "I'll bet they have other security measures in place, so let's assume they already know we're here. After the events three weeks ago, they must be on high alert. Have you ever heard of the Carroways, Gloria?"

Mrs. Crandall shook her head. "Either it's a false name or they're a branch-off family."

Jax knew some Transitioners traced their ancestry straight back to legendary figures, like Riley to King Arthur and Deidre to Morgan LeFay. But others had branched off and diverged into new talents over the fifteen hundred years since their ancestors had cast the Eighth-Day Spell. "Isn't there a directory of some kind?" Jax asked. "With all your names and talents and marks?"

Mrs. Crandall snorted. "Anyone who tried to collect that information wouldn't last long. Transitioners like their secrets."

"I want you to stay in the car," Riley told Evangeline.

"But I'm the only one they're likely to trust," she protested.

"Someone with an itchy trigger finger might shoot at you before they realize who you are. They know the Eighth-Day Spell was attacked, and they have an Emrys heir. If I were them, I'd be nervous if Kin approached the house."

Evangeline frowned at him. "You look more threatening than I do." She indicated Riley's heavily tattooed arms.

"I'll go," said Mrs. Crandall.

That was no good. Mrs. Crandall was six feet tall and dressed in army fatigues.

"I'm the one who has to go," Jax said. "I'm the most harmless looking out of all of us, and they probably won't shoot me on sight." *I'm useful. You don't want to send me away.*

"He's right," Riley admitted.

"No," Mrs. Crandall objected. "Riley, he—" She bit off her words in frustration.

Riley pulled Jax aside. "It might be hard to find the house. That's the Carroway talent."

"No sweat. Information is *my* talent, right? I'll find the house, explain who we are, and come back to get you."

"We need a signal," Riley said. "So I know you're not under duress."

"How about *Riley, you suck*?"

Riley laughed. He'd once signaled Jax with the phrase *Jax, you idiot.*

At first Jax had trouble finding the right street. He pictured where it had been on the map and turned a corner that didn't seem like the right one, but *had* to be. Then, he couldn't find the house. There was a 15 and a 19, and a 16 and 18 on the other side of the street. But no 17—and no space for one, either. Jax gripped the hilt of his dagger and stared *hard* at the place where it should be, calling on his talent for information. Suddenly number 17 appeared: large and white with turrets and a wraparound porch.

"Hold it right there, boy!" a voice rang out from the house. "I've got a rifle scope aimed at your head. Hands in the air!"

Jax threw up both hands. "I come in peace!" he shouted. *Crap. That sounded stupid.*

"You're not alone," the voice called.

"No, but my friends are staying back till you say they're welcome."

Jax sensed movement behind him and turned just in time to be body slammed by somebody twice his size. This man grabbed Jax's right hand, twisting it behind his back and away from his honor blade. Then he grabbed Jax's left arm and turned over his wrist.

"He's an inquisitor," the man shouted. "Don't recognize the family, though."

The scroll and the eye on his tattoo named his talent. Jax had figured out that much. An eye and a scroll meant *inquisitor*, just like the crown on Riley's meant *command*. The arrangement of the symbols and how they were combined with others were unique to each individual family. Riley's mark was famous enough to be known on sight, while Jax was nobody important.

"No questions out of you!" ordered the man from the house. "I'm a good enough shot to take you out without hitting my son."

"I don't want to ask questions. I came to see Addie." Jax gave the nickname Evangeline had used, thinking it might carry more weight.

The man's grip on Jax tightened. "We don't know any Addie."

"Yeah, you do," Jax said. "The Taliesins gave us your name. I've got Addie's sister with me and someone else. Someone important."

"What's her name?" hissed the man holding Jax. "The sister."

"Evangeline. She's sixteen. Addie's thirteen, and there was a younger brother, Elliot." Jax searched his memory for other personal information about the Emrys family. How could he prove he was a friend?

The man untwisted Jax's arm but kept a grip on him and pushed him forward. "Start walking."

"Uh, could you tell the guy in the house to take his rifle scope off my head?"

"Dad doesn't have a rifle on you. We don't keep guns in the house. Too many kids."

There certainly were a lot of children. Jax stared at them in surprise. He'd never seen little kids on the eighth day before, since Transitioners didn't experience their first Grunsday until they were at least ten.

But these were Kin children.

They dashed out of sight when he was escorted through the house, all except for a toddler who sat in her diaper and nothing else in the middle of the floor. But they came back to sneak looks at him when he explained who he was and why he'd come.

The elder Carroway and his wife were in their sixties.

Their son was probably near forty. Seated in the back corner of the room, a Kin woman nursed an infant and listened silently.

"I don't sense any harm in him," said Mrs. Carroway. "Nor in the others. They're anxious, but not hostile."

Jax nodded. She was a sensitive. Riley had predicted they'd have one for security. "They're probably worried about me, and Evangeline wants to see her sister."

"How do we know Addie's sister wasn't the one who tried to break the spell?" Carroway Jr. addressed his parents. "Do we dare trust her here?"

"Look," Jax said angrily. "I'm tired of people thinking the worst of Evangeline when she almost died saving the world." That crazy lord Wylit had wanted to wipe the seven-day timeline off the face of the earth and had needed an Emrys heir's cooperation to finish casting his spell. He'd hurt Evangeline and threatened her, but she had refused to help him. And after Wylit was dead, Evangeline had repaired the damage he'd already done to the spell—with some help from Riley and Jax and all their friends. Jax was proud of his liege lady; she was brave and selfless and deserved a lot more respect than most people gave her.

Mrs. Carroway exchanged a glance with her husband and gave him a small, discreet smile. Jax suspected his feelings had just been read and his indignant defense of

Evangeline had won the old lady over. But as he looked around, Jax realized something else was wrong here.

The children who kept peeking around the corner had pale skin, silvery-blond hair, and blue eyes, but none of them appeared to be a thirteen-year-old girl with a personal interest in Jax's story. "Doesn't Addie get a say in this?" he asked. "Where is she? Aren't you going to tell her that her sister's here?"

Carroway Jr. sighed. "Addie's gone. She left here over a month ago."

6

"A WAY STATION?" Riley stared at Mr. Carroway incredulously. "You had an Emrys heir here while operating a *way station?*"

Evangeline had taken the news about Addie bravely but sadly, as if she hadn't really expected a happy reunion today. When the diapered Kin toddler waddled over and lifted her arms like a demanding queen, Evangeline scooped her up and buried her face in the little girl's hair. Jax was pretty sure she was hiding tears.

"Residents don't share their family names," Mr. Carroway said defensively. "That's one of the rules. If they want to stay here, they remain anonymous."

Really? Little kids were expected to keep secrets? Jax saw Mrs. Crandall shake her head and guessed she was thinking the same thing he was: that the first thing kids did when out of sight of adults was say, *Guess what I'm not supposed to tell you.*

Riley was blunt about it. "She must have told someone, or they figured it out."

Mrs. Crandall put a hand on Riley's arm to quiet him. "What you're doing here is a very kind and generous thing," she said more tactfully. "But considering the importance of keeping Adelina Emrys safe and out of sight . . ."

"Addie lived here for over thirty years, and there was never any problem," Mr. Carroway said. "Refugees came and went, and no one noticed the one little girl who stayed."

All the Kin staying here had either been driven out of their homes by Transitioners or were forced to leave by events in the Normal world. Jax had never considered how hard it must be for the Kin, with their extended lives, to find a safe place to live. Buildings were remodeled or torn down when they got old. Sometimes they caught fire or fell into disrepair. And Jax hadn't really grasped the fact until now that a lot of Transitioners had a strong dislike for Kin. Transitioners were the jailers, and the entire Kin race were their prisoners, sentenced for crimes committed long ago. The most hated and evil Kin families were imprisoned even within the eighth day, and the others . . . well, Jax guessed they were like ex-convicts. Allowed out on their own in a limited way, but not really trusted, and nobody wanted them living next door.

The woman nursing the baby had been chased out of her long-time home. She and her children were staying with the Carroways until her husband found a new place. Some of the kids here were orphans, Mrs. Carroway said. Others had been left here by parents who could find no other safe place to keep them.

And six weeks ago, Addie had run away from this house with a teenage Kin girl she'd befriended.

"How do you know she went willingly?" Riley asked.

Mrs. Carroway looked tearful, and her husband said, "Because she left us a letter."

After an awkward pause, Carroway Jr. said, "We love Addie. But let's face it. She's . . ." He paused.

Evangeline lifted her face from the little girl's head. "Difficult."

He sighed in relief. "Exactly."

"Do you have anything that belonged to her?" Evangeline asked. "I could scry for her."

Jax didn't know what that meant, but apparently Mrs. Carroway did. "She took everything she owned," the old woman said regretfully.

"Even a hair would do."

"The house is full of blond hairs. I don't know how we could tell if one was Addie's."

"You said she left a letter," Mrs. Crandall reminded them. "Do you still have that?"

Mrs. Carroway twisted her hands together. "I'll get it." She left the room, and after a moment, her husband followed.

As soon as they were gone, Carroway Jr. said, "Take it easy on my parents. They did right by Addie, and they've been really worried about her, especially after the attack on the spell."

"I'm sure they did their best," Evangeline replied.

"She's been part of our family as long as I can remember," he continued. "She was my big sister, and then my little sister, and then she was like a daughter to me." He took a deep breath. "I have my own daughters now, and I know they go through stages. But Addie's stages lasted *decades*. We got older, but she didn't."

The elder Carroways returned, and the wife handed folded papers to Evangeline with a shaking hand. Evangeline took them eagerly. But after scanning them, she frowned. Jax leaned over her shoulder to catch glimpses as she read:

> *. . . you sent me to bed early even though it was Jimmy's fault.*
>
> *. . . I always got blamed.*
>
> *. . . Jimmy got chocolate cake for his birthdays and I always had to have vanilla even though I kept telling you I wanted chocolate.*

Jax glanced at the forty-year-old Carroway. If he was *Jimmy*, Addie Emrys had kept some childish grudges a very long time.

Mrs. Carroway waited with fingers pressed against her lips for a reaction to this list of injustices. Finally, Evangeline looked up. "I see Addie hasn't changed a bit," she remarked, ripping a strip off the first page. "May I use a metal pan of water, please, and saffron if you have it?"

Mrs. Carroway exhaled in relief. "With all the Kin in this house? Of course I have saffron."

Jax watched in fascination as Evangeline set up her spell. Her talent was very different from his. He could call on his inquisitor magic at any time, but it was only good for gathering information. Evangeline could perform a wide variety of magical acts, but she needed symbolic objects and rituals to activate them. She set the pan of water on Mrs. Carroway's kitchen table, then cast the paper with Addie's handwriting into it. Once the surface of the water grew still, Evangeline placed two golden threads of saffron on her tongue, closed her eyes, and murmured a spell. Opening her eyes, she leaned over the pan and stared into the water. Jax held his breath.

"I don't see her," she whispered, her eyes fixed unblinking on the water.

"She's blocking you." The Kin woman with the baby

spoke for the first time, causing Jax to jump. He'd forgotten she was there.

"No," Evangeline said. "I don't get that sense."

"Keep your eyes on the water." The woman handed her infant to Mrs. Carroway and approached the table. "Open your mouth." Evangeline did, and the woman placed more saffron on her tongue. Then she covered Evangeline's hands with her own, lending strength to the spell.

Evangeline tried for a minute longer. Then she collapsed into a chair and buried her face in her hands. "Addie's not out there. I think she must be dead!"

Mrs. Carroway burst into tears, and her husband and son rushed to her side. Jax shuffled his feet uneasily and looked at Evangeline and then at Riley, hoping *he* knew how to comfort a crying girl.

Apparently not. Riley made a move as if to pat Evangeline's head or give her a hug, but then he chickened out and did neither. Mrs. Crandall elbowed him out of the way so she could put an arm around Evangeline.

The Kin woman, meanwhile, cleared away the pan of water and saffron, then folded the remaining pages of Addie's letter and pressed them into Evangeline's hand. "You're overwrought. Try again when you're fresh. You were blocked."

"No one was fighting me," Evangeline argued. "I'd know."

"Not if she was shielded by wards."

Evangeline inhaled sharply. "It could've been wards."

Now *wards*, Jax knew about. They were protection spells placed on objects or places. Last week, Evangeline had designed wards based on Kin symbols for their cabin in the mountains, and A.J. had spent all week working on them.

Everybody jumped on the idea that Addie was safe and secure behind wards somewhere, comforting both Evangeline and Mrs. Carroway. Meanwhile, Jax slipped out of the kitchen and wandered off to the front room of the house, the one with windows facing the porch. He didn't want Evangeline to see how disappointed he was in this failure.

Addie had left here six weeks ago. That was only six days for the Kin. Evangeline had missed her sister by *six days*. Not only had the sisters failed to reunite, but Addie had no way of knowing that villainous Transitioners like the Dulacs would be hunting for her because of the near miss on the pyramid. And how were Riley and Evangeline supposed to find her first with their limited resources? They couldn't call her or text her or send her an email because no technology with a computer chip worked on the eighth day. Addie Emrys would never have used a phone or a computer in her life. *How do people live that way?*

Jax glanced back toward the Carroway kitchen. He and Riley and Evangeline must be some kind of cursed trio. Riley had lost his entire family in a devastating explosion. Evangeline's brother was dead, and now her sister had vanished. And since the death of his father eight months ago, Jax's only relative was Naomi, a cousin of his mother's, and she was a Normal. There was a time when Jax would've given anything to live with Naomi and her family—to live in a home with parents and cousins who'd be the siblings he'd never had.

Now that he knew Mrs. Crandall and Riley were actually planning to send him there, Jax balked. Those people didn't feel like family anymore. They were practically strangers, and they could never know anything about Jax's secret day or his magical talent.

Jax wanted a family he didn't have to keep secrets from. A family where he fitted in.

He lifted his head, sniffed suspiciously, and turned around. "You. I thought so."

The Kin toddler held up her arms.

"No way. You stink."

"Brigit likes you."

Jax jumped at the voice. The Kin woman who'd helped Evangeline stood in the doorway. "Sorry," Jax said, embarrassed. "I think she needs changing."

The woman crossed the room, picked up the girl, and set her on her hip. "Brigit likes you *and* your liege lady. I take great stock in that." She examined Jax with her very blue eyes. "It's rare for a Transitioner to swear to Kin."

"Yeah, well . . ." Jax didn't know what to say to that. He hadn't known it was unusual when he'd done it, and he wouldn't change it even now that he did know.

"May I see your mark?"

Jax held out his arm and let her take his wrist with her free hand. She ran her thumb across his tattoo, and Jax shivered. "You're not who you think you are," she said.

"Huh?"

She lifted her face, and Jax saw that her eyes had gone glassy, her pupils unfocused. "You're not who *they* think you are, either. You're something new."

"What do you mean?" The woman swayed, and Jax grabbed her shoulder, worried she was going to drop her kid. "Who do you think I am?" he asked. "Who are *you*?"

The Kin woman leaned toward him and whispered into his ear: *"Oath—an oath falls to Lear today."* A moment later, she slipped away from Jax's grasp like water. "Let's take care of your diaper," she said brightly to her child, apparently unaware of the last few seconds.

She turned and walked away, while Jax stared after her. *What was that about?!*

7

IT WAS NEARLY MIDNIGHT on Grunsday when they got back to the Pennsylvania mountains. The ride home took longer than it should have, because Riley decided along the way that Evangeline needed driving lessons as a survival skill.

"What about me?" Jax demanded. "What if I need to make a getaway on a Grunsday?"

"Let's wait until you're old enough to see over the steering wheel, squirt."

That was lame. Jax was just as tall as Evangeline. But he suspected Riley was really trying to distract Evangeline from her disappointment and worry. If so, it didn't work much. Evangeline tackled driving the way she did everything, with determination and competence, but she didn't seem to take any joy in it. It wasn't *fun* for her, the way it would've been for Jax.

A.J. greeted them at the cabin door and didn't need to ask if they'd been successful. Their faces said it all, and they obviously didn't have an extra Kin girl with them.

"No luck?" called Mr. Crandall from the second-floor loft.

"Not a lot," Mrs. Crandall said, heading directly for the stairs and her bedroom.

"Sorry, Evangeline," said A.J. She gave him a smile, but her eyes filled with tears. "Hey," he added quickly. "Come see what I did." He motioned her into the main room of the house, where he'd painted protection wards on two opposite walls. "North and south," A.J. pointed out. "There's one on the west wall in the kitchen, and I put the east ward in the little room where you'll sleep instead of on the stairwell above it. I thought that might give you a little extra protection."

Evangeline surveyed the convoluted symbols A.J. had painted, one above the fireplace and the other between two windows. To Jax's eye, they looked like giant knots—interesting to look at, but meaningless. "You altered the design I gave you," Evangeline said.

A.J.'s face fell. "Yeah. Dad gave me heck for that and wanted to paint over them and do them himself. I said, 'At least wait till she sees 'em.'" He sighed. "But I know. I shouldn't mess with Kin symbols. I'll start redoing them tomorrow."

"No. Don't." Evangeline looked perplexed. "What made you change them?"

A.J. shrugged. "Thought they looked better this way."

"I think you've made them stronger," Evangeline said. "These wards will obscure our presence from sensitives. They'll repel magical attack and physical assault."

"Wish you'd had that at Mrs. Unger's house," Jax said. A lot of things might have been different if Evangeline had been invisible to sensitives there. Especially one orange-haired scent sensitive who had caused them a lot of trouble. But Evangeline couldn't have painted weird symbols on Mrs. Unger's walls. The poor old lady would've called an exorcist!

"Me too," Evangeline said. "But wards made by me wouldn't be as potent as these anyway. It takes a gifted artisan like A.J. to invoke this much power from a symbol."

A.J. beamed.

Jax and Riley glanced at each other. Probably nobody, not even A.J.'s mother, had ever called him *gifted*.

"Will they protect us from scrying?" Riley asked.

"Yes," she admitted. "And that may be why I couldn't find Addie today. I should have thought of that myself, but I panicked." Evangeline sank down in a chair and rubbed her eyes with her fingers. She wasn't the crying type usually, but this had been a long, discouraging day.

"I haven't given up, you know," Riley told her. "I have

a trick or two up my sleeves."

"I thought all you had up your sleeves were tattoos," Jax said. Riley made sure Evangeline wasn't looking, then smacked Jax in the back of the head.

"What time is it?" Evangeline asked from behind her hands.

Jax checked the cheap Timex watch he wore on Grunsday. "You've got ten minutes."

She lowered her hands and looked up at her friends glumly. "Where do you want me? In the car or in the house?" Wherever Evangeline was when midnight came, that was where she'd remain until next Grunsday.

Jax hated seeing her so miserable. "We want you to *stay*. I wish we had handcuffs."

"They wouldn't work," Evangeline said.

"You don't know that," Jax protested. "I took that bank robber to Grunsday, and he didn't belong there." It hadn't been Jax's idea—getting handcuffed to a criminal—but he *had* dragged the guy to the eighth day.

"But Normals aren't *forbidden* to enter the eighth day," A.J. said. "They just don't have a way to get there, normally. With Evangeline, it's different, especially after she repaired the spell on the pyramid. *Even if it imprisons me for the rest of my life*." He shook his head at her. "Did you have to say it that way? Couldn't you have given yourself parole or something?"

"I was trying to save the world, A.J. I wasn't thinking of anything else."

"But you know, Jax is right," said Riley, which is something Jax had never heard him say before. "We won't know for sure unless we try. I mean, *Jax* can't do it. He's a newbie and barely trained." Okay, that sounded more like Riley. "But maybe *I* can do it."

"How do you figure?" A.J. demanded.

Riley unsheathed Excalibur. "This is a pretty potent magical artifact itself, and it was used in the spell—both times. Plus there's my talent." He looked at Evangeline. "I could command you to stay."

"Do you actually have handcuffs?" Jax asked.

"It doesn't have to be handcuffs. Any kind of binding should do it." Riley walked out of the room and into the kitchen. They heard him opening and closing drawers. A few seconds later, he returned with a roll of duct tape. "Let's experiment."

"Are you sure?" Evangeline stood up, looking hopeful.

"What's the worst that can happen? You guys can stand to be without me for a week, right?"

"Longer," Jax said, making sure he was out of head-smacking range.

"Just in case"—Riley pulled his phone out of a pocket and handed it to A.J.—"call in that favor, like I told you."

"Okay," said A.J. "Gimme the tape and hold her hand."

Riley took Evangeline's hand. She blushed and looked everywhere but at him while A.J. wrapped the tape around their wrists. Bound together in this physical manner, they had to stay in the same timeline. They couldn't be separated.

Riley checked his own watch, then balanced Excalibur on the palm of his free hand. "Look at me," he said, and she did, but her cheeks got even redder. "Evangeline Emrys, I command you to stay with me for Thurs—"

Then they were both gone.

A full second passed before A.J. said, "Well, that went the way I expected."

Mr. Crandall was furious—especially because A.J. didn't tell him until morning.

As if he could've yanked Riley back if he'd known earlier.

"*What* is that boy thinking?" he roared. "I mean, I *know* what he's thinking, but he's never lost his head over a girl before."

Mrs. Crandall dumped a fresh stack of pancakes onto the table. A.J. and Jax both stabbed their forks into the pile. "If you give him a hard time, Arnie, you're only going to make it worse. You know how stubborn he is."

"I've got nothing against the girl," Mr. Crandall said apologetically to Jax. She was his liege lady, after all. "But there can't be anything between them. You know why."

Jax nodded. Evangeline lived on a different timeline. Riley and everybody in this room would probably be dead and gone before she aged ten years. Jax was surprised to discover that the idea of getting old didn't bother him as much as the thought of Evangeline being left behind.

"Anyway, we've got instructions for while he's missing." A.J. brought out Riley's phone. "We keep on looking for Adelina Emrys." He thumbed through the menus until he found what he wanted, then stabbed at a key and put the phone to his ear. He grinned at Jax, although Jax had no idea why.

"Yeah, hi," he said after a moment. "No, it's A.J. Crandall." Pause. "Riley's not here. He's gone to the next Grunsday with Evangeline." Pause. "They tied themselves together, trying to pull her into . . . Well, I didn't think it would work either, but . . ." Pause. "Hey, forget about Riley. Aren't you going to ask about *Jax*?"

Jax froze with a forkful of pancakes halfway to his mouth. Who the heck was A.J. talking to?

A.J.'s eyes grew wide, and he held the phone away from his head for a moment. Then he brought it back to his ear and said, "How does a girl your age even know words like that? Put your father on."

Jax groaned. *No, no, no. It can't be. . . .*

"Gimme that," growled Mr. Crandall, taking the phone from his son. He waited a moment, then bellowed, "Donovan? It's Crandall."

"Are you crazy?" gasped Jax. "You're asking the Donovans to help us?"

Mrs. Crandall put the final batch of pancakes on the table and slapped her son's hand away so she could serve herself. "We already discussed this with Riley. The Donovans have proved they can sense Kin on any day of the week and identify families by scent. We need them to track down Adelina."

"But you can't trust them!" Jax protested.

"Payment?" Mr. Crandall was yelling into the phone. "Wasn't my son just talking to your daughter? Remember who got her back alive for you? My liege lord, in case you forgot. You *owe* him!"

Jax threw up his hands. "A.J. wards the house against enemies, and then you *invite* the worst people you can think of?"

"It's already settled," Mrs. Crandall said. "Riley banked on this as Plan B."

He'd never told Jax. None of them had discussed this with Jax.

Jax shoved his breakfast plate away, his appetite gone.

These people didn't consider him part of their clan or

their family. He was temporary and disposable and not even worth consulting on important decisions.

And now he was going to have to put up with Tegan Donovan.

Super.

8

DORIAN WRINKLED HIS NOSE in distaste. The house in southwestern Pennsylvania where Jax Aubrey had lived with the Pendragon guy was a dump. It didn't even have a full second story, just a bathroom and two small bedrooms with sloping ceilings. Sloane refused to put a foot over the threshold.

The furniture was still there—ugly and sagging and stained. But all the personal items of the residents had been removed. Dad's eyes were as dark as thunderclouds when he and Dorian came down from the second floor. "The house has been thoroughly vacuumed; sheets and towels are gone," Dad reported to Sloane. "Not a hair left behind." Hairs could've been taken back to their clan spell caster, Dr. Morder, for use in a locater spell.

Albert Ganner, head of security for the Dulacs, was overturning cushions and examining every cranny in the sofa. Aunt Ursula had insisted he accompany them as her condition for allowing Sloane to enter *enemy territory.* "They knew what they were doing when they vacated here," Ganner said.

"They didn't know how to clean the windows or get stains out of the carpet, though." Sloane stood on the front stoop, as if afraid grime was catching. "Albert, there's a cellar door and a shed in the yard."

"I'm on it," Ganner said. "Maybe they overlooked something." He didn't sound hopeful.

"I'm going to talk to the old woman next door. Dorian, come with me." Sloane turned and walked down the front steps, trusting Dorian to follow like a dog.

Heel, Dorian.

Dad cast one last glowering look around the house. "I'll question the other neighbors."

Earlier in the week, Dorian and his dad had visited a town in northern Delaware to confirm that "Rayne Aubrey" really had been Rayne Ambrose. Neighbors had recognized him immediately in the photographs Dad showed them, even though the pictures were over twenty years old. And if that wasn't enough proof, almost every one of the neighbors had added without prompting, "Your son looks a lot like Jax."

It gave Dorian a weird feeling in his stomach to think there was a Dorian doppelganger on the loose.

Rayne had been a widower, apparently, and his late wife's nearest relative, Naomi Stevens, had been the one to take Jax in after Rayne's car accident—at least until Pendragon had showed up with legal documents naming him Jax's guardian. Dad interrogated Naomi thoroughly, but she hadn't been able to tell them anything about Pendragon—or *Pendare*, as she called him. She got confused when asked how old he was and couldn't explain why no one had challenged the custody order.

"He used the voice of command on her," Dad told Mom over the phone.

"If the prisoner was correct about his age," Dorian heard Mom say, "he must be Philip Pendragon's son or one of his nephews. Did the Pendragon boys go to Bradley Prep? Sloane might know him."

"Doesn't matter who he is," Dorian's father had replied grimly. "If he's the last Pendragon, he's the clan leader—and he's got my nephew."

Dad wanted to take the investigation directly to Pendragon's house after finishing up in Delaware, but Aunt Ursula insisted he return to New York to deal with some crisis that had occurred on the eighth day. Not even Dorian's secret method of spying had enabled him to find out what had happened. Everything was *hush-hush* and *need-to-know* only. Aunt Ursula was called to an emergency meeting of the Table, and Dad had narrowly escaped being sent to the U.K. to deal with whatever it was that had everybody upset.

Dorian caught only one conversation between Dad and Aunt Ursula before she left for her meeting. "If the reports from Wales are accurate, this could be a crisis of epic proportions. That makes it more important than ever for me to catch up with Rayne's son," Dad told her. "If he's really sworn to the oldest Emrys girl, he's our best chance at finding her."

"Yes, I see the point, Finn." Aunt Ursula had been more terse than usual.

"Someone else can conduct the search in Wales. Only *I* can handle finding Jax."

There'd been a long pause, and for a few seconds, Dorian wondered if they'd walked out of hearing range. Then Aunt Ursula said, "Deal with it, then. And Finn—I *am* sorry about Rayne. I always hoped we'd get him back someday."

Dad was grief stricken that he'd located his long-lost brother only to find out he was dead. Dorian had never met Uncle Rayne, so he couldn't tell anyone why he felt so connected to his uncle—or at least connected to the *teenage* Rayne. Mom and Dad didn't know that Dorian had discovered why Rayne ran away from home a week before his sixteenth birthday, when he would've been expected to swear allegiance to Aunt Ursula. And Dorian wanted to keep it that way.

Sloane ran lightly up the steps to the house next to Pendragon's and rang the bell. Dorian mounted the stairs behind her.

The door was answered by an old lady with a cane who listened intently to Sloane's pitch about collecting money for sick children. The woman fetched her wallet and offered them twenty dollars so quickly, Dorian felt ashamed. But he accepted the bill, brushing his hand against hers to enhance his talent through physical contact with the subject.

"Thank you, ma'am." He handed the twenty to Sloane. "Do you know the guy who used to live next door?"

"Why, yes! Jax?" The old woman's face lit up immediately. "Or Riley?"

"Riley," said Sloane.

Finding Jax might've been Dad's first priority, but Aunt Ursula and Sloane seemed very interested in this Pendragon who'd turned up alive. He hadn't been a Bradley student, according to Sloane, but she knew acquaintances of the Pendragons, and *Riley* had been the name of their leader's son. "Where did Riley move to?" Dorian asked.

"I don't know. I'm sorry," the old woman said unhappily, the compulsion of Dorian's magic making her apologize for not being able to answer his question. "I wish I could tell you."

Dorian switched his focus. "Did you know them well?"

"Oh, yes!" Now she smiled. "Jax ran errands for me. And Riley fixed my electrical box so I could have a generator when the power went out. He wouldn't let me pay him, either."

Sloane tipped her head to one side and smiled. "I hope you don't think this is odd, but I have a gift for seeing things others can't. When I rang your doorbell, I had the strangest feeling there was a *presence* here. Something otherworldly."

71

Dorian delivered the question Sloane wanted him to ask. "Have you ever felt like there was an unexplained presence in your house?"

The old woman's face fell. "I did—for a long time. But I think she's gone now."

There didn't seem to be anything else this woman could tell them. Dorian nudged his cousin. "You're not going to keep the money, are you?"

Sloane plastered another smile on her face and reached out to grasp the old woman's arm. Her other hand slithered into an inner pocket of her jean jacket where Dorian knew she kept her honor blade. The nice old lady's face took on a slack, dazed look. Her mouth fell open, and her eyelids fluttered as the Dulac talent took hold of her memory. Dorian shuddered, imagining what was happening in her brain.

When Sloane released her, the woman stared for a moment at the wallet in her hand, then beamed. "How nice of you to return my wallet! I didn't realize I'd lost it!"

"Don't forget this." Sloane handed her the twenty.

The woman offered them each a five-dollar bill as a reward. Dorian refused, but Sloane stuffed hers into a pocket. *That's my future liege lady—not too proud to steal five bucks from an old lady.* Of course, Dorian didn't say that out loud. Instead he followed his cousin down the front steps like a . . . what? Loyal minion? Mindless henchman? Coward was more like it.

The only thing necessary for the triumph of evil is that good men should do nothing. That was the quote that had gotten Dorian's favorite teacher at Bradley Prep fired, he was pretty sure. Dorian thought debates about the rights and wrongs of the past and how they applied to the present made history class more interesting, but some of his classmates had complained to their parents, and one day, Mr. Brand was gone—replaced by a woman who taught strictly by the approved course outline.

"The Emrys heir lived in that house. Pendragon set up the generator for *her*, not the old woman," Sloane said to Dorian. "Emrys and Pendragon with an alliance. Very interesting. It's like the good old days with King Arthur and Merlin."

Right, thought Dorian. *Except in the good old days, Sloane's ancestor was on the same side as Arthur and Merlin.* "What's next?" he asked.

"We find them. Your father wants Jax, and Grandmother wants Emrys and Pendragon."

"What for?"

"For protection, of course. You know what Wylit almost did with the girl."

That explained why Aunt Ursula wanted one, but not the other. Dorian felt a chill. Nobody believed a random gas explosion had taken out the entire Pendragon family. Unexplained explosions were *always* assassinations. Dorian had that on good authority. But *who* had arranged it and *why* . . . no one had been able to prove that conclusively.

"Aunt Ursula seems really worked up about what happened in Wales on the eighth day," Dorian said. "Is that why finding these people is so important?"

Sloane stopped in her tracks. "What do you know about Wales?"

"What do *you* know?" Dorian tried to indicate with his eyebrows that he was in on all the juicy details.

"Nice try, Dorian." She saw right through his bluff. "I could tell you, but then I'd have to kill you."

"Jax! Hey, Jax! Wait up!"

Dorian and Sloane turned around. A boy ran toward them, waving his arms. "Hey!" He skidded to a stop with a frown. "Oh. Sorry, dude. I thought you were somebody else."

"You thought he was Jax Aubrey, didn't you?" Sloane elbowed Dorian.

Dorian stuck out his hand. "I'm Dorian Ambrose, Jax's cousin."

"Billy Ramirez." The boy stared at Dorian's hand like it was a dead fish, and Dorian dropped it, feeling stupid. "Do you know where Jax is?" Billy asked.

"We were hoping you could tell us," Sloane said.

"I haven't seen him since the night of the fire in town, when all that weird stuff happened," Billy replied.

Dad, who'd heard the boy call out Jax's name, crossed the street toward them. Albert Ganner appeared as well, drawn by their voices. "This is my dad," Dorian said. "Jax's uncle."

"Finn Ambrose." Dad put out his hand, and because that was expected from an adult, Billy took it.

Just like that, he was theirs.

"What happened the night you last saw Jax?" Dad asked.

Billy told them everything he knew, eagerly and rapidly— how a suspicious fire gutted a house in town and a hearse drove away with Jax inside. He told them about the unconscious man on the sidewalk who turned out to be the father of a kid from Billy's school. "Thomas wouldn't let anybody call 911, and then his dad woke up just as Riley got here—smelling like smoke, like he'd been *in* the fire—and the two of them almost had a fistfight on the lawn. Riley's friend, A.J., and some guy I think was A.J.'s dad broke it up. Riley told me to go home, and I haven't seen any of them since."

"What do you know about Riley Pendare?"

Billy gushed. "He's so cool! He's got this classic motorcycle and the most awesome tattoos." The kid launched into a description of the tattoos, but Dad cut him off.

"Do you have a way to contact Jax?"

"He doesn't answer my calls." Billy pulled a phone from his pocket. "He texts me, but he won't say where he is. It's like he and Riley are in some kind of"—a flicker of suspicion passed through the boy's dark eyes—"trouble." Dorian could almost see their compulsion over him waver. "Jax never said anything about an uncle," Billy said, frowning. "Just a grown-up cousin, Naomi. And her kids were real little." He took a step backward. "How did you say you were related?"

75

Dad looked at Sloane. "We need him."

"I see that." Sloane flashed her most winning smile. "Billy, you're going to be a big help to us." Then she nodded at Albert Ganner.

Billy took two more steps backward, but it wasn't going to do him any good.

Dorian looked away.

9

ON MONDAY, THE INTERNET connection at the cabin was finally activated, and Jax spent a couple hours searching through multiple (and often contradictory) Arthurian legends. "Was King Lear a member of the Round Table?" he asked Mrs. Crandall when she passed by with a laundry basket.

"King Lear is a character from Shakespeare, Jax."

"Yeah, well, I thought King Arthur was just a character, too," Jax muttered.

"Why do you ask?"

"The Kin woman at the Carroways' talked about somebody named Lear." That was his impression, anyway, that she'd been talking about a person. Of course, most of what she'd said made no sense.

Mrs. Crandall set down the basket. "Do you mean L-L-Y-R?" Mrs. Crandall took the mouse from his hand and hit the back button. "You're looking in the wrong place.

The Round Table is *us*—Transitioners. If you're looking for Llyr—who are Kin—you need to look *here*." She typed in *Welsh Gods and Myths* and selected the first result. A list of familiar names appeared. *Emrys. Wylit. Taliesin. Arawen. Llyr.*

"Gods?" Jax said incredulously.

"To the Normals of that time period, the Kin were powerful enough to be gods. The Llyrs in particular were set on enslaving the Normal population. They were the *reason* the Eighth-Day Spell had to be cast. The family has mostly died out by now, and what few of them are left are safely under lock and key very far away."

"Wait a minute. I know this." Jax rummaged in the box of notebooks and papers Melinda had brought from

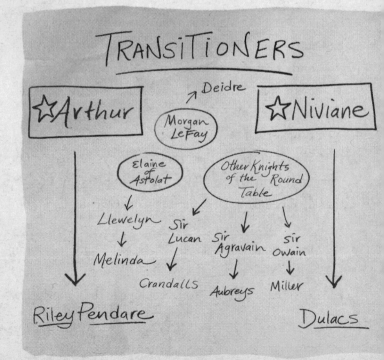

Riley's old house. And there it was—a rumpled piece of paper with a child's crayon drawing on one side, a chart in colored pencil on the other.

"What's that?" Mrs. Crandall asked.

"The cheat sheet Melinda gave me." Jax flattened out the creases with his hand. Melinda, his tutor in all things magical, had listed names of Transitioners and Kin when he was having trouble keeping them straight.

Mrs. Crandall surveyed the list and sniffed. "Melinda left out a few important people." Jax wondered if she was talking about herself.

Then he grunted "Huh," as he spotted *Llyr* listed under Kin adversaries. He hadn't realized how that name

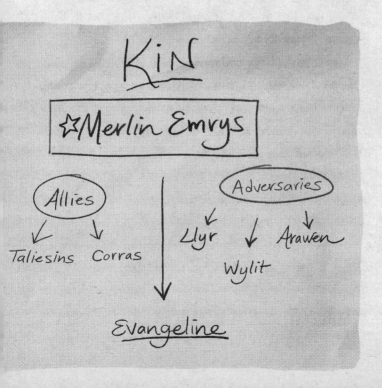

was pronounced. Melinda had told him those people were imprisoned in the eighth day—and also imprisoned *inside* the eighth day.

"What did this Kin woman say about the Llyrs?" Mrs. Crandall asked.

"Something about an oath," Jax said. "Her eyes went all funny when she talked to me, and afterward I don't think she remembered what she said."

That seemed to disturb Mrs. Crandall. She picked up a cell phone from an end table. "I'll text Deidre to see if she's heard of any unusual activity at the Oeth-Anoeth fortress. Thank heavens she's still willing to be our eyes and ears."

"I guess it's a good thing Deidre didn't really care about marrying Riley."

Mrs. Crandall looked up from the phone, startled. "Oh, Jax," she said. "I think she cared very much." Then she took her basket and headed for the laundry machine while Jax wondered why Deidre was still helping them if Riley had hurt her feelings.

Girls don't make any sense, he decided, turning back to the computer to read the descriptions of the so-called Welsh gods who apparently represented specific and very real Kin families. Like Transitioner families, each seemed to have a specialized talent for magic. *Emrys* was called a wizard, although Jax knew Evangeline preferred the term spell caster. Merlin Emrys was named as if he'd been the only one, but Jax had been told that Merlin was one of many Emrys leaders. *Taliesin* was a bard, and that matched what Evangeline said about their family. *Wylit* was a prophet, although it didn't mention him also being a complete whack job. Maybe that only applied to the Wylit Jax had had the misfortune to meet.

Arawen was supposed to be lord of the dead, and *Llyr* was the name of a weather god.

Then Jax froze, information buzzing in his head. *Imprisoned inside the eighth day. Under lock and key very far away. Unusual activity at the Oeth-Anoeth fortress.* The words of the Kin woman fell into his brain like a puzzle piece finally snapping into its correct spot. The phrase she'd whispered to Jax had been: *Oeth-Anoeth falls to Llyr today.*

"Whatcha looking at?"

Jax jumped out of his chair. Thomas Donovan stepped backward, hanging on to a bowl of cereal.

"Where'd *you* come from?" Jax yelped.

"The kitchen," said Thomas around a mouthful of Cap'n Crunch. "Duh."

"There's no outside door to the kitchen! What'd you do, climb in a window?"

Thomas shrugged unapologetically, as if that was a perfectly normal way to enter someone's house. Probably for him, it was.

Jax had begun to hope he wasn't going to see the Donovans at all. After Mr. Crandall's phone call on

Thursday, they'd gone straight to Vermont and the Carroways' to start their search for Addie. But apparently they'd decided to come in person to deliver a report. Jax heard the front door open, and Michael Donovan and Mr. Crandall walked into the living room with Tegan and A.J. trailing behind.

"You didn't tell me the trail was six weeks old, Crandall. And now you say she's *warded*? What're we supposed to do with that? From outside the house, I can't even smell the Emrys you've got living *here*, thanks to those things." Michael pointed to the wards.

"Are you telling me you've come up with nothing?" Mr. Crandall asked.

"There's the scent of Emrys at that house and on the Carroways themselves, but otherwise, nothing," Michael said.

Tegan glanced in Jax's direction and added, "The stink of Kin in that place is so deep, there's no telling who she left with."

Jax glared at her. Tegan never passed up a chance to take a dig at the Kin and seemed to especially resent the fact that Jax was sworn to one. Just then, his phone vibrated on the desk as a call came in. Of course, it was Billy. Jax hit the ignore button.

"Unless we happen to cross the girl's trail, there's nothing we can do," Michael said. "And if she's warded, there's not much chance of that."

Now Jax's phone buzzed repeatedly. He sighed and clicked into his texts to read them.

```
Billy: hey jax call me ive been kidnapped
Billy: they say they want to talk to YOU
Billy: this is so cool
```

"It has to be a trick," Mr. Crandall insisted. "To flush us out of hiding."

"Billy's a moron. It's probably a prank," said A.J.

Meanwhile, Tegan was looking online for news reports about missing boys. Jax wanted to tell her to get off his computer, but she was searching faster than he could have.

"Call the boy's house," Mrs. Crandall suggested.

"If he's really been kidnapped, they'll have police listening on the line," Donovan warned them. "They'll trace the call."

"Jax can call from his email account," Tegan said. "It makes voice calls."

"What are you doing in my email?" Jax demanded.

"Can they track us through the service provider?" Mr. Crandall turned on his son. "I *told* Riley it was a bad idea to get a connection."

"Not a problem." Tegan's fingers flew across the keyboard as she leaned forward, her tangled orange hair a curtain around her freckled face. "Jax is using a service provider out of New Zealand right now."

"I'm *what*? What'd you do to my computer?" Jax peered over her shoulder, totally mystified by the windows of codes and nonsense symbols whizzing by. He guessed she was hacking into computers on the other side of the world, and although he was surprised to see Tegan demonstrate this kind of skill, he probably shouldn't have been. "Are you stealing credit-card numbers while you're at it? Draining bank accounts?"

Tegan stood and offered Jax the chair. "Shut up and make the call."

"No," Mr. Crandall said firmly. "No calls."

"They can't trace this computer," Tegan insisted. "I've hidden it." Then she launched into an explanation involving *encrypted open proxy servers*, *dynamic IP addresses randomly routed through fifty different countries*, and *automatic port shuffling*. Mr. Crandall listened with his mouth hanging open, then looked at her father.

Donovan shrugged. "She's smarter than you and me combined, Crandall. If Tegan says it's safe, it is."

"This is a terrible breach of security," Mr. Crandall growled. "Riley picked a fine time to jump over seven days!" But he waved a hand, giving permission.

Mrs. Ramirez was delighted to hear from Jax. She exclaimed about how much Billy had missed him and how Jax was welcome to visit anytime. The more she talked, the more everybody in the room relaxed, because no way was this the mother of a kidnapped boy.

"Can I speak to Billy?" Jax asked.

"Billy's at golf camp. He won a scholarship after someone saw him play at school. I always knew he had a gift for it," Mrs. Ramirez said. "His father and I are so proud of him."

The Donovan twins glanced at each other. "Billy almost knocked himself out swinging a golf club in gym class," Thomas whispered. Tegan nodded.

Mr. Crandall made a *cut* gesture, and Jax ended the call as fast as he could. "Someone's altered her memory," Mr. Crandall said.

"Dulacs," A.J. agreed. "It's gotta be."

"Why? What's the Dulac talent?" Jax asked.

Everyone stared at Jax like he didn't know the name of the U.S. president. "Dulacs can change a person's memory," Mrs. Crandall said.

"Like Miller Owens?" Miller had been one of Riley's vassals working undercover among their enemies, and Jax had experienced firsthand the unpleasantness of having Miller's memories stuffed into his head. Specifically the memory of pain.

"No," said A.J. "Miller could *insert* memories, but you knew they weren't your own. The Dulacs can change what you remember and believe. They can change who you are, practically."

Jax felt a chill throughout his body. "I gotta call Billy,"

he said to Mr. Crandall.

Mr. Crandall looked around the room unhappily. He was used to sharing his opinion—loudly and repeatedly. But Riley usually decided what was right for the clan, and that wasn't going to happen today. "Go ahead," he said finally.

Jax entered Billy's number into the computer. After several rings, a familiar voice answered. "Yeah?"

"Billy? It's Jax."

"Jax? This isn't your number."

"I'm calling from my email. Are you okay?"

"From your email? Cool! I've never tried—"

"Billy, are you okay?"

"I'm fine. But I'm so *mad* at you! A secret day of the week? Why didn't you tell me?"

"Where are you? Were you kidnapped or not? Who's got you?"

"I'm in New York City, and, well, I was *sort of* kidnapped. But it's not that bad. They explained why they needed me, and I agreed to go with them. This is so cool!"

Mr. Crandall made a twirly gesture next to his head.

Jax wasn't sure. This sounded pretty normal for Billy. "Who are *they*?"

"Your relatives."

"My cousin Naomi kidnapped you?" Maybe Mr. Crandall was right.

"No. The relatives on your dad's side."

Coldness swept through Jax's body again. "I don't have any relatives on my dad's side."

"Yeah you do. That's why we want to get you on a video call. Because they need to show you their tattoos. And they want to see yours."

Mr. Crandall yelled some more about what a terrible idea this was. Shouting seemed to make him feel better about being stuck with the final decision. "Arnie," his wife quietly interjected into his tirade, "we need to know for certain who has the boy. If he was kidnapped, it's because of us. We're responsible for what happens to him."

Mr. Crandall muttered unhappy words under his breath and pointed his finger in Tegan's face. "Are you *sure*? And don't bother telling me about proxy port decryptions."

Tegan cringed at his mangled terms. "Not even the government could trace this call," she assured him. "Maybe, if they put all their resources on it, they could track the connection over six months. But only if it was in constant use."

"Keep it short then," Mr. Crandall barked.

Thomas laughed. "Less than six months, Jax. Got it?"

A.J. and his father rearranged the furniture so Jax could sit in front of a blank wall that gave no clue to his location. Jax stood off to the side and watched.

His dad had lied to him. Outright, barefaced lies.

There was a lot of stuff his dad had failed to tell him—such as what the tattoo on his wrist meant. Or how Jax had a 50 percent chance of being a Transitioner. He'd never mentioned his life was in danger, or that he'd signed custody of Jax over to a stranger in the event of his death. Jax had spent months fuming over all those untold truths. But because he'd learned that his father had wanted to protect Evangeline, he'd slowly been getting over it.

Now there were lies on top of the omissions, and Jax was seething with rage.

A hand fell on his shoulder. "Are you okay?" Mrs. Crandall asked.

"Yeah. Fine."

She sighed, and Jax belatedly remembered her truth-telling talent. "Put two chairs in front of the computer," she told A.J. "I'm sitting with him."

"You don't have to," Jax said.

"I'm not letting you face this alone."

So he ended up sitting with Mrs. Crandall in front of the computer, his stomach flipping somersaults while an electronic bleeping signaled the incoming video call. His hand shook as he clicked ANSWER on the screen. Then he expelled his breath in relief, because it was just Billy.

"Dude!" they said at the same time.

"You jerk!" Billy exclaimed. "An eighth day. You should have told me!"

"I couldn't! Are you okay? Your parents think you're at golf camp!"

"I know, right?" Billy laughed. "Hey, where's Riley?"

Jax didn't need the chopping gestures from Mr. Crandall and A.J. to know he wasn't supposed to talk about Riley. "Billy, are they keeping you prisoner?"

"If you can call it that when they've got a *huge* TV and a billion channels." Billy dropped his voice to a whisper. "And one of your cousins is *hot.*"

"Dude," Jax protested. "Ew."

"Look, they want to talk to you. But later, I want to know *everything.*"

Billy moved offscreen, and several people took his place. A man and a boy sat down in front of the screen. A woman and a girl stood behind them.

Jax had to grab the edge of the desk. The man looked so much like his father, it hurt.

Before speaking, the man held up his left hand so Jax could see his mark. It was identical to his dad's mark—probably done by the same tattoo artist. The boy showed his mark too, but Jax barely glanced his way. The man absorbed all his attention.

"Jax, I'm Finn Ambrose, your dad's older brother. I know this must come as a shock, since Billy tells me you didn't know your father had living relatives."

Not as shocking as you kidnapping Billy. Jax wanted to

say that, but he couldn't make his mouth work. And it would've been a lie anyway. Seeing the ghost of his father in this man's face was more shocking than Billy's abduction.

Because Jax had been kidnapped twice since becoming a Transitioner, but he'd never seen anybody come back from the dead before.

10

"THIS IS MY SON, Dorian," Finn Ambrose said from the computer screen. "My wife, Marian, and my daughter, Lesley."

The woman showed her mark. "Hello, Jax. My word, you certainly are an Ambrose. Anyone can tell by looking at you."

Lesley, who was probably about fourteen years old, gave a brief wave but didn't show her mark. Dorian said, "Hi, Jax," and stared through the screen like he was surprised by what he saw. Still stunned by the whole situation, Jax couldn't think at first why the boy looked so familiar, and then he realized where he kinda-sorta knew him from. The mirror.

Oh, crap. He looks like me. Jax found his voice. "My name's Aubrey, not Ambrose."

"No," said Finn. "That's a made-up name. It might be on your birth certificate, but you're an Ambrose. Although

I do need to see your mark to be sure."

Jax tried to swallow, but his mouth was too dry. *My name is a lie, too.* He held up his left hand for the webcam.

Finn and Dorian leaned close to the screen. "Is that an eagle?" asked Dorian.

"Rayne let someone change your mark?" Finn sounded shocked.

Jax glanced at A.J., who shuffled his feet. It was supposed to have been a falcon, but A.J. thought a bald eagle was *cooler*. "No, Dad wasn't . . ." Jax broke off even before Mrs. Crandall nudged him. He didn't want to explain how his dad had died before he was marked, leaving him totally ignorant of his heritage.

"But you have the inquisitor talent," Finn pressed him. "That's what I've been told."

By who? "Yeah," said Jax.

"The Ambrose talent wasn't affected, then." Finn sat back in his seat.

The Ambrose talent. Was he *really* Jax Ambrose? That name sucked. Suddenly he was furious again. "You kidnapped my friend."

Finn laughed. "We *invited* your friend to come to our home in Manhattan and help contact you. He seems to like making an adventure out of everything, though."

Jax had to admit this was true. But Mrs. Crandall said, "Kidnapped or not, his mother doesn't know where he is."

"We couldn't tell his parents the truth." Finn eyed Mrs. Crandall through the screen. "Are you going to identify yourself?"

She held up her hand. "Gloria Kaye," she said, which was the first time Jax had ever heard her family name instead of her married one.

Finn nodded, as if he wasn't surprised. "And is Pendragon going to show himself?"

Holy crap. They not only knew about Riley, they knew who he really was.

"You'll be dealing with me today," Mrs. Crandall said. "And we won't be negotiating at all unless you send the Ramirez boy home."

"We'll do that after you bring my nephew to New York."

"My dad told me he was an only child," Jax said. "He told me he had no family. He changed his name. Why would I want to have anything to do with you?"

A look of pain crossed Finn's face, and his wife put a hand on his shoulder. "There was a disagreement between Rayne and his father many years ago," Marian Ambrose said. "It causes my in-laws a lot of grief that Rayne held a grudge so long. But there's no reason you should go without a family because a teenage boy once got really mad at his parents."

Jax thought his father must've been a lot more than *really mad* to do what he'd done.

"Send Billy home, and we'll discuss letting you meet Jax," said Mrs. Crandall.

Dorian spoke up. "Billy's okay. I promise. He's been hanging out with us, playing our video games, and asking a million questions."

"He's pretty annoying," Lesley muttered. "I vote we send him back." Dorian elbowed his sister, and she shoved the back of her brother's head.

Jax watched them tussle with a strange twinge. *I have cousins.*

Meanwhile, Finn called out, "Billy, do you want to go home?"

Billy shouted from somewhere nearby. "No! I want to stay until Jax gets here." Finn smiled as if that proved his point.

Mrs. Crandall shook her head. "Meaningless. You didn't just lie to Mr. and Mrs. Ramirez. Somebody altered their memories. You're an inquisitor, and your wife is a healer. So who manipulated the Ramirezes? Sounds like a Dulac talent to me."

Finn folded his hands on the desk. "We *are* Dulac vassals."

Jax blurted out a curse word. Not only were these people his relatives, they were Riley's enemies.

Finn raised his eyebrows at Jax's outburst and cleared his throat. "I don't know what you've been told, Jax. Probably a lot of lies. But we're not just vassals to the

Dulacs, we're family. My mother, your grandmother, is a Dulac. She's the sister of our clan leader."

Suddenly a hand grasped Jax by the back of his neck and yanked him out of his chair. Mr. Crandall sat down in his place and thrust his left hand at the screen for the Ambroses to see. "Arnold Crandall. You'll be dealing with me now, and I'm not letting Jax anywhere near you."

"You have no claim to him," Finn replied coldly. "I understand Pendragon has custody papers, but he's barely old enough by law to be Jax's guardian, and he's not a blood relative."

"Don't talk to me about the law. *Your* liege lady assassinated *my* liege lord and all his family." Mr. Crandall spoke through clenched teeth. "You aren't fit to have custody of Jax."

Standing to one side, Jax had a view of the monitor but could no longer be seen by the web cam. He watched his uncle dismiss his family. Dorian alone hesitated, peering at the corners of the screen as if he might be able to see where Jax had gone before clearing out of the way. Finn Ambrose pulled his chair to the center and spoke directly to Mr. Crandall. "Ursula may never have gotten along with Philip Pendragon, but she had no reason to want his bloodline wiped out. Someone else did that."

"Lies," said Mr. Crandall.

Finn pointed at Mrs. Crandall. "Ask Kaye. I'm telling the truth."

Mrs. Crandall said nothing.

"Your current liege lord is very young, with no family. That makes him vulnerable," Finn went on. "On behalf of the Dulacs, I'm prepared to offer him the protection of our clan. Furthermore, I understand you're providing shelter to an Emrys girl who took on my nephew as her vassal even though he's far too young for it. We can overlook that breach of courtesy if she will also place herself under our protection."

Jax felt that sweeping cold again, and his knees wobbled. *They know about Evangeline. They know everything. How? Who told them?*

"This conversation is over." Mr. Crandall stabbed the power button so hard, he tipped the monitor off the desk.

Jax watched it fall without moving. He didn't react when Tegan caught it, or when Mr. Crandall started pacing the room like a caged tiger, cursing and roaring about murderers and criminals. He watched everyone in the room as if through a fog.

Once again, he'd led the enemy straight to his friends. Billy was in the hands of ruthless killers. They wanted Riley and Evangeline, too, and worst of all, Jax was related to them. *That man looked just like my dad. That boy looked like me.*

Mrs. Crandall put an arm around Jax's shoulders and turned him away from the living room. She propelled him into the kitchen and planted him in a chair. Then she ladled soup into a bowl and plunked it down in front of him. "Eat. It's the best remedy for shock."

He stared at the soup without interest. "Did Riley know?"

"Of course not. All Riley knew about your father was that he acted as an informant for *his* father."

In the living room, A.J. was telling Mr. Crandall to *calm down and think things through.*

Jax turned his hand over and stared at his wrist. "Why didn't he recognize my mark?"

"Riley wasn't even fourteen when he went into hiding and not much involved in clan business. He wouldn't have met the Ambroses or had occasion to see their mark. They're a small family. Your grandfather moved here from the U.K. and married into the Dulac clan. Trust me, Jax. Riley had no idea."

She seemed very certain. And Jax realized why. "You and Mr. Crandall knew."

For a long minute, Mrs. Crandall was silent. Then she said, "Arnie didn't know until just now. But yes, I knew from the start."

11

"I'M SORRY, JAX, BUT I couldn't tell you. I took an oath."

Jax stood up and turned his back on her, putting his hands on the kitchen counter and staring blankly at the open window where Thomas had climbed in.

"Riley's father swore me to secrecy back when he first started using your dad as an informant—when Rayne was a teenager. Only a few of Philip's vassals were trusted to meet him, and we swore to protect his identity because his family was looking for him."

"Why? What happened between them?"

"Philip may have known. I never did. When Rayne approached Riley last year, it'd been almost a decade since I'd last seen him, but I was still bound by the oath I made twenty-five years ago. And when you came to us—well, the oath chose to protect you as well. I couldn't tell Riley or even my husband who your father really was."

Jax turned around. "What do you mean, *the oath chose*? How does an oath choose?"

"Magic follows rules of its own, Jax. You saw that with the basketball and the bike. You saw it when Riley went to next Grunsday, instead of Evangeline coming to Thursday. An oath will demand obedience in ways you can't antici-pate." Mrs. Crandall gently turned Jax back toward the table. "Now that your secret is known, I seem to be released, which is a relief." She put him back in front of the soup.

"This is why you wanted to get rid of me," Jax said. He'd been a poisonous snake among them, a danger to the last remaining Pendragon, his identity protected against Mrs. Crandall's will by a twenty-five year-old oath. "I *heard* you trying to convince Riley to send me away."

She didn't look surprised that he'd been eavesdrop-ping. "Jax, I had your best interests at heart. I assume your father trusted you with us because Riley was hiding from the Dulacs, just like he was. You were only supposed to be in our care a few months, until we could confirm you were a Normal. I didn't consider it a problem. But then, you weren't a Normal, and worse, you swore on with Evangeline. When Riley said he wanted to claim his seat at the Table, I realized the correct thing to do was to send you back to your Normal relatives as soon as possible. If we came out of hiding, it would only be a matter of time before someone recognized your mark and informed the Dulacs, which is the last thing your father wanted. As it is, I'm pretty sure Deidre has guessed who you are. She *must* know the Ambroses, and your mark is only slightly different."

Jax remembered Deidre's warning to be careful. "Yeah, she knows." Why hadn't she told Riley? *She must think he already knows. 'Cause what kind of idiot shelters his enemy without knowing it? When Riley finds out . . .* Jax was surprised to discover how much Riley's opinion mattered to him. "When my"—Jax swallowed hard—"my *uncle* said the Dulacs had nothing to do with what happened to the Pendragons, was he telling the truth?"

"I detected no lie in anything he said. But your uncle may not know the truth." Mrs. Crandall put a hand on Jax's arm. "None of us will judge you for what they did, Jax. I certainly don't, and I lost family in that explosion, too."

"Were you there?" Jax croaked. The Pendragons had been killed at an engagement party for Riley's sister, when the entire family and their vassals had been gathered in one place.

"No. Arnie and I were at home because A.J. had the chicken pox. Melinda happened to be on her honeymoon, so she wasn't there either. Out of the family members and vassals present, there were only two survivors."

"Riley and Miller Owens," said Jax. Mrs. Crandall nodded. "I didn't know your name was Kaye. That's like Sir Kay, right?" He'd been reading about the Knights of the Round Table most of the afternoon, and Sir Kay had been Arthur's foster brother.

Mrs. Crandall said, "My family has served the Pendragons a long time."

That was for sure. "What are we going to do about Billy?" he asked.

"Leave that to us."

Jax didn't like that answer. Not when he was the cause of the problem.

Jax ate enough soup to satisfy Mrs. Crandall, then slipped off. When he passed through the living room, Michael Donovan was criticizing Mr. Crandall's proposed plan. "I'm not a fan o' the frontal assault," Donovan was saying, "but if you're set on confronting them head-on, you're gonna need the voice of command."

"We won't have Riley back for two more days. Are you suggesting I leave the Ramirez boy with them that long? Who knows what they'll do to his head in the meantime?"

Jax skirted around the edge of the room and upstairs to the bedroom he was sharing with A.J. and, normally, Riley. There were two beds, both claimed by the older boys. Jax had been making do with a sleeping bag on the floor until Riley disappeared. Then he'd thrown the dirty clothes off Riley's bed and taken it over.

Now he flung himself down and stared at the ceiling in misery.

Who the heck am I? Jax Aubrey or Jax Ambrose?

He was surprised by how quickly the answer came to him.

Names change. That's what Evangeline said. But I'm her vassal no matter what.

He didn't have fifteen hundred years of tradition behind his vassalhood, like Mrs. Crandall, but he knew who he was.

Dad told me a lot of lies, but what do I know is true?

When his father was in danger, he'd asked Riley to be Jax's guardian. Not his own brother.

So I'm not going to trust Uncle Finn. But Mrs. Crandall didn't detect any lies in what he said today.

And Jax's uncle said they would let Billy go when they got Jax.

What would Riley do?

That was easy. When Evangeline and Jax were abducted by Wylit's vassals, Riley had delivered himself bound and gagged into enemy hands, just to get close enough to rescue them.

Riley had traded himself out of loyalty to his friends. Put it like that, and Jax's course of action seemed clear.

A.J. snored so loudly, Jax didn't have to be quiet sneaking out of the room. He was a little more careful in the loft, because Mrs. Crandall had sharp hearing. But downstairs,

Donovan was sleeping on the sofa, and he made almost as much noise as A.J.

Jax didn't know where the twins were. *Probably burglarizing neighboring houses.*

He rode his bike five miles down the mountain road to the convenience store/bus station, where he purchased a ticket for the last bus departing for New York City, the time of which he'd checked on his computer earlier that evening. Nobody in that smoke–filled place questioned why a boy was buying a ticket for a bus mainly used by late-shift employees from local casinos and resorts, but Jax took a seat in the back of the bus and curled up out of sight, in case someone thought better of it and decided to intervene. When the bus started moving, he dozed with his head resting on his backpack.

About an hour into the ride, someone pushed his legs off the seat and sat down beside him. "Wanna doughnut?" Thomas offered him half a slightly squashed bear claw.

Jax banged his head on the window sitting up. "What the—where—have you been on the bus this whole time?"

"What d'ya think?" Thomas said. "We dropped in from the sky?"

"We?" groaned Jax.

Tegan appeared over the back of the seat in front of him. "You really don't observe your surroundings much. It's a wonder someone hasn't robbed you already."

Jax grabbed at his backpack, just to check, and glared

at her. "How'd you get to the bus station?"

Tegan shrugged. "We 'borrowed' some mountain bikes from a cabin down the road. What d'ya think you're doing?"

Jax held up his fingers one at a time, counting the steps. "One, meet my uncle. Two, get Billy sent home. Three, make like my dad and run away from them."

"That's your plan?"

"It's better than Mr. Crandall making a *frontal assault*. Someone'll get killed." Jax had seen that happen when Riley and Miller had rescued him and Evangeline on the pyramid, and he didn't want to see it again. Not when he could prevent it. He didn't know how Riley was going to react when he found out who Jax really was, but Jax knew he'd have an easier time facing his guardian if he cleaned up his own mess.

Especially since it was Jax's stupidity that got them into the *last* mess.

Of course, the Donovans had helped create that one. Jax glared at the twins. "Why do you care, anyway? Don't you have stuff to do? Banks to knock off? People to swindle?"

Thomas looked at his sister and grinned mischievously. "Well, *I* didn't want to go to New York City, but Tegan made me come. She was worried that without someone looking out for you—"

"I have an idea." Tegan silenced her brother with a

threatening glare and pulled out her phone. "Which is more than either of you two numbskulls can say. I'm calling Smitty. I'm sure he's in New York."

"Oh," said Thomas. "That *is* a good idea."

"Who's Smitty?" Jax asked.

"An associate of my dad's." Tegan searched through her contacts.

An associate. She meant another crook. "Great," Jax said sarcastically. "I'm sure I'll love him."

Tegan hit the dial button and grinned just like her brother. "Actually, I'm pretty sure you'll hate him."

12

DORIAN'S TEACHER WASN'T HAPPY when his father yanked him out of class in the middle of the day, especially since he had finals tomorrow. But she didn't protest too loudly. All the teachers at Bradley Prep knew that when students were pulled for *family business,* it was best not to argue.

Besides, Dorian wasn't the only student pulled out early this week—or missing entirely. *There's something big going on,* Dorian thought, *and other clans know about it even if no one's talking about it. They can't all have long-lost relatives coming into town.*

Jax was waiting for them at the Port Authority bus station, just where he'd told Dad he'd be. He was taller than he looked on the video call, about two inches taller than Dorian. He carried a backpack over one shoulder, and, as they approached, he scowled at them from beneath tousled hair, looking tough and angry.

Dorian, wearing his school uniform with his short hair neatly parted and combed, felt like a geek by comparison. There was definitely a resemblance between him and Jax, but all it did was make Dorian look like the shorter, weaker, dweebier cousin.

"Where's Billy?" Jax demanded.

"At home," Dad said.

"Making my sister watch *Doctor Who*," Dorian added. Lesley's public school had already let out for the summer. There weren't a lot of things to be envied about Lesley's life, but having a long summer vacation was one of them.

"That's not what we agreed on over the phone," Jax said.

"If I put Billy on a bus today," Dad replied, "you'd have no reason to come home with us. You'd get on the bus with him."

Jax's scowl deepened. Dorian guessed that was exactly what Jax had been planning.

"Your aunt's making dinner to celebrate your homecoming. Please come with us." Dad extended his hand in welcome and bumped into a boy in a hoodie who was too busy on his phone to pay attention to where he was going. Dorian watched his father grin and bear the collision instead of snarling at the kid the way he normally would've done. When Jax didn't move, Dad shot Dorian a look. This was why he'd been yanked from school: to make Jax feel safe and welcome. But what was Dorian supposed to say?

Run, Jax. If I had any guts, I'd tell you to run.

But Dorian didn't have any guts, and in the meantime Jax had apparently made up his mind. "All right," he said. "Let's go."

On their way to the street exit, they passed through a knot of people. A girl with gnarled curls of orange hair pushed her way between them, elbowing Dorian in the ribs and knocking the backpack off Jax's shoulder.

"Watch where you're going, jerk," said the girl.

"Same to you," Jax replied, picking up his backpack.

Dad hailed a taxi, and the boys climbed into the back together while Dad sat in front with the driver. Jax flung himself into the far corner and looked at Dorian. "You always dress like that?"

Dorian realized he'd been wearing the same clothes on their video call. "It's my school uniform." Jax wrinkled his nose and turned away to look out the window.

When they arrived at Central Park West, Dad discovered his wallet was missing. "Pickpockets," he growled, waving down the doorman to come pay the cab driver.

Jax, meanwhile, tipped his head back to stare at Dorian's apartment building. "Holy crap!" he exclaimed. "Is this the place from *Ghostbusters*?"

"No, that's down the street," Dorian said. Jax glanced at him skeptically, but it was the truth. "This one belongs to the Dulac clan."

"The building's full of Dulacs?" Jax stopped in his tracks, like he was about to enter a vampire lair. "How many of them are there?"

"Not just Dulacs. Their relatives and vassals, too," Dorian clarified. "Everyone who lives here is part of our clan." Everyone who worked here, too, down to the doorman and the security guards. But Jax looked spooked enough, so Dorian left that out. "There are a few buildings along Central Park owned by Transitioner clans. You can tell which ones because they're some of the oldest—no electronics in the elevators—but they all have solar panels on the roofs. To make and store electricity for the eighth day."

"You don't try to hide it?" Jax asked.

"Why would we?" Dorian and Jax looked at each other, equally confused. Then Dorian remembered the dinky little house where his cousin had been living with the Pendragon guy. Flying under the radar and hoping not to be discovered. "It's perfectly safe here," Dorian assured Jax. As if anyone would mess with the home base of the Dulac clan!

Once inside, Dad patted down his pockets and cursed under his breath. "Keys are gone too," he muttered.

"I'll have to report that, Mr. Ambrose," said the doorman, using his own key to let them on the elevator. "We can't afford any lapses in security, especially now."

"Of course not," Dad agreed, but he jerked his head toward Dorian and Jax with a warning look, as if to remind the doorman not to talk about the big secret in front of the children. Dorian practically ground his teeth together in frustration. *Does everyone know except me?* Then the elevator jerked to a start, and Dad made the effort to paste a smile on his face for Jax's benefit. "Welcome home," he said as the elevator climbed to the fifth floor. "This is where your father and I grew up."

Jax had abandoned his swagger now and seemed completely overwhelmed. He faltered when they entered the Ambrose apartment, looking at the vaulted ceiling and the crystal chandelier as if he must be in the wrong place. Then he spotted his friend and heaved a sigh of relief. "Dude! You had me worried!" Jax left Dorian and Dad behind to hurry down the steps leading from the foyer to the sunken living room.

Billy stood up to meet him, grinning. "I told you I was okay."

Jax grinned back, heaved his backpack off, and hit Billy playfully in the arm with it.

All the color ran out of Billy's face. He staggered backward.

Mom crossed the room swiftly, putting herself between the two boys. "No roughhousing in the living room," she said, brushing a hand against Billy's elbow. Then she grabbed Jax's face with both hands and planted a big kiss on his head. "Jax, honey, we're so happy to have you here." She pushed his hair out of his face and looked him in the eyes. "Did those people take good care of you?"

"Yeah, I'm fine." Jax pulled out of her hands. Dorian was impressed. Not many people got away from Mom that easily. By now, Billy was seated on the sofa again with the game controller, perfectly at ease.

"Lesley, have you said hello to Jax?" Mom prompted.

Lesley glanced up from the game she was playing with Billy. "Hello, Jax."

Dorian saw the exact moment when Jax noticed what was different about Lesley. His eyebrows came together, and he opened his mouth to say something.

Not here. Not now, Dorian begged silently. *Please don't embarrass her.*

Then Jax clamped his lips shut and went back to looking around in disbelief at the apartment and the view of Central Park from the picture windows.

"I hope you're hungry," Mom went on. "I may have gone a little overboard, but it's not every day we celebrate a family reunion. Your grandparents will be here any minute."

Panic crossed Jax's face, and Dorian couldn't stand it anymore. "You know, Mom, we kinda forced Jax into this. Maybe we should stop acting like everything is normal and give him a break. Do Gran and Gramps *have* to come right away?"

Jax shot Dorian a look of gratitude while everyone else responded at the same time.

"Ya think?" That was Lesley, agreeing with him.

"Dorian . . ." A low growl from Dad.

From Mom with hands on her hips: "Do *you* want to call your grandparents and tell them to stay home?"

Billy put down the game controller and looked up at Jax, mortified. "Does he mean you only came because of *me*? I was trying to help. Don't you remember how many times you told me you wanted to be with a family? Well, *this* is your family."

That was when the grandparents burst in, Gramps yelling, "Is he here? Is the boy here?"

Gran wore her pearls. And her diamonds. And a pressed linen suit. She'd had her hair permed for the occasion. "Dear heavens!" she exclaimed. "Wait until I tell Ursula. He looks just like Rayne!" She reached for Jax with both hands, intending to hug or kiss him.

Jax scrambled behind Lesley's armchair. "You're the one who's a Dulac, right? You're not touching me."

An awkward silence fell over the room, and Dorian cringed.

Gran straightened her shoulders with dignity. "Now I *know* he's Rayne's son. He needs a haircut," she said in an aside to Mom, who nodded vigorously. Then she turned back to Jax. "Young man, I don't know what you've been told, but Dulacs do *not* use our talent on everyone we meet and certainly not on family members!"

Dorian stared at the floor. That was a lie. A big, fat lie.

"Did Pendragon come with him?" Gramps shouted. He

must have had his hearing aid turned off again. The volume of his voice wiped out the charm of his high-class British accent.

"He came alone," Dad answered in an equally loud voice. "But we'll get the custody worked out, don't worry."

"Whoa." Jax put up his hands defensively. "I'm here for *a visit*. If you send Billy home tomorrow morning, I'll agree to stay a couple days. That's it."

"I'm not going home tomorrow," Billy protested. "I want to stay for the eighth day!"

"You can't get into the eighth day," Jax said.

Dad cleared his throat. "Actually, there's a way to bring him . . ."

"I know how to do it," Jax interrupted. "But I don't want my friend in danger. *Bad things* happen on the eighth day."

There was another moment of silence, and then everyone burst out laughing.

"Bad things?" Gramps hollered. "What's he mean—*bad things*?"

"Well, I've occasionally made bad business deals on the eighth day," Dad admitted.

"I've heard some bad bands at Rockefeller Center," Lesley added.

"I've had bad meals at Sardi's," Gran said. "All their best chefs are Normals."

Jax looked more confused than ever. Billy crossed his arms and said, "I'm staying."

"O-kay," Jax said, frowning. "We'll stay until Thursday."

But Dorian could practically see the wheels turning in his cousin's head. Jax wasn't planning on staying a second longer than he had to.

13

DORIAN DIDN'T THINK THE "family reunion" could get any more awkward, but dinner proved him wrong. Jax ate plenty but responded to all questions with one-word answers or stony silence. Billy spilled information like a waterfall, but Billy didn't know anything he hadn't already told them.

Jax tensed when asked a question about Riley Pendragon or the Emrys girl. And despite his obvious discomfort, Dad and Gramps kept bringing them up. Dorian wondered if this persistent interest in Jax's guardian and liege lady had to do with the *crisis of epic proportions* Dad had predicted after whatever it was that had happened in Wales.

Occasionally, without warning, Gramps or Dad would throw inquisitor talent behind some question. Each time Jax deflected it expertly.

Jax relaxed only once, and it was thanks to Lesley.

Gramps had just blurted out, "What kind of name is *Jax*

anyway? Spelled with an *x*, they tell me? I've never heard of such a thing."

Lesley covered her face with her hands, then peeked between her fingers at Jax. "Officially dying of embarrassment now. If you want to run for the door, I'll cover you."

Jax broke out in his first genuine smile.

Because Lesley was so honest. So Normal.

After dinner, Dad and Gramps disappeared into Dad's office for about an hour. Dorian tried to sneak off and listen at the door, but Mom snapped her fingers at him and motioned for him to stay put. Meanwhile, Gran tortured poor Jax with a photo album, showing off pictures of his father until it looked like Jax was about to climb the walls to get away from her. Finally, Dad and Gramps reappeared, and Mom rescued Jax, nudging the grandparents toward the door and sending the boys to their room. Dad pinned Dorian with another meaningful look as they were leaving.

Yeah, yeah, he got the message. He was supposed to bond with Jax.

Billy took his borrowed pajamas and went into the bathroom to change, and Dorian groped for something to say. "I hope tonight wasn't too bad."

Jax turned cold eyes on him. "Best dinner with kidnappers I've had yet."

Bonding fail.

"Your sister doesn't have a mark," Jax said.

Dorian nodded unhappily. At least he'd waited until they

were alone. "She's a dud."

"What does that mean, exactly?"

Was he kidding? "It means she never transitioned to the eighth day," Dorian said. "She has no talent."

"No eighth day, no talent, right?" Jax said as if repeating something he'd been taught, instead of something every Transitioner knew. "You can't take her there with handcuffs?"

"We can, but it doesn't help. She still hasn't developed any talent."

"Maybe she needs a mark," Jax suggested.

"Which one? Mom's or Dad's? Giving her the wrong one would ruin any chance of her developing talent, and our clan artisans refuse to take the risk. It's a sore subject around here. Dad's disappointed he couldn't give Aunt Ursula more than one talented child for the clan." Dorian didn't like remembering the dark days in the Ambrose family when Lesley passed her thirteenth birthday without transitioning. Dorian had transitioned two years ago, at age ten, which shamed his older sister all the more.

"Ursula's the Dulac leader, right?"

"Yeah. She's Gran's older sister." Dorian couldn't stand it anymore. He had to ask. "Is it true you're sworn to Kin? To an Emrys?"

Jax's scowled returned. "Yeah."

That was creepy and fascinating all at the same time. "Did you really kill a Wylit?"

"Not me personally."

"But you were there, right? What was it like?"

"People were trying to murder me, my liege lady, my guardian, and most of the world. What do you think it was like?" Billy came back into the room, and as if by agreement, Jax and Dorian dropped the subject. "Where am I sleeping?" asked Jax. "The floor? 'Cause I'm tired and want to go to bed."

That seemed unlikely, but Dorian answered, "Billy's got the lower bunk. You can have the top. I'll sleep on the futon. It folds out."

"Fine," said Jax, throwing his backpack onto the top bunk. "G'night."

"Are you kidding?" asked Billy. "It's barely ten o'clock."

Jax wasn't kidding. He climbed into the bunk fully clothed and didn't say another word to anyone. Billy sighed and got into the lower bunk, moving stiffly.

Dorian pulled the futon out into a bed and turned out the lights. Once it was safely dark, he opened two dresser drawers. From one he removed pajamas, and from the other he carefully extricated a journal that was hidden beneath old school papers, awards, and report cards. Covering the journal with the pajamas, he carried the whole bundle with him to the bathroom.

He didn't intend to change his nightly routine, especially now.

Hunched over the sink, Dorian read yesterday's entry. Then he opened to the next blank page and wrote:

Yesterday matches what I remember.

Today I met Jax. He came to NYC to trade himself for his friend. But Dad won't send Billy home, and of course Billy refuses to leave. Jax says they'll stay until Thursday, but I bet he'll try to talk Billy into making a run for it sooner. Maybe he can do it, but he's up against Mom's and Sloane's talents, so I doubt it.

I like Jax. He's smart and brave. He doesn't trust us, but he was nice to Lesley anyway.

Nobody tried to change Jax's memory today.

I don't think anyone changed my memory today.

When Dorian returned to his room with the journal wrapped up in his clothes, he slipped it back into its drawer, on top of the one he'd found a year ago in his grandparents' apartment, the one that had belonged to Uncle Rayne.

Then he lay down on the futon to watch and listen.

Half an hour later, a phone lit up on the top bunk. It flickered like Jax was moving through screens, maybe checking his messages. In the quiet of the room, Dorian could hardly miss it when Jax suddenly started cursing under his breath.

14

JAX STARED AT HIS phone.

```
Thomas: sent of emrys on yr uncle
```

The message was hours old, texted only minutes after Thomas had bumped into Uncle Finn at the bus station. Assuming Thomas meant *scent*, he was saying that Finn Ambrose had the smell of an Emrys on him. And since Jax knew the man had been nowhere near Evangeline, it meant he'd been in contact with Addie.

Jax swore under his breath with every curse word he could think of and texted both twins.

```
Jax: tell crandalls asap
```

A few seconds later, replies appeared.

```
Tegan: already did.
Thomas: crandalls really ticked at u.
```

Yeah, Jax knew that. He'd just scrolled through a total of seventeen messages from all three Crandalls.

```
Tegan: I walked around your building. cant
smell girl. is it warded?
Jax: maybe
Thomas: you & billy breaking out 2nite?
```

That had been Jax's plan: to grab Billy and get out in the middle of the night. Now he'd have to scrap that.

```
Jax: cant. if addies here I have to stay &
find her
Tegan: did you get the keys?
```

Jax hadn't had a chance to see what Tegan had shoved into his backpack. A quick search turned up a ring with several keys on it but no sign of his uncle's wallet. Well, the Donovans *were* thieves.

```
Jax: got em. thanx
```

There was no reply. Jax guessed the twins were having a night on the town, courtesy of Finn Ambrose's wallet.

That was okay. They deserved it. Picking Uncle Finn's pockets had been Thomas's idea. And when Jax had first arrived in the city, before he'd called Billy to arrange the meeting with his uncle, Tegan had introduced him to her dad's friend Smitty. Together, they'd set up a fallback plan Jax hoped they'd never have to implement—but which he was glad to have in reserve.

He turned the phone off, wishing he could call Riley and get him to command Billy out of this place. Mr. Crandall was right. These people had done something to Billy. His friend was geeky, not stupid. Even if the Ambroses had fooled him into thinking they were nice, Billy should've picked up on Jax's urgency to leave. And the way he looked like he was going to pass out when Jax hit him with the backpack . . . Something was wrong with him, although Jax couldn't prove it with Dorian watching them like a creepy little owl.

Jax was certain Dorian was awake and spying on him right now. *If I thought I could get Billy out of here tonight, I'd jump you and tie you up with your stupid school tie, cuz.*

But now Billy wasn't his only responsibility. If there was a chance Addie was in this building, he had to search for her. Jax fingered the keys Thomas had stolen from his uncle's pocket. Both the doorman and Uncle Finn had looked upset about the loss of these keys. *I need to search tonight, before they replace the locks.*

He lay in the top bunk waiting for Dorian to fall asleep

and occasionally stabbing himself in the palm with the keys to stay awake. It had been a long night already, facing his relatives and fending off their questions. Looking at photos of his father as a young teen had almost made him sick. That Dulac woman—*my grandmother?!*—had shown him pictures of Dad skiing, boating, and golfing with people whose existence his father had denied.

You never took me skiing, Dad. Not even once.

Here was an instant family—the kind Jax had been longing for—and he wanted nothing to do with them. Lesley seemed okay, but the rest of them creeped him out. They'd asked about Evangeline and Riley repeatedly during that torturous dinner, and he'd had to repel their inquisition talent. *Not good. Not good at all.* Jax wished he could be long gone before Riley and Evangeline reappeared tomorrow night, but if Addie was here, he couldn't leave without her. *And if I wait long enough for Addie to appear, I run the risk of Riley coming to New York to "rescue" me.* Jax was going to have to scope out the situation, figure out if Addie was here at all, and then call the Crandalls and make sure they *and* his guardian stayed in the mountains. It was one thing for Riley to present himself to the Table in front of all the Transitioner clan lords; walking up and ringing the doorbell of Ursula Dulac's lair was another thing altogether!

Jax waited long past the point when he was sure Dorian was asleep. He needed the adults to be asleep too. When his phone said 2:15 a.m., he removed his honor blade from inside his backpack and strapped the sheath around his waist. He hadn't worn it on the bus, and bringing it out for dinner seemed more hostile than necessary. No one in the Ambrose family had been wearing a blade, although some Transitioners carried them concealed. But now he was going to need it to enhance his talent. He lowered himself from the top bunk and removed his shoes. Stocking feet were quieter.

Slipping out of the bedroom and across the apartment, Jax let himself into the fifth-floor hallway and approached the elevator. Instead of the normal up and down buttons, there was a keyhole. He fumbled through Uncle Finn's keys until he found two of the right size. One didn't work, but the other caused the elevator shaft to whir into mechanical life. When the elevator arrived, Jax opened the gate—something he'd only seen on television—and went in.

Now what?

He drew his dagger and balanced it on his left palm. *I need to find Addie, if she's here.* Just because Uncle Finn had been in contact with her didn't mean she was in the building. And Addie wouldn't be *anywhere* until Grunsday. But Jax could sense Evangeline's location even on days she wasn't physically present. If Jax was an Emrys vassal, he technically served Addie too.

Before he knew what he was doing, Jax punched the

button for the first floor. The elevator shivered down five floors and shuddered to a halt at the lobby. Jax froze, wondering what to do next. Hard-soled shoes rapped across the tiled floor as the doorman started over to investigate why the elevator had come down but no one was getting off. Jax's eyes fell on the separate elevator button labeled B with its own keyhole. *Down, down, down,* pounded his heart.

He shoved the other key of the right size into the lock, stabbed the B button, and the elevator lurched downward. His head passed out of sight just as shiny black shoes appeared on the lobby floor above him.

The elevator stopped with a jerk and a clanging sound at the basement level. Jax opened the gate and cautiously stuck his head out. From the elevator, he could turn left or right and travel a short distance in either direction before reaching a corner. No one was in sight, but he heard dull footsteps on concrete flooring not far away—coming from the right. Slapping a random elevator button with one hand, Jax shoved the gate closed from the outside and took off *left* in his stocking feet. Gears ground loudly as the elevator started up again, covering any sound Jax made as he pelted down the short hallway and right at the corner. A much longer corridor lit by yellow fluorescent lights stretched in front of him. There were doors spaced along the walls on either side, and Jax fingered the ring of keys as he ran.

This door. This key.

He fell through a doorway midway down the corridor and whirled, pulling the door closed behind him. A few seconds later, footsteps passed outside. Jax glanced at the key in his hand, in awe that he'd randomly picked the right one for this door.

When he was scared and desperate, his talent guided him. On math tests, not so much.

He groped for a light switch. Tubular light bulbs flickered eerily, then came on one by one, illuminating tables and computers as well as a solid steel rack of cages and a bank of refrigerators with glass doors. Jax screwed up his face in distaste as he approached, but the closer he got, the more he was sure. The refrigerator shelves were filled with trays holding vials of blood.

Or tomato juice. *But I'm thinking blood.*

Painted on the wall above the refrigerators was something that looked like the symbol Evangeline had taught A.J. *Aha!* These people did know how to create Kin wards and might be using them to shield Addie, as well as this laboratory. But there were no wards on the other three walls, which was strange, because Evangeline said a place needed warding on all sides for the protection to work. Then Jax turned to look into the cages and leaped back with a startled yelp.

A dozen faces stared back at him.

Furry flat faces with black, glittering eyes.

Brownies.

Some chattered at him, baring their sharp incisor teeth. A large brownie with a tuft of white fur on its head shook the cage door like a jailed criminal. Its thin, dexterous fingers gripped the bars, and Jax noticed that brownies had hands, not paws.

What were brownies doing here on a Tuesday? Or rather, a very early Wednesday morning? Weren't they eighth-day creatures?

The solid metal sides of the cages were marked with wards similar to the single one painted on the wall of the lab. Even the tops of the cages were marked, as well as the placard on the front of each barred door where someone might normally stick a label. Were the wards holding these eighth-day creatures in the seven-day world? Jax glanced at the vials of blood. What was going on here?

Did it matter? *Using animals in experiments sucks and so do the Dulacs!*

Jax unlatched the cages and threw open the doors. The brownies leaped to the floor. Jax planned on opening the corridor door next, giving them access to the rest of the basement. Hopefully they'd make like rats and disappear into nooks and crannies until Grunsday, when they could transition back to their own timeline. But instead, the brownies all made a beeline across the lab toward the opposite wall . . . and vanished into the cinder blocks.

Jax gaped at them. The last brownie, the one with the white-topped head, paused to look back. Its round little

ears twitched and rotated, like the creature was considering Jax with interest. Then the brownie curved the fingers
of its hand toward its body before diving into the wall.

Did that thing beckon me to go with it?

Jax ran his hands over the cinder blocks. Rough, cool,
a little damp—just what he expected until he reached the
spot where the brownies had disappeared. Those blocks
felt spongy. Jax pushed firmly, and his hand vanished into
the wall.

After a few seconds of groping blindly, he pulled back
his hand and examined it. No harm done.

Jax stuffed his head in.

Weird. When he was outside, he couldn't see his hand
inside. With his head inside, he couldn't see his body outside, but he *could* see the rest of the lab—dimly. It was
like peering through tissue paper, if tissue were elastic
and smooth to the touch. Straight ahead, a narrow tunnel
passed through the wall and into a room full of furnaces.
He took an experimental breath. There seemed to be air.
Should he go in? What if it closed behind him and he
couldn't get out?

The brownie had motioned for him to follow.

"What the heck," he muttered, and climbed in.

The first thing he did was confirm he could get back
out. Then he stood up and took a couple of steps forward.
There was some give to the substance around him, but he
couldn't push through it except for that one spot on the

laboratory wall. When he passed into the furnace room, he couldn't get out there, either. He had to follow the path of the tunnel, which went all the way through the room like a tube in the kiddie play zone of a Chuck E. Cheese. Only this one was transparent and made of magic instead of plastic.

The tunnel led him across the furnace room before swerving through a wall and into the basement corridor. Here Jax's hand, groping along the side of the tunnel, felt a spot where the elasticity of the walls gave way to an actual hole. He didn't stick his arm through to test it, though. There was at least one other person in this basement who might see it if he did; Jax had heard the footsteps. He was pretty sure he was invisible as long as he kept all parts of his body inside this tunnel. The brownies had disappeared when *they* entered it. However, he also suspected that from inside, he couldn't see anyone on the outside—the same way he couldn't see the rest of his body with his head inside the tunnel. There might be a guard walking down the corridor right now, and Jax wouldn't see him.

On a hunch, Jax took out his phone and wasn't surprised when it wouldn't turn on. Phones didn't work on Grunsday because computer chips didn't recognize the eighth day. Was the tunnel outside the seven-day timeline? It was charged with magic. Jax knew that much. The sensation was similar to the time Evangeline had given him a spell to hold. His whole head buzzed with talent.

Jax grinned. Whatever this tunnel was, it was perfect for searching the basement unseen. *Do the Dulacs know it's here?* Jax wondered. With an entranceway right in their research lab, how could they miss it? He had to assume they knew.

The tunnel cut across the corridor and into another room, and Jax's heart rate sped up. There was a bed, a sink, and a toilet. This was a cell. It appeared to be empty, but if his theory was correct, anyone outside the tunnel was in a different timeline than he was. Of course, if this was Addie's cell, she wouldn't be there on a Wednesday anyway.

Jax had no sense of an Emrys presence, but maybe the magic in the tunnel was blocking his vassal bond. When he patted along the wall, his fingers slipped into another hole. He got down on his knees and thrust his hand through experimentally, but he couldn't even see his hand groping around. He needed to exit, he realized, and then perhaps he'd be able to detect whether Evangeline's sister had been imprisoned in this room.

No sooner had he stuck his head through the hole than a hand grabbed him by the hair and yanked him bodily out. He hollered and fought, but somebody stronger than he was dragged him to his feet and pushed him against a very solid cinder-block wall.

Jax looked up into a face he'd hoped he would never see again.

15

"AUBREY?"

Angus Balin must've been just as surprised as Jax, because his grip loosened. Jax wrenched sideways and dived for the tunnel entrance. He bashed his forehead on the wall of the cell first, but found the hole and stuffed his head and torso inside.

Hands clamped around his ankles.

Jax clawed at the tunnel walls, but there was nothing to hold on to. Balin hauled him backward, then wrapped his huge hands around Jax's neck and shook him like he was no bigger than a kitten. Jax kicked and pounded his attacker with his fists. He might as well have been hitting the wall.

"I'm going to enjoy choking the life out of you, Aubrey." Balin's grip tightened. Jax panicked and clawed at the hands around his neck. Then a puzzled look passed over the man's face. "But how did you get in here?"

Jax pointed desperately at the wall. Balin eased up on Jax's throat enough for him to gasp, "Tunnel . . . invisible . . ."

Balin shifted his grip to Jax's T-shirt and felt with one hand down the wall.

Jax sucked in air. "Are they holding you prisoner? You can escape!" Surely Balin would want to escape more than he wanted to choke the life out of Jax.

"That's a brownie hole," Balin growled. "I can't get in there. How did you?" Grabbing Jax with both hands, Balin thrust him in the general direction of the tunnel. Jax's head and shoulders banged repeatedly against the wall while Jax flailed helplessly. An arm went in and part of a shoulder; then Balin pulled him out again.

When Balin touched the wall, however, it was solid. He cursed and threw Jax off to one side, standing between him and the only means of escape.

Jax sucked in lungfuls of air. "It's because you're a Balin," he croaked. Magic didn't work on the Balin family. They had heads like rocks.

"No, it's not. That's a *brownie hole*," Balin repeated. "Humans can't use them. What *are* you?"

"I'm human!" Jax protested. "Riley said so!" He'd *asked*, back when all this started.

"Whatever you are, I'm going to take my time killing you. I've got nothing else to entertain me."

"You don't want to kill me." Jax scrambled to his feet

and backed away. "I've got . . . Look, I've got . . ." He tried to fish the keys out of his pocket, but his hands were shaking.

This was how the Ambroses knew so much about Jax—that he'd been on the pyramid and that he was Evangeline's vassal. Angus Balin had told them. Jax had spent days in a car driving to Mexico with this man, who'd despised him on sight and offered repeatedly to *take him out back and shoot him*. It was the older brother, John Balin, who'd protected Jax, trying to recruit him for Wylit's cause right up to the moment Jax had betrayed him.

"You killed my liege." Balin reached for him with his big, meaty paws.

"I didn't kill your liege!" Jax protested, dodging. "He fell down the side of the pyramid!"

And got stabbed by Riley's dagger.

Which was in Evangeline's hand.

Probably better not to mention that.

"You played your part," Balin growled.

"I defended my liege lady! Just like you defended your lord. We each did what we had to, according to our oaths." Jax kept backing up, but the cell was small and lacking in places to shelter from maniacs. "How'd you end up here anyway? I thought you were . . ."

"Dead?" Balin bared his teeth in an unfriendly grin. "Captured by Morgans?"

One of those. But Jax lied. "Got away. Back to your

clan." There'd been more Balins at the farmhouse where they'd temporarily held Jax—and other families sworn to Wylit. They had been the strangest group of Transitioners Jax had ever met, more like some weird cult than a clan like Riley had, or Deidre, or what he'd seen of the Dulacs.

"I had to make sure my people got away," Balin said. "That required sacrifice."

Balin had traded his freedom for the safety of others, Jax realized, and he was startled they had that in common. "You probably want to join them," he said, retrieving the keys from his pocket. "I can get you out of here."

Interest flickered in Balin's cold eyes, but he said, "Even if you have a key, there's no keyhole on this side."

"Yes, but—"

"I'm here because of *you*," Balin interrupted. "They've kept me here for days, all so Ambrose can stick me with drugs and ask more questions about *you*. Where we found you. Who you lived with. What I know about your liege lady and where she might be now. It's all been about *you*, Jax Aubrey. Breaking your neck will be a real pleasure, if it ends their questions."

"They won't be happy to find me dead in here with you," Jax pointed out.

Balin laughed. "I don't care what they do to me." He grabbed Jax by the shirt. "They're not going to let me out of here alive anyway. Because of your father."

Jax didn't bother to fight as Balin drew him closer.

"Are you the one who ran his car off the road?"

"No," said Balin. "He did that himself. When he saw he couldn't shake us, he gunned the engine and drove right over the railing, into the river."

Jax shook his head. "No."

"Yes, boy. We wanted him alive. He knew where the Emrys girl was."

Jax's knees gave way. Balin laughed nastily and threw Jax up against the wall, where he slid to the ground bonelessly, feeling light-headed.

Dad drove his car off the road deliberately.

He left me.

Balin moved in a leisurely fashion, surveying Jax as if deciding what it would be fun to do next. Jax felt such despair, he was tempted to let him do whatever he wanted.

But his head buzzed with leftover magic from the tunnel, refusing to let him succumb to grief. What had Balin said? They kept asking questions about Jax's liege lady and where she might be.

They have Addie and they want Evangeline. They want both Emrys heirs.

It's not about a stupid family reunion at all.

Jax held up the ring of keys shakily. "We have a common enemy. The Dulacs and the Ambroses."

"They're not your enemy. They're your blood relatives."

"My loyalty is to my liege lady, not my relatives," Jax

said. "They want her, and I have to protect her. Let me go, and I'll use the brownie tunnel to go around and unlock your door."

"You expect me to trust you?"

"I'll swear an oath on my bloodline."

"Miller Owens swore his loyalty to my lord and still betrayed him! You people always find a way to slip your oaths." Balin spoke as if the words left a bad taste in his mouth.

"Miller was immune to oaths"—which was what made him such a valuable double agent, Jax thought—"but I'm bound to mine, just like you are to yours. Let me go, and I swear to come back and free you."

Balin *did* have people worth living for. Jax could see it in his expression. There was probably a Mrs. Balin and some mini-Balins—a horrible thought, but maybe useful now. A moment later, the man's face returned to stone. "It's no use. There are guards in the hallway. They aren't going to let you walk up and open the door."

Guards. More than one. That made it tricky, invisible tunnel or no invisible tunnel. "It won't be tonight," Jax admitted. "But I'll figure out a way to get you out of here."

"What's in it for you? If I let you go, why would you come back?"

"I'd be compelled to." That was the point of making an oath.

"With no time limit to complete the bargain?" Balin

laughed shortly. "I see your trick, you worthless little—"

"I think there's another prisoner down here," Jax blurted out. "I might need help getting her out. There's no trick. I let you out. You help me and my friends."

"Define *friends*."

Balin was bargaining now. That was a good sign. "Billy Ramirez," Jax said. "He's a Normal who's here with me. And—" He didn't want to specifically name Addie. Who knew if Balin would agree to help an Emrys? "Anyone who's part of my clan. You don't hurt us. You help us if we need it, and we all get out of here alive."

"Stand up," Balin demanded.

Jax climbed to his feet and faced Balin, who held out his hand expectantly. "They took my blade. I'll have to swear on yours."

"You're not going to stab me, are you?" Jax drew his dagger warily.

"Tempting. But I have a clan to return to—and another liege lord who needs me."

Another Wylit? *Oh, great.* But Jax kept that thought off his face as Balin wrapped his hand around Jax's with the dagger between them.

16

MINUTES LATER, JAX STAGGERED through the magic tunnel so weak-kneed he kept losing his balance and falling into the walls.

After his encounter with Balin, he'd almost turned around and gone back the way he'd come. But if he didn't finish exploring tonight, when would he? They might change the locks because Uncle Finn's key had been stolen, and he needed to find where they were keeping Addie so he could make a move to rescue her as early as possible on Grunsday. *If* they were keeping Addie. Jax was beginning to doubt his own judgment. So many things he'd believed had turned out to be a lie.

Dad. Pain pierced his chest. His father had sacrificed himself for what . . . to keep the secret of Evangeline's location? Was that why he'd left his son an orphan?

Balin could've been lying. He'd wanted to hurt Jax. It might've been a lie.

The tunnel took him upward through a wall thicker than the others and out to the street where it continued toward Central Park, shimmering and transparent. It did not return to the building. His exploration of the basement was over, and he'd only seen a small section of it.

Jax stood in the middle of the multilane Central Park West, staring up and down the street. He didn't see a single car. Even if this was the middle of the night, there ought to be traffic. On a Grunsday, he would see cars frozen in transit, stuck in the moment between Wednesday and Thursday. But inside the tunnel, he saw no cars at all.

Where am I in time?

He looked around and felt the tunnel walls with his hands, but didn't find any of the puckered openings he'd come to recognize as exits. There might be one in the park, though. He could keep looking. He could escape into Central Park, call the Crandalls, and say, "Come get me." He could let the adults take over and handle the whole thing.

But Michael Donovan's words came back to him. *I'm not a fan o' the frontal assault, but if you're set on confronting them head-on, you're gonna need the voice of command.*

That was how Riley and the Crandalls would handle this: an armed assault with Riley leading the charge. The last time they'd done that, to rescue Jax and Evangeline, they'd lost Miller. Who would they lose this time? One of the Crandalls? Riley?

Jax had to admit he didn't want to see the Ambroses hurt either. Whether he liked them or not, they were his relatives.

It was going to take cleverness, not a frontal assault, to locate Addie and get her and Billy out of that building before Riley and his vassals came charging in. If Jax wanted his guardian and his liege lady to remain safely out of Dulac hands, he was going to have to handle this himself. He'd go back and make the Ambroses believe they were winning him over. It was like the thing with John Balin all over again. Jax rubbed his face wearily. His dad had been a sort of spy. Jax was only following in his footsteps.

Returning to the building, he wished the buzz of magic in the tunnel gave him physical energy, because he was bone tired. *I've got to get back before they miss me. If they know I've been snooping, they're never going to trust me.* The need to hurry drove him forward. He passed by Balin's cell with only a glance. He could see the room but not the man—which reminded him that emerging from the tunnel would be tricky. Jax might step out and find himself facing an armed guard. Or his uncle.

Once again, he relied on his talent, waiting by the exit that opened into the basement corridor until instinct told him to climb out. He glimpsed the back of someone turning a corner twenty yards down the hallway and took off in the other direction, toward the narrow end of the building and the elevator. But he couldn't resist looking back over his shoulder as he ran. There was absolutely no sign of the tunnel—no shimmery wall, no puckered opening. It was completely invisible. Jax counted the doors on the hallway to fix the location of the brownie hole in his mind.

He made it into the elevator, punched the button for the fifth floor, and pressed himself into the corner to avoid being seen by the doorman while passing through the lobby.

The Ambrose apartment was just as quiet and dark as when he'd left. He crossed the foyer, then stopped at the steps to the sunken living room and pulled off his socks. They'd served him well for silence, but now they were filthy. It wouldn't do Jax any good to have left and come back in secret if he tracked dirty footprints across Aunt Marian's snow-white carpet.

He crept down the hall to Dorian's bedroom and turned the knob. There was no movement inside, and before entering, Jax checked his phone to see how long he'd been gone.

It was 2:23 a.m.

He'd been gone eight minutes.

That was impossible! Even if his time in the tunnel didn't count—even if that had been outside the normal timeline—it had taken way more than eight minutes to get down to the basement, explore that lab, and talk Balin out of killing him.

Dorian sat up on the sofa bed. "Jax?" he said sleepily. "What're you doing?"

Jax shoved the phone into his pocket and pulled the door closed behind him. "Bathroom." He climbed into the bunk and lay real still. Dorian remained sitting up for a few more seconds, then flopped down again, apparently satisfied with his explanation. After all, Jax had only been gone eight minutes.

Impossible though that seemed.

It felt as if Jax had barely fallen asleep when Uncle Finn banged on the door. "Breakfast in ten, boys! Dorian, you need to be at school by eight thirty."

"School?" Dorian whined. "But Dad! Jax is here and—"

"You've got finals, Dorian."

"You're still in school?" Jax rubbed his bleary eyes. He'd assumed Dorian wore that stupid uniform because he liked showing it off.

"Bradley Prep goes year round," Dorian said glumly. "With three weeks of vacation four times a year."

Billy's head popped out from the bottom bunk. "Sucks to be you, dude." Then he grinned at Jax, his dark hair standing up from his head like a bird's crest. "Right, Jax?"

"Yeah." High on Jax's to-do list today was getting Billy alone and trying to break through that happy, clueless bubble he was in. It was freaking Jax out.

The smell of eggs, bacon, and homemade waffles rejuvenated him. Once again, Aunt Marian had put out a spread. Well, Jax had no objections to eating if she wanted to cook. He was on his second waffle when Aunt Marian exclaimed, "Jax, what happened to your head?"

Startled, he put his hand to his forehead and felt around.

"You've got a lump as big as an egg," said Lesley.

"Hit my head on the bathroom door in the dark," Jax said. He suspected there was another knot on the back of his head, but luckily it was hidden under his hair. He couldn't very well say the door had ambushed him from both sides.

"Jax, look at me," his aunt said. When he did, she placed her hands on both sides of his face. Immediately, the pain of his bumps and bruises subsided, and a wave of energy washed over him. That was followed by a sensation of safety and love, like hot chocolate after playing in the snow or a welcoming fire after being drenched by rain.

Jax pulled out of her hands and scowled at her. She had tried this yesterday too, when they'd first met. She kissed him and cast some calming magic over him, which he pushed out of his mind instinctively. He had to keep an eye on his aunt. She was trickier than she looked.

Aunt Marian frowned back at Jax as if she'd done nothing wrong. "You really shouldn't fight what's good for you." And then, as if it explained his unmannerly behavior, she added gently, "I'm told you lost your mother at a young age. To cancer, was it?"

"Yes," he replied in a surly voice, picking up his fork. He didn't know whether he was annoyed by her nosiness—or angry because it suddenly occurred to him that this might have been another of his dad's lies. Except he remembered . . . "My dad took us all around the country, visiting doctors, but never at doctors' offices. Always at their homes. I was only four, but I knew that was weird. Now that I look back, I guess they were healers, huh? Like you."

"Very likely," Aunt Marian said sadly. "But I've never met a healer who could cure a chronic illness or aggressive cancer. We're best at alleviating symptoms and accelerating the healing of injuries."

Jax glanced at Billy, who was wearing a borrowed long-sleeved shirt and shoveling eggs into his mouth. Lesley leaned across him, reaching for the syrup, and Billy cringed away from her, pulling his left arm into his lap.

Uncle Finn cleared his throat. "Jax, you and I have an appointment with my liege lady at nine this morning."

"What if I don't want to?"

Next to Jax, Dorian stiffened, while Lesley, across the table, caught Jax's eye and shook her head. Realizing he might have crossed the line, Jax turned toward his uncle.

Finn Ambrose gazed at him expressionlessly. "If your

liege lady asked you to do something, what would you do?"

"Do it," Jax replied.

"My liege asked to meet you," his uncle said evenly.

"Okay. Sorry, sir."

His uncle accepted the apology with a nod. "And tonight," he announced to everyone, "we'll take Jax out on the town. I'm not sure he understands what an eighth day in Manhattan means."

Billy looked up with an excited grin, and Lesley asked eagerly, "Me too?"

"You too," her father agreed.

Just then, Dorian bumped a glass of orange juice. It spilled between Jax and Dorian, over the edge of the table and onto the floor. Aunt Marian ran to the sink for a sponge. Dorian grabbed a handful of napkins and dragged Jax under the table to help him.

"Ursula Dulac," hissed Dorian under the table.

"Yeah?" whispered Jax.

"Don't let her touch you." Dorian stared at Jax with big, worried owl eyes, and then his mother appeared beside them. They blotted juice and said no more.

17

THE ELEVATOR SHIVERED ITS way up the building toward the twentieth floor and the penthouse. Jax stood stiffly beside his uncle, trying not to conjure images of Darth Vader taking Luke Skywalker to meet the Emperor.

Uncle Finn glanced at his nephew and sighed heavily. Jax rolled his eyes. He knew he didn't measure up to Ambrose quality control. Aunt Marian had even offered to "help" him with his hair. Jax assumed she'd already provided that service for Dorian, who left for school with his hair parted and combed flat against his head. But no matter how geeky Dorian was, his frantic warning under the breakfast table had bumped him up a notch in Jax's opinion.

What does it say about Ursula Dulac that her own clan is afraid of her?

As with the basement, reaching the penthouse required a special elevator key. Uncle Finn had borrowed his wife's keys this morning, but Jax knew it was only a matter of time before all the locks were changed, making the ones he had useless.

On the twentieth floor, the elevator opened directly into the foyer of the penthouse apartment. A man was waiting for them.

"Daniel," said Jax's uncle in greeting.

"Finn."

They followed Daniel past a library with floor-to-ceiling bookshelves and leather chairs, where a maid in an actual uniform was dusting. Jax saw a dining room with a table large enough for twelve, and a living room with a high ceiling and two fireplaces, before he was led out to a glass-walled terrace overlooking Central Park.

Jax had been picturing Ursula Dulac as a cross between Cruella De Vil and the evil queen from *Snow White*. Since meeting his grandmother yesterday, he'd added pearls and a perm to his mental image. But the woman sipping coffee on the terrace was nothing like he'd imagined. She was supposed to be older than Jax's grandmother, but she didn't look it. A headband held back her loose gray hair, and she was dressed casually in a blouse, slacks, and sandals.

A teenage girl with long, honey-brown hair sat beside her, busily texting on her phone. She wore the same school uniform as Dorian, except with a short skirt instead of pants. It didn't look as dorky on her.

Jax worried that Ursula Dulac would offer her hand for him to shake and he'd have to refuse. His uncle would be furious. But instead she laid her coffee aside and smiled without getting up. "My sister was right. He looks like Rayne."

"Jax." Uncle Finn laid a hand on Jax's shoulder. "This is my liege lady and your great-aunt, Ursula Dulac."

"Hello, ma'am," Jax said.

Ursula indicated the tall man who'd escorted them and the teenaged girl. "This is my son Daniel and his daughter, Sloane, my heir."

Daniel nodded briefly. The girl dropped the phone into a pocket of her school blazer and raised her left hand with a cool and distant smile. "Nice to meet you, Jax."

Jax raised his own left hand automatically, showing his mark. Ursula and Sloane both leaned forward to get a better look, then glanced at each other. "That's not the Ambrose mark," Ursula said.

Uncle Finn sighed. "It's been altered."

"It's a bald eagle instead of a falcon," Jax said. "The guy who did it said they were both birds of prey and it didn't matter." Why was everyone making such a big deal about this?

"*It didn't matter?*" repeated Ursula. "What kind of cut-rate amateur did Rayne take you to? Does he have the Ambrose talent, Finn?"

"I believe so, although I haven't had the chance to—"

"He wasn't cut rate." Jax surprised himself by defending A.J. "And he wasn't an amateur."

Uncle Finn gripped Jax's shoulder and squeezed, which Jax interpreted as: *Don't interrupt me, and don't talk back to my liege lady.* Jax closed his mouth but didn't apologize.

"I'll look into it," Uncle Finn said. "Perhaps it can be repaired."

It's not broken. Jax glared at his uncle but didn't speak the thought out loud.

"Hmm." Ursula nodded toward the empty chairs across from her. "Please, sit down." She picked up her cup and held it out to her son. "Daniel, ask Maria to pour me another. Finn takes his coffee black, I think. Jax, would you like something?"

"No, thank you." Jax chose the chair farthest away from her.

"Sloane, anything for you?" Daniel asked.

"Iced tea," the girl said. "Thank you, Daddy."

Jax watched curiously as the man went off to wait on his mother and his daughter, while Uncle Finn addressed Sloane. "No finals this morning?"

"Not until eleven." Sloane turned to Jax. "You'll like Bradley."

Jax thought she meant a person until his uncle said, "I'll have to reserve a place for him in the fall."

"After you've tested him," Ursula murmured.

They were talking about sending him to Dorian's

school, Jax realized. "What is this place? A prep school for Transitioners?" Could there be enough Transitioner kids to fill a school?

Sloane looked slightly insulted. "Not *any* Transitioners," she clarified. "Not riffraff."

A mental image of the Donovan twins as the dictionary definition of *riffraff* popped into Jax's mind at the same time that his uncle explained, "It's a very small, elite school. Personalized attention. Flexibility for our needs. The perfect thing to catch you up."

"Lesley doesn't go there?" While Dorian was shuffled off to class in his uniform this morning, Lesley had thrown herself on the sofa to watch Billy play Zelda. She wore an SPCA T-shirt and running shorts, her dark hair in a messy, crooked ponytail.

Uncle Finn's face darkened a bit. "Lesley wasn't happy there," he said gruffly.

Because she has no talent, Jax guessed. He wanted to tell these people that he'd only agreed to a short visit and had no intention of going to their snobby school. But he didn't. *I have to play along. I've got a mission here.*

"Jax, I understand your father never told you about your heritage," Ursula said.

"No, ma'am. And nobody's told me why he left, either. There must've been a reason."

"Not a very *good* reason." Ursula pursed her lips.

"Rayne didn't get along with his father. They were like oil and water."

"Wasn't there a blow-up over a girl?" Jax's uncle frowned. "I can't recall exactly."

"It wasn't just that. They argued over Rayne's grades and his behavior, even his hair." Ursula's gaze wandered toward Jax's head, and he fought the urge to comb his hair with his fingers. "I suppose Rayne believed running away was the ultimate act of rebellion. I don't know why he never came back and made amends like a man. Except . . ." Here she peered intently at Jax. "He left before taking his oath as a vassal and by all accounts flitted around aimlessly thereafter. What kind of business did he run? Stealing secrets from small, unimportant people and selling them to other small, unimportant people?"

Jax bristled. He wanted to say, *My dad worked for Philip Pendragon, and* he *wasn't small and unimportant—or you wouldn't have had him killed.* But he kept his mouth shut.

"Taking the oath of allegiance would have given Rayne a sense of purpose," Ursula went on. "It was something he desperately needed, and something I suspect he never found. But, you, Jax, are too young for such an oath. Never mind that by heritage, you were promised to me—what was the Emrys girl thinking, taking on a thirteen-year-old boy?"

Promised to *her*? Jax gripped the seat of his chair with

both hands. "She saved my life. If she hadn't sworn me on, I'd be dead right now."

"She should have released you when the danger was past."

"I didn't want to be released!"

"Ja-a-ax," Uncle Finn growled, dragging out his nephew's name.

Jax flinched. How many times had Jax heard his father say his name exactly that way? *Ja-a-ax . . . can you explain this 43 percent on your science test? Ja-a-ax . . . why is your bed full of Halloween candy wrappers?*

Daniel returned to the terrace with the coffee and iced tea. "Thank you, dear," Ursula said. Then she returned her attention to Jax. "Although the circumstances are unusual, you can be our intermediary with the Emrys girl. We want to bring her here, where she'll be safe."

Aware of his uncle's gaze and not wanting his father's voice resurrected again, Jax spoke carefully. "Thank you for your offer, Mrs. Dulac, but she's already safe."

Ursula smiled. "You can call me Aunt Ursula. Mrs. Dulac is not accurate." Sloane snickered.

Jax didn't know what was so funny. Wasn't she married?

"This point is not negotiable," Ursula went on. "A month ago, one unbalanced Kin lord nearly destroyed the seven-day timeline. There are others out there, *dangerously sane ones*, who have similar designs. We can provide the girl with protection—and she need not be alone anymore, the very last of her family."

With difficulty, Jax managed not to show his alarm on his face. Why did they say Evangeline was the last when they knew she wasn't?

Had they killed Addie?

No, they can't have! Something sent me down to the basement last night. My talent drove me there. She's not dead; they just don't want to give away that they have her.

"Your liege must come to us," Ursula repeated. "It's safest for everyone that way."

Jax struggled not to show his fear for Addie or how little he wanted Evangeline in this woman's hands. His great-aunt and his cousins and his uncle were all watching him intently and—oddly enough—making a point not to look at each other. *There's something they all know and don't want to reveal,* he thought. *More than just Addie. Something that makes them want both girls very badly.* "I'll speak to her about it," he said finally.

Apparently, Ursula was satisfied by his answer. "Let me know what comes of your tests," she said to Finn, signaling the end of the interview. Jax's uncle rose without finishing his coffee and led the way back through the penthouse.

Jax waited until the elevator dropped before turning to his uncle. "Can I ask you something?"

Uncle Finn looked pleased. "Yes, of course."

"Why is Aunt Ursula's granddaughter her heir instead of her son?"

"Are you kidding?"

"No."

"Magical talents are gender linked, and the Dulac talent runs strongest in females. Daniel is a Dulac, but Sloane is more talented and the rightful heir. Ursula's other sons inherited their father's talent and took his last name, Bors. He passed away some time ago, but the Bors sons and their families all live in this building, too." Uncle Finn seemed puzzled and disturbed. "Did Rayne teach you *nothing* about how talents are passed through families?"

"Dad died. Before I transitioned the first time." He was plenty mad at his father, but if Jax didn't defend him, who would? "I didn't transition until I was thirteen. He must have thought I never would."

"It was still wrong to leave you uneducated," Uncle Finn said. "And even more wrong to put you in the hands of a boy who apparently didn't do any better."

"Riley was having me trained," Jax replied indignantly. "But then we got kind of busy, saving the world and stuff."

His uncle made a huffing noise and opened the elevator cage door. "We're getting out here." Jax looked at the dial above the door. Floor twelve. "I'm taking you to see our clan artisans," Uncle Finn explained. "About your mark."

18

THE DADE BROTHERS HAD somehow made their luxury Manhattan apartment look like somebody's basement. Jax wasn't sure if it was the movie posters plastered over the picture windows, the torn vinyl furniture, or the thumping bass from their massive speakers.

The Dades were either twins or close enough in age that they might as well have been. And they didn't agree on anything. "A little ink can turn that bald eagle into a falcon. We just have to color in the head," said Dade #1.

"A dark head doesn't turn an eagle into a falcon. They're completely different birds," Dade #2 argued.

"Maybe *you* can't do it, but *I* can."

"If you change his mark, you might screw up his talent."

"We don't even know if he has any talent with a mark like that."

Jax muttered under his breath and drew his dagger.

Everybody wanted to know if he was really an inquisitor. *Fine.* He concentrated, balancing the blade on the palm of his left hand. Uncle Finn sat back in his chair and watched.

Twenty seconds later, Dade #1 was spilling the PIN of his debit card, all his computer passwords, and—on an impulse that flashed into Jax's head—the name of the first girl he'd ever kissed (Megan) and the place (homecoming dance, senior year).

Unfortunately, Megan had been the date of Dade #2 at that homecoming dance.

The Dades erupted into name-calling. One of them threatened to kill the other's World of Warcraft character in retaliation for "stealing the only girl I ever loved."

Uncle Finn took Jax by the shoulder and steered him out of the apartment. "That was uncalled for."

"You wanted to know if I had any talent," Jax said smugly. "I just proved it."

"It's discourteous to use your talent to embarrass your clan members."

They're not my clan. "I don't want those guys touching my tattoo."

"It doesn't seem necessary," his uncle said. "You're obviously an Ambrose." Then he made a noise that caused Jax to glance at him in surprise. Jax couldn't tell if it was a snort or a laugh or even a sob, but Uncle Finn was looking at him with strangely moist eyes. "Rayne would've done the same thing."

Jax grinned. And his uncle grinned back.

"How did it go?" Aunt Marian asked before they'd gotten all the way in the door.

"Very well," Uncle Finn said. "Ursula is pleased we've brought Jax home."

Jax looked into the living room. Lesley was painting her toenails, her bottom lip caught between her teeth as she focused on each brushstroke. Jax passed his aunt and hurried down the steps into the sunken living room. "Hey," he whispered. "Where's Billy?"

"Bathroom?" she suggested without looking up.

Jax glanced at his aunt and uncle. They were headed toward a room he thought was his uncle's office, seemingly as anxious to talk outside his earshot as he was to catch Billy outside theirs. So he lurked near the bathroom until he heard the toilet flush. When the door opened, he reached out to push Billy back inside.

Billy flinched, avoiding Jax's touch.

Deep down he knows something's wrong, Jax thought. With Jax blocking the doorway, Billy, looking puzzled, backed into the bathroom. Jax followed him in and shut the door.

"What—"

"I need to talk to you alone," Jax said.

"Dude, this is weird."

"You have no idea. What happened the day you were kidnapped?"

"I wasn't kidnapped," Billy said with a laugh.

"You said *kidnapped* in your text."

"Did I?" Billy scratched his head. "I was just being funny."

Jax shook his head. "I don't think so. Tell me what happened."

"O-kay. Your uncle and cousins were asking questions around the neighborhood. When they found out I knew you, they invited me to help them find you. They told me everything."

"Everything," Jax repeated. "They told you about the eighth day, and you believed them."

For a moment, Billy seemed puzzled. Then he broke into a stupid grin. "Yeah."

"Your parents think you're at golf camp."

"That was your cousin's idea. We couldn't tell them the truth."

"Dorian?"

"No. Your *hot* cousin. Sloane."

Of course. His cousin Sloane, the Dulac heir. "I don't think it happened the way you remember. What's wrong with your arm?" Jax pointed at Billy's left arm.

"Nothing. What are you talking about?" Billy edged

around him. "Let me out of here."

Jax pressed his back against the door. "Do me a favor. Roll up your sleeve."

"I don't want to." Billy's eyes darted nervously around the bathroom.

"Okay then." Jax bunched his hand into a fist and pretended he was going to punch Billy in the arm. His friend backed away so hastily, he tripped over the tub, and when he used his arms to break his fall, he gasped in pain. His face went gray. "Roll up your sleeve and look at it," Jax urged him.

Hesitantly, Billy pulled up his left sleeve. Livid purple blotches covered his forearm, and there was a neat row of stitches just below the elbow. Billy stared at his arm like he'd never seen it before, his eyes bugging out of his head. He tried to speak, but his lips trembled, and he stared at Jax, bewildered.

"I don't think you went with them willingly," Jax said. "They kidnapped you, just like you said. And they must've gotten rough."

"Is it broken?" Billy whispered, moving his arm experimentally.

"I dunno, but my aunt's a healer. What'd she say at breakfast—that she can make injuries heal faster? She must be using her talent to fix you up as quickly as she can—and I think she's been sedating you. When she touches you, she can make you feel happy, safe . . ." *Loved.*

"But I don't remember getting hurt." Billy swallowed. "Every time I changed my clothes, I never saw this."

"Sloane changed your memory. That's her magic talent. Between the false memories she gave you and my aunt's magic, I guess you didn't see what they didn't want you to see. Don't let Aunt Marian touch you. Or Sloane. Or my grandmother. Maybe most of the people in this building. They're dangerous."

"Are they not really your relatives?"

"No, they are." And they were horrible. Jax couldn't believe he'd almost had *a moment* with his uncle in the elevator. "I don't want them to know we're on to them," Jax said. "So you have to pretend nothing's wrong. We have to stay here a bit longer, because there's something I need to do before we can leave."

Billy nodded and rolled his sleeve down, looking shaken.

Jax removed his phone from his back pocket. There were more texts from the Crandalls, but instead of reading them, he called up the Crandall least likely to yell at him.

"Jax? You idiot."

"A.J., you suck."

"*I what?*"

"It's code for *everything's okay*," Jax explained. "It's what Riley and I picked at the Carroway house to— Oh, never mind. Did Tegan and Thomas tell you Evangeline's sister might be here?"

Billy gaped at Jax. "Tegan and Thomas *Donovan*?"

On the phone, A.J. replied, "Yeah, we heard. That's the only thing that kept my dad from going up there yesterday to bust you out."

"I don't need to be busted out. Things are under control."

A.J. exhaled doubtfully. "My mom drove to New York and met with the twins. She's nearby and wants you to contact her ASAP. Which you'd know if you'd answer your texts. Dad and I are waiting here for Riley, to see how he wants to handle this."

"Make sure Riley doesn't do anything stupid," Jax said. It was bad enough that Mrs. Crandall had come to New York. He didn't want to put anyone else in danger. "Hang tight and wait to hear from me. Now, I've got something else to ask you. What's a brownie hole?"

"Brownie hole? Are you sure they haven't scrambled your brains?"

"Just tell me."

"They're . . . well, they're how brownies get around."

"Brownie?" whispered Billy. "You mean, like a little hobgoblin?"

Jax nodded. It figured Billy knew the word. He'd probably read every fantasy book ever written, played every game, seen every movie. "Do brownie holes cross timelines?"

"How would I know?" A.J. said impatiently. "Nobody's

ever been in one. Look, Jax, forget brownies. I gotta tell you what Mom found out from Deidre. There's bad stuff happening in Wales. Serious trouble."

Jax suddenly remembered the Kin woman's warning, or prediction, or whatever it was. "I got something to tell you, too."

A loud knocking made both Jax and Billy jump. "Boys," called Aunt Marian. "You okay in there?"

Billy's eyes got wide again, and he held his injured arm close to his body. Jax hung up on A.J. and stuffed the phone into his pocket. "This is going to look weird," he muttered before opening the door.

Aunt Marian peered in. "Goodness, boys. If you want to make a phone call, you don't have to hide in the bathroom. That's silly. Come out of there."

What did she hear? Jax left the bathroom first, shielding Billy, who slunk out and kept his distance. But her attention was all on Jax. "Were you calling your guardian? We'd like to meet him. Is he in the city?"

"No," said Jax.

"Too bad. We're taking you out to dinner tonight before the transition. He could've joined us." While Jax tried to imagine Riley sitting down to dinner with the clan that had murdered his family, Aunt Marian put her arm around him and guided him into Dorian's bedroom. "I notice you didn't bring any nice clothes . . ."

Jax made a strangled sound when he saw his backpack open on the floor—every compartment zipped open and emptied. "You went through my stuff?"

"I put your clothes in the wash," she said, as if she was perfectly justified. "They needed it. But I didn't find anything appropriate for dinner."

It was a good thing he'd kept the stolen keys in his pocket.

"We can squeeze Billy into something of Dorian's, but you're too tall. I'm going to have to take you shopping."

Jax slithered out from under her arm. "Aunt Marian," he said, "I'd rather you *torture* me than take me shopping."

Their eyes met. For a moment Jax saw something hard in her expression and wondered if he'd spoken too bluntly. Then she smiled, and it was gone. "Well, this is a big clan. I'll call around. There must be a family with a pair of decent trousers and a shirt in your size. If not, I'll order clothes delivered, and you can just live with it if they don't fit right."

"Oh, the horror," Jax deadpanned, and it must've been the right thing to say, because Aunt Marian laughed and pinched his cheek before leaving the room.

It was just in time. Billy collapsed on Dorian's futon, shaking violently. "Holy crap, Jax. Is your aunt a nice lady or a conniving witch?"

"Both," Jax said. "Are you okay?"

"No. I've been *kidnapped*. This sucks."

It took a couple minutes for Billy to pull himself together. Jax tried comparing this adventure to Billy's favorite movies. He mentioned the damsel in distress who needed rescuing—and left out the big, scary killer they also had to rescue.

"So this Evangeline," said Billy. "You're like her knight?"

"Yep."

"And the sister—she's pretty?"

"Gotta be."

"Okay, I'm in."

When Billy finally stopped shaking, they went out to the living room, where Lesley was hobbling after her father, walking on her heels while her toenails dried.

"Can Valerie come over?"

"No." Her father was headed for the apartment door.

"Can I go over to Valerie's?"

"No, Lesley. We have guests."

"But they don't need me."

Uncle Finn whirled around and looked his daughter in the eye. "*I* might need you this afternoon, after I meet with Dr. Morder."

Lesley froze. Her father looked up and spotted Jax and Billy. "Make yourselves at home, boys. Lesley and Marian will get you anything you need." Then he walked out.

Billy plunked himself onto the sofa in the same spot

as this morning and picked up a game controller. Jax watched, worried false memories would reclaim his friend and he'd revert to cluelessness, but Billy toyed with the controls idly, surveying the apartment with new, alert eyes.

Lesley sank down beside Billy. "You want to play something?" she asked the boys listlessly.

Jax fidgeted, but there wasn't much else he could do right now. "Guess so." He sat down.

Billy looked out the wall of windows. "We could take a walk in the park instead."

"With my mom?" Lesley clicked through the game menus.

"Without her," Billy said forcefully. "Like, right now."

"I don't have an elevator key."

"What if there was a fire?" Billy demanded. "Are you telling me you can't get out? That's against the law."

"There are stairs," Lesley said, staring at the TV. "But there's a guard at the bottom, and when you came here, they put a guard on our floor, too. Right on the other side of the fire exit."

There was a long, silent moment.

"Sorry," said Lesley. "Did you want me to go on pretending you guys weren't prisoners?"

"Not really," Jax replied.

She faced him, and he saw that her eyes were filled with tears. "If it makes you feel any better, I'm a prisoner too. And I'm not even important."

"If it makes *you* feel any better," Jax said, "you're the only person here I like."

Lesley turned back to the TV. "Mario Kart?"

Jax picked up a controller. "Sure."

19

OH HIS WAY HOME from Bradley Prep, Dorian's phone chirped out a text notification.

```
Lesley: dads with dr morder
```

He sucked in his breath and typed a response.

```
Dorian: ill check on them
Lesley: pls pls pls D, i cant keep doing
this
Dorian: i got it L
```

He broke into a run. Dad meeting Dr. Morder and Lesley in a panic could only mean one thing: more experiments. And nothing upset Dorian more than experiments that involved his sister weeping in the brownie tunnel while his father yelled at her. Even worse was when Dad enlisted Dorian as an accomplice—forcing him to go in and "help" her.

"Help her *out*?" Dorian had asked the first time.

"Help her learn to use the magic." Dad's face had been livid. "The brownie tunnels are incredibly charged with magic. It has to affect her. It *has* to!"

"She's scared, Dad."

"She's a *coward*. Get in there and stop her crying!"

Dorian had found his sister a few feet inside the tunnel, huddled in a ball, sheltering her head with her arms—because, he learned later, she thought the walls were collapsing in on her. Although Dorian could see her perfectly—and could see through the walls of the tunnel to the outside physical space—Lesley was in utter darkness. His sister was an Ambrose, and thanks to the spell Dr. Morder had discovered, she could enter the brownie tunnel, but she didn't have enough magic to do anything else.

That didn't stop Dad from attempting to "cure" Lesley through prolonged exposure to the time tunnel. Handcuffing her and tethering her over to the eighth day hadn't caused her to develop any talent, but Dad had high hopes for this new procedure. He kept at it for months, and eventually Lesley started having night terrors, complete with ear-piercing screams and random sleepwalking.

Because her nightmares were usually on Wednesday nights, Dad concluded Lesley was close to transitioning after all. He pushed her harder. Once he even left her in the time tunnel for five hours straight. Dorian was sure she'd suffered through every minute of those hours. Lesley didn't know how to make the tunnels shift her in time to end the torment, although Dad thought she might learn if provoked enough. Instead, she came out catatonic with fear. Mom had sedated her and put her to bed. That had been the Wednesday night before the eighth day when Dorian stood on the street with his clan watching the sky crack open—the night they feared the Eighth-Day Spell had been broken and the world was ending.

But Thursday arrived after all, and when Dorian and his parents returned to their apartment, they found Lesley out of bed and standing in the living room in her nightdress, drenched with sweat, trembling violently with her eyes wide open but unaware of where she was. After that, Mom begged Dad to leave her alone, and until today, he had. The nightmares hadn't gone completely away—there'd been another one last week, in fact—but Dorian had hoped that Dad had given up tormenting her.

"Finals go well?" the doorman asked Dorian, letting him into the elevator when he got home.

"I think so." Dorian would've chosen the floor he wanted, but the doorman leaned in to press the button for him. Courtesy—or control? Dorian was never sure. "I want three," he said quickly. "I'm visiting Gran and Gramps."

When the elevator stopped on the third floor, Dorian got off, passed his grandparents' door, and pushed straight into a wall.

Dorian had discovered he could enter the brownie holes by accident last fall when he'd caught a glimpse of Dr. Morder emerging from a solid wall just beyond his grandparents' apartment. At the time, Dorian hadn't understood why humans could suddenly use brownie holes, but he had started exploring that very day. When Dad had finally let him in on the secret, Dorian had been navigating the tunnels for weeks without anyone knowing.

The one on the third floor was mostly a dead end and, as far as Dorian could tell, served the sole purpose of letting Dr. Morder peek inside the apartment of a clanswoman he'd once proposed marriage to who'd turned him down. *Stalk much?*

But brownies burrowed vertically too, and this tunnel had a chute that connected to the basement. Sliding down was kind of like being swallowed. It wasn't pleasant, but when Dorian needed to get to the basement undetected, this was how he did it. The invisible walls of the tunnel hugged his body and slowed his fall until he plopped out at the bottom.

It usually frustrated Dorian that the tunnel didn't extend farther into the basement, because there were some places he couldn't explore. Brownies were able to make the tunnels go *where* they wanted *when* they wanted. Dorian was getting good at shifting in time, but still hadn't figured out how to shift his location. Today, however, it was enough that he could follow the tunnel to the lab. If Dad and Dr. Morder were down here, that was where they'd be.

When he arrived, the lab appeared to be empty. The tunnel existed outside of time, according to Dr. Morder, and events happening in real time could not be observed from inside it. But Dorian had learned a few tricks. Sitting on the floor of the tunnel, he felt for the opening and pried it apart with his fingers like it was a hole in a sack. An eye peering out of the wall might be spotted, but an ear was just a dark hole if one was very careful.

". . . how they got out," his father was saying.

"I assume they were released," Dr. Morder replied in a dry voice.

"By whom?"

"By their own kind."

"You can't tell me they organized a breakout. They're animals!"

Dorian recognized the frustration in his father's voice, even though he was trying to hide his temper in front of Luis Morder, scientist and spell caster for the Dulac clan.

The Morders were descended from Sir Mordred, disgraced knight of the Round Table and supposed killer of King Arthur. Dorian didn't know if that legend was true, but he did know Mordred's descendants had mixed their line with Kin, who were more gifted in magic than other races. Dorian could tell just by looking at Dr. Morder's pale skin and startling blue eyes that he had Kin ancestors. It creeped Dorian out, but it had also enhanced the Morder family's natural talent. Most of the prominent Transitioner clans included vassals with some type of spell-casting talent, but Luis Morder was the only person Dorian had ever heard of who could combine science and magic so well.

"Have you done anything with the blood I brought you?" Dorian's father asked.

"It's hard to work with blood that disappears for seven days at a time."

"What? The brat *bit* me while I was collecting those samples! Don't tell me it was for nothing! Are you sure the test tubes didn't get mixed up?" Dorian heard the sound of glass rattling and knew his father was rummaging through the refrigerated cases.

"All my samples are carefully labeled," Morder said levelly. "The ones in that case are for the next batch of families to be admitted to the tunnels." The refrigerator door thumped closed. "What did you expect, Finn? We're talking about Emrys blood. It reinforces the existence of the Eighth-Day Spell."

"But if it can't be used in the seven-day timeline, it won't be any help to us! I expected that we'd be able to store it, use it indefinitely . . . *afterward*. . . ."

Afterward? Dorian frowned. *After* what*? And where did they get Emrys blood?*

"I need the magic in that blood, Luis." Dad's voice was strained. "The brownie tunnels are not a solution for Lesley. I accept that. She can't navigate them, and they haven't activated any latent talent in her. This blood is pretty much the last option we have for curing her condition."

"Patience, Finn. Research can't be rushed. You've seen that with the time tunnels. If we'd given up at the first obstacle, we wouldn't have what we have now."

What do *we have now?* Dorian wondered. Dr. Morder had discovered a spell that granted human families access to the brownie holes when blood from that family was sent through the tunnels. For over a year, Morder had been capturing brownies and releasing them a few at a time with test tubes of spelled blood strapped to their bodies. This gave select family bloodlines a key to the time tunnels. The Dulacs. The Ambroses. The Ganners and other families who provided security for the clan. Morder himself.

But what they planned to do with the tunnels remained a mystery to Dorian. *Besides stalking Dr. Morder's ex-girlfriend and spying on my dad, what good are they?*

"Give me time to experiment with the Emrys blood, and I'll see what I can do for your daughter," Morder said. "There are a lot of options to explore—scientific and magical. I don't believe anyone's ever studied the effect Kin blood has on the talent of Transitioners—let alone blood of the Emrys family. It will be groundbreaking research."

"We don't have much time, Luis. Ursula will to want to push forward with the final stage of our plan as soon as Jax brings us the other Emrys girl."

Dorian sucked in his breath. The *other* Emrys girl? Meaning they already had one? Dorian had forgotten there were two, and he would never have guessed one of them was a prisoner here. *The brat bit me*, his father had said.

"Ursula's manipulated your nephew into cooperating, then?" Morder asked.

"No, I asked her to let me work on him. I want to bring him to the clan without coercion."

"I'm surprised she agreed to wait," said Dr. Morder. "Given the circumstances."

"Tell me about it. And it's worse than you think, because our search in Wales turned up nothing. We think they left the country immediately."

"You think they will come here?"

"It hardly matters where they go. We'll see the effects of their freedom within a few weeks, even with them restricted to one day out of eight. Things will get ugly fast, and the two Emrys girls are the ultimate weapon against them."

"You would condone it, then?" Dorian detected an edge to Morder's normally mild voice. "Two girls—not much older than Dorian and Lesley? And the consequences?"

"I don't *enjoy* the idea, Luis. But we'll do what we have to do." While Dorian pondered what that meant, Dad continued softly. "Ursula thinks the timing may actually work in our favor. No one will question our decision if we appear to make it under threat of war. And if other Transitioners want to regain what they've lost, they'll have to come to us."

Cold prickles ran across Dorian's skin. He didn't understand exactly what his father meant, but he didn't like the sound of it at all.

20

DORIAN LEFT THE TUNNEL his usual way, through the exit in the park. It was guarded, but Dorian knew the man and had long since convinced him that he was running errands for his father.

Lesley leaped to her feet as soon as Dorian entered the apartment, and he gave her a thumbs-up. "Hey, Les. Everything's cool." *Not really . . .*

Jax, who'd been sitting next to Lesley, asked, "Something wrong?"

"No," Dorian said sharply. Lesley sat down again, her knuckles white as she gripped the game controller. Jax didn't look convinced.

Billy glared at Dorian with a suspicious expression very different from the dopey grin he'd been wearing since Sunday. *La-la Land wore off? Well, good. You should be suspicious of us.* Dorian didn't think he'd ever forget the sight of Albert Ganner tackling Billy in the street—not to mention the broken bone sticking out of Billy's arm afterward. Dorian had gagged at the sight—while Sloane proved just how powerful she was. She'd moved fast, needing only one touch per person to wipe the memories of every Normal witness.

Dorian went straight to his room. He pulled off his blazer and tie, balled them up, and hurled them at the floor. Then he sank down at his desk and buried his face in his hands.

What was he going to do?

He wasn't brave like Uncle Rayne must have been. At fifteen, Rayne had refused his oath and defied his clan. Secretly, Dorian had always imagined his uncle coming back one day and doing *something*—making a *difference*. Instead, Rayne had spent his life in hiding, and according to Dad, he'd become a petty criminal. It was the word *petty* that was the insult, because the Dulac clan was full of criminals—*important* ones who had their own private bankers and had reserved tables at Manhattan's finest restaurants.

Uncle Rayne had run a shady business, and now he was dead because he'd cheated a Kin lord. Was that someone to look up to?

Dorian slipped Rayne's journal out of its hiding place. He'd found it in Gran and Gramps's apartment, stuffed inside a history textbook on a shelf in Rayne's old room. It started out as a notebook, half filled with history notes. Not far in, a page had been ripped out. More history notes followed, and then the ripped-out page appeared, stuffed into the back:

A girl from Bradley died the week before school started. Amie Bruin. Her family's yacht caught fire and the engine exploded. The newspapers said it was a gas explosion, but everybody knows unexplained explosions are always assassinations. I wondered who did it, because I saw Amie in the Hamptons over the summer. I didn't know her well, though.

But today I found an unfinished letter in a pocket of my chinos. From me. To Amie. I don't remember writing a letter to Amie, but here it is. And it's like we're in love or something. I talk about being with her on her boat. <u>On her boat.</u>

Did my mom do this to me? Or Aunt Ursula? Dad's in on it, of course, but I don't think Finn is. He's too wrapped up in his girlfriend, Marian, to notice anything strange going on.

Amie, I'm sorry. I barely remember you.

The rest of the journal was written in the back of the notebook. History notes stopped after February, where the ripped-out page had been inserted and the notebook had been converted to another purpose.

February 3, 1990—OK, I just found this page in my notebook. It's not dated. But it must have been written right after school started, and it's six months later now. I don't remember writing it. I can't find a letter to Amie Bruin anywhere in my stuff. If this wasn't in my handwriting, I wouldn't believe it. But it is. That means they've changed my memory <u>more than once.</u>

They made me forget I remembered. What did they do before that? Did they make me forget about Amie Bruin after she died? Or did they make me fall in love with her in the first place and then change me back?

<u>Did I have anything to do with blowing up the boat?</u>

I better hold it together. Because last time I must have confronted them, and look what happened. Six months of forgetting.

I've been fighting with everybody nonstop for weeks over stupid stuff. Deep down, I guess I knew something was wrong. They can change my memory, but they can't change <u>me</u>.

Gonna be a lot more careful this time.

After that, Rayne wrote daily. The entries were brief, just a quick outline of his day, and each one ended with the statement: *I don't think anybody changed my memory today.* Occasionally, he mentioned "the plan," but he was careful not to put details on paper. Dorian leafed through the pages quickly, wanting to get to the last entry.

May 17, 1990—It's now or never. I'll be 16 in a week, and they'll make me swear allegiance to Aunt Ursula, and I'll be stuck forever.

I've got money stashed away. Not a lot. I _do_ have a plan about _who_ to ask for help, but I'm not going to write it down. Because I'm leaving this notebook here as The Rayne Ambrose Legacy for whoever finds it.

Finn, if it's you (and I hope it is) <u>this is why</u>.

If it's somebody else, <u>take this as your warning</u>.

Rayne had run away from his family, and while that meant he was free of them, his desertion hadn't served to change the clan in any way. It hadn't made life better for the niece and nephew he'd never known. True, he'd left the journal behind as a warning, but there were no solutions suggested in its pages other than the one Rayne had chosen.

Dorian didn't have the luxury of running away. Jax was here, and Aunt Ursula was going to use her magic on him if he didn't turn over his Kin-girl liege. Meanwhile Dad wanted to experiment on Lesley using the blood of another Emrys girl apparently imprisoned in this building. And Aunt Ursula was planning to use both girls for a plan that made even Dr. Morder squeamish.

Dorian covered his face with his hands again.

What was he going to do?

21

DINNER WAS LATE. NOT late as in *not on time*. Late as in *after nine o'clock*. Worse, it was in the fanciest restaurant Jax had ever seen. There were too many forks and plates, including a special one he apparently wasn't supposed to eat on. The waiter gave him a dirty look over his mistake.

"*This* was your bread plate," Uncle Finn said, pointing out a small plate off to one side. He sounded amused.

Jax tugged self-consciously at his collar. He was dressed in the clothes of some Dulac clan kid. *Funeral clothes*, his dad would've said—a thought that only brought back memories of the last time he'd worn a suit: his dad's memorial service. Jax squirmed in his chair, obliterating the memory by looking around.

The restaurant was full of rich people, many of whom stopped to say hello to either Jax's aunt and uncle or his grandparents. Jax could tell if they were Normals or Transitioners by the way they greeted one another. Normals shook hands; Transitioners showed their mark.

He was shocked by how many were Transitioners.

"Are there a lot of people like us?" he'd once asked Riley.

"A few," Riley had replied. He'd never mentioned that many of them lived in Manhattan and seemed a lot wealthier than Riley and his vassals.

"Sheila is intent on conversation with Calvin," Jax's grandmother commented, looking across the restaurant. "Do you think they have news from Wales that's any different from ours?"

The appetizers arrived, thankfully, because Jax was beginning to think he'd have to eat his napkin. He snatched a fried something off a serving plate before the waiter even set it down.

Meanwhile, Jax's grandfather leaned closer to his wife and yelled, "What did you say?" in an accent that made him sound like a deaf and slightly senile James Bond.

"I said," Gran replied in a louder voice, "Sheila Morgan is meeting with Calvin Bedivere."

Jax looked up from his food.

"Huh," grunted Gramps. "Interesting."

Jax pushed a whole stuffed mushroom into his mouth, listening intently while pretending not to. The person they were talking about was Deidre's mother. He scanned the restaurant, trying to spot her. *Which woman looks like she's carrying a small arsenal?*

"I'd give my eyeteeth to know if they've found anything more useful than our people have," Uncle Finn muttered. "We're getting nothing but stories about the Girl of Crows appearing at Oeth-Anoeth. What claptrap."

"You should've gone yourself," Gramps said.

"I had business here, Father."

Jax's phone vibrated. Glancing around, he decided the adults were busy with their own conversation. He slipped his phone out of his pocket and checked his message.

```
Thomas: u wanna b bustd outta there? big
destracshn?
```

Jax decoded the spelling error and looked warily around the restaurant. He did *not* want the Donovans making a big distraction.

```
Jax: no!
Thomas: rlly?
Jax: how did u find me?
Tegan: followed you from the dulac building
dummy
```

He wondered if Mrs. Crandall was with them. She'd

given up texting him and was probably as mad as a hornet that Jax wouldn't respond. But he really didn't want to get yelled at.

> Tegan: need to talk to you. can you ditch
> them?
> Jax: theyre taking me to rockefeller center
> later
> Tegan: get alone. ill find you
> Thomas: woo woo
> Tegan: shut up tommy

"He certainly keeps a tight rein on you," Aunt Marian remarked from across the table. It took a second for Jax to realize that Aunt Marian had spotted him texting under the table. Her comment caught Uncle Finn's attention.

"It's not him," Jax said. Did they really think he'd contact Riley in their presence? How dumb did they think he was?

"Then who is it?" Without any warning, Uncle Finn grabbed Jax's phone.

Resisting would have caused a scene. But before Jax let go, he punched a button to delete the texts. Instead, he accidentally called up Tegan's profile—her number and a blank avatar.

"Who's Tegan?" Uncle Finn raised an eyebrow.

"My girlfriend," Jax blurted out. What else could he say?

Billy choked on a cocktail shrimp and burst into laughter, spraying the table with seafood. "Dude!" he exclaimed. "Really? Aren't you afraid her brother'll beat you up?"

Jax's cheeks burned, but his obvious embarrassment and Billy's teasing did the trick. Uncle Finn handed back the phone. "Like father, like son."

Gran frowned. "The boy's too young for girls."

"You think so?" Uncle Finn apparently found that funny. "Don't you remember Rayne's girlfriend who wore the leather skirts? That was in eighth grade."

"Pink hair," Gramps grunted disapprovingly.

Uncle Finn counted on his fingers for his mother. "There was the girl with the horses, the girl with the Rollerblades . . ."

"The girl with the boat," Aunt Marian added.

"The girl with the beach house," Uncle Finn went on.

Jax's face felt hotter and hotter, and it wasn't the lie about Tegan or the fact that his father had been some kind of teenage Romeo. What was much worse was how casually his uncle had taken his phone and how easily he could have looked through all the information stored on it. Phone numbers, call records, texts. His uncle had just held all that in his hand.

Giving back the phone had been an act of showing off. *See,* Uncle Finn was telling him. *I can overpower you and choose not to. Because I'm such a nice guy.* It was just like Aunt Marian, going through his backpack and not even bothering to hide it.

Jax had been careless and stupid, carrying so much information with him. He'd put both Riley and Evangeline at risk, and he should've known better, after all the commotion Mr. Crandall had made about Jax calling Billy on his computer! Beneath the cover of the table, he popped out the data card, dropped it on the floor, and crushed it beneath his heel. Then he put the disabled phone back in his pocket. It would be useless in a couple of hours anyway.

Meanwhile, his grandmother was denying that Rayne had spent his teenage years dripping in girls, but she did admit he liked loud rock music, dyed his hair absurd colors, and kept vermin as a pet.

"The brownie," groaned Uncle Finn.

"Stink!" exclaimed Jax's grandfather.

"Of course it stank," said Gran indignantly. "Don't they all?"

"No, that was its name, Mother. Stink."

"Did *he* call it that?" Aunt Marian asked. "I know that's what the rest of us called it." She turned to Jax. "My family lived on the seventh floor, and my mother hated that brownie with a passion! It ran amok all over the building, turning up in everyone's kitchens, overturning garbage, and annoying the whole clan. And heaven forbid anyone try to kill it. Rayne would've had a fit."

"I don't suppose you ever saw it?" Uncle Finn looked at Jax.

"Uh, no," Jax said.

"Thought it might still be around. Those things live forever." Uncle Finn sighed. "Unlike the rest of us." He picked up his wineglass and held it out across the table. "To Rayne."

Aunt Marian clinked her glass with his. "To Rayne."

Gran put her fingers to her lips with one hand, as if overcome with emotion, and lifted her glass. Gramps did too.

Dorian grabbed his glass of soda and joined in the toast. "To Uncle Rayne."

"To Dad," Jax said, his voice close to breaking.

Spending time with these people was like walking across a fun-house floor that bucked and tipped beneath his feet. One moment he hated them; the next, he didn't.

By the time they finished dessert, it was almost midnight. Jax's grandparents parted ways with them outside the restaurant. "I need to be at the Stock Exchange early tomorrow," Gramps said.

"The Stock Exchange is open on the eighth day?" Jax asked.

"The Secret Stock Exchange," Dorian muttered. "The

one where deals are done privately, prices fixed, takeovers planned . . ."

"Isn't that illegal?" Billy asked.

"Shh! We don't talk about it like that." Lesley glanced at her father, who was trying to hail a cab for his parents. Jax frowned. Lesley had been jumpy and tearful for most of the day. Dorian had come home from school upset about something. There was all kinds of stuff going on here, but Jax reminded himself that his cousins were not his problem. His job was to get Billy and Addie out of Dulac hands—and keep Riley and Evangeline as far away from Aunt Ursula as possible.

A weird contraption that was part carriage and part bicycle stopped to pick up Gran and Gramps. "What the heck is that?" Jax asked.

"Pedicab," said Dorian. "They can't use a taxi this late on a Wednesday. They'll get stuck at the change. The blue pedicabs are run by Transitioners—or Normals tethered over to do the job."

Uncle Finn saw his parents off, then rubbed his hands together. "Everybody ready?"

Manhattan at midnight was not as crowded as it was at noon, when Jax had arrived yesterday, but the streets were still full of cars. The roads would be impassable on Grunsday, with all those vehicles frozen and going nowhere for twenty-four hours. Jax saw several blue pedicabs on their way to Rockefeller Center. Tourists stopped to take pictures of themselves in front of fountains and landmarks. A street performer strummed his guitar with his case lying open in front of him, hoping for donations.

Uncle Finn produced handcuffs from inside his suit coat pocket. "You want to do the honors?" he asked Jax, nodding toward Billy. Meanwhile, Aunt Marian fished another pair out of her purse, and Lesley held out her wrist.

Nobody around them batted an eye when Jax handcuffed himself to Billy's good arm—except for Billy himself. "Should I brace myself?" he asked.

"Not really."

Two seconds later, the cars stopped in the streets, the sound of engines cut off like someone had flipped a switch. The fountains died away, and the lights of the city dimmed, reduced to the afterimage of leftover light. More than half the people on the sidewalks vanished, although some of the tourists continued to take pictures with disposable box cameras.

The guitarist didn't miss a beat, but a voice joined in with him. A young woman had appeared beside the musician—a woman with fair skin and silvery blond hair, her voice as clear as a bell. She took up the song in the middle as if continuing from where she'd left off last week.

Billy gaped at the changed world around him. He

turned in a circle, dragging Jax with him. "Uh," Jax said to his uncle. "The keys?"

Uncle Finn took Jax's wrist and turned the cuff around, showing him a button on the side. "They're trick cuffs. Special order, so we don't have to worry about losing a key." The cuff fell open, releasing Jax's wrist. "We use these more than you might think."

Jax glanced around the plaza and remembered what Dorian said about the pedicab driver. "Not all these people are Transitioners."

"No, not all. Just as we've trusted your friend Billy with this secret, other Transitioners have trusted their friends—or business associates—or employees." Uncle Finn surveyed the crowd with a critical eye. "It would be better if fewer people knew. Many Transitioners in Manhattan have become . . . careless."

Jax watched his uncle shrewdly. *You think you should be the one to decide, don't you? You and the Dulacs.*

"Look," exclaimed Billy. The sound of generators replaced the silenced engines as all around Rockefeller Center, stores and vending carts powered up. Lights came on in some of the shops that had been dark a few seconds ago. At one café, someone in an apron rolled up the iron security gate while a waitress lit candles on the streetside tables.

The twang of an electric guitar came through an amplifier, followed by a brief drumroll. "One . . . two . . .

three . . . testing . . ." a voice said through a microphone.

"Dude, there's a band. Did you know there was a band?" Billy shook Jax's arm.

"I had no idea." Nothing Riley had ever told Jax would have led him to imagine Transitioners and their Normal friends making secret use of Manhattan on Grunsday.

"Can you spare some change?" Jax looked down and realized he'd almost passed a homeless man without acknowledging his existence or noticing he was Kin. Looking into those piercing blue eyes, Jax fumbled in his pockets for money before remembering these weren't his pants. Then he thought, *A rich kid's clothes are more likely to have cash in the pockets than mine!* He started checking the suit coat pockets.

"Come on," Uncle Finn said roughly, taking Jax by the back of the neck and directing him away from the man crouched on the sidewalk. "He's using his magic on you."

Was he? Jax looked back. The homeless Kin man met his eyes, then turned away. Meanwhile, the guitarist and his Kin girlfriend were being ordered to move on by an aggressive Transitioner wearing a band T-shirt. The musician hurried to get his guitar back in the case, while the girl cowered behind him.

"This is awesome," Billy whispered, his attention directed in front of them. "Retro nirvana." Vendors unfurled tents, revealing temporary storefronts. Most of them targeted Transitioner needs—including out-of-date technology, which was the only kind that worked on Grunsday. Mechanical clocks. Vacuum tubes. Ham radios.

Jax stared at racks of VCRs and 8-track players from the seventies and eighties. "Do these actually work?"

The vendor standing beside the cart looked insulted. "You think I sell stuff that doesn't work?"

"I mean, do they work on the eighth day?"

"You been living under a rock?" Then the man grinned. "Oh, you just turned. These are early models. Before computer chips. They'll work, same as cassettes and record players."

Jax looked at a bin of VHS tapes. Evangeline had never seen a movie. Jax had more important things to think about right now, but he stared at the movies hungrily, wishing he could give Evangeline something she'd never had.

Uncle Finn leaned against the cart beside him. "Want one?"

Jax snapped out of it. "No."

"We'll take that one." Uncle Finn pointed out a VCR for the vendor. "I need it delivered to my building."

"No thank you, Uncle Finn," Jax repeated firmly.

"Consider it the first of thirteen birthday presents I owe you." Then he grinned, and Jax wished he wouldn't, because he looked like Jax's dad when he did. "Let me buy my nephew a gift. Pick out some movies to go with it."

This is silly. When I leave, I won't be carrying a VCR. But

Jax selected some VHS tapes anyway, playing along. Uncle Finn gave his address to the vendor and paid cash from a new wallet. Remembering who had Uncle Finn's old wallet, Jax looked around. Billy was down the street, investigating other carts and asking Dorian questions. Lesley was negotiating with her mother for the right to go listen to the band. And Uncle Finn, apparently, was sticking to Jax like glue. How was he going to meet Tegan?

"Can I look around?" Jax asked his uncle.

"That's why we brought you here."

"No, I mean alone." When Uncle Finn frowned, Jax put on his *I'll be honest with you* face. "Look, this family thing is freaking me out. I'm trying, really, but if you want me to trust you, then you can start by trusting me."

They faced off for a long moment. Finally, Uncle Finn said, "I'm sorry, Jax. We've gone to a lot of trouble to find you, and I don't want to lose you."

"Okay, no trust then." Jax reached inside his borrowed suit coat. The Dulac kid had a reinforced pocket sewn inside it, just for carrying an honor blade. Handy. "I'll swear it. On the Aubrey name—uh, *Ambrose*," he corrected when he saw his uncle's face. "Ambrose, Aubrey, whoever I am, I swear on my bloodline that I'll go back to your apartment with you tonight."

That seemed to satisfy him. "Very well. Take a walk around. We'll meet you back here in an hour."

As Jax put away his dagger and hurried to catch up

with Billy, he thought back to last Grunsday and the Kin woman at the Carroway house. His oath, sworn on two names, brought her words back to him.

You're not who you think you are.

That was for sure.

You're not who they think you are, either.

No, he certainly didn't intend to be.

22

JAX AND BILLY NAVIGATED the perimeter of Rockefeller Center. As they passed the summer gardens, Thomas Donovan vaulted over a low wall into their path. He threw an arm around Billy's neck, bent him over, and rubbed his knuckles across Billy's scalp. "Hey, Ramirez. How's it goin'?"

"Urgh." Billy struggled to escape.

Tegan appeared from behind a tree and grabbed Jax by the lapels of his suit coat. She hauled him close and leaned her head next to his, sniffing. Jax had always been skeeved out by the Donovans' smelling talent, but this time, for some reason, it didn't seem that bad.

Her hair smelled like tangerines.

Then she shoved him backward. "He's all right," she said to Thomas. "Nothing's changed, except I smell a couple new oaths on him."

Okay, no. It *was* creepy.

Thomas let go of Billy. "Ramirez is messed up. Not a lot, but they hurt him."

Billy staggered, recovering his balance. "I can't believe you guys are part of this."

Jax felt a looming presence behind him and turned to face Mrs. Crandall. "I should put you over my knee," she said, glowering at him, and the twins grinned like that would be loads of fun to watch. Mrs. Crandall snapped, "Your phone," and held out her hand expectantly.

"I disabled it." Jax handed it over anyway. "Right after texting Tegan, I realized it was a security risk. I shouldn't have been calling A.J. on it."

Mrs. Crandall grunted. "If you'd bothered to read *my* texts, I tried to instruct you on how to contact us with less risk. Jax, what possessed you—"

"Riley's last order was to ask the Donovans to find Addie, and they did!" Jax interrupted. "Or at least, they tracked her to my uncle. I'm your best shot at finding out where she is. They're making nice with me while they try to talk me into giving them Evangeline."

Mrs. Crandall sucked in a breath. "They won't be able to get around your oath to her, that's for sure. But I'm not surprised they want to track her down after what happened last week, probably more than they want Riley right now." Jax frowned. That might make Mrs. Crandall feel better, but it didn't comfort Jax. "What that Kin woman told you—"

"Oeth-Anoeth fell to the Llyrs. Right?"

Thomas looked surprised. "You already knew?"

Jax recalled the Kin woman's glassy eyes and faraway gaze. "I think I got a real-time report of it." He turned to Mrs. Crandall. "You said there were only a few of them left. How'd they break out?"

"They had help," Mrs. Crandall said. "Possibly from Kin who came from *this* country."

"Dad thinks they'll be coming here," Tegan said.

"Oh, you've talked to your dad, have you?" Mrs. Crandall put her hands on her hips. "He disappeared after we got to New York, and just like Jax, he won't answer my calls."

Tegan shrugged. "He has stuff to do, investments to protect. Especially if the Kin are going to rise up and start the next apocalypse."

"Look," Jax said to Tegan, "I know you don't like Kin, but—"

Thomas barked out a laugh. "It's not *all* Kin she has a problem with. Just *one* she can't stand." He waggled his eyebrows at Jax as if expecting him to guess who he meant.

Tegan punched her brother in the stomach hard enough to double him over.

Mrs. Crandall grabbed each twin by the scruff of the neck and separated them. "This is too dangerous a time for you to play spy, Jax, even if you think the Dulacs are being nice. Trust me: they won't be for long. The Llyrs have a unique and powerful talent, and now that they're free, things could get deadly fast. Securing the two Emrys girls is the surest way to prevent the Llyrs from tampering with the Eighth-Day Spell. That's why Ursula wants them."

"You'd almost think she was trying to do the right thing," Jax muttered. "Except if she had good intentions, she would've told me Addie was here."

"Glad you see my point," Mrs. Crandall said. "That's why you're leaving here with us. Now."

"I don't think so." Jax was pretty sure that if she picked him up and threw him over her shoulder, Mrs. Crandall still wouldn't be able to leave the area with him. "I swore an oath to my uncle that I'd go back to his apartment tonight."

"Jax!" she exclaimed.

"But you can take Billy," he said.

"What?" Billy looked hurt and betrayed.

"My uncle will be mad, but at least you'll be safe."

"What about the damsel in distress?" Billy demanded. "I thought I was going to help!"

"It'll be better if I only have one person to worry about," Jax said apologetically. "I'm going to take another stab at finding Addie in that building. I've got less than twenty-four hours to figure out if she's there . . . and smuggle her out if she is."

Mrs. Crandall grimaced in disapproval but gave in.

"Since you swore an oath to go back there, you've left us with no choice. We'll take Billy. If you get Adelina out of that building, you can meet us in Chinatown, where we're staying with *friends* of the Donovans."

By the tone of her voice, Jax already knew what she meant by *friends* even before Tegan corrected her. "Not friends. *Associates*. And they won't want us bringing trouble to their hideout. We'll use the Balto statue as a meeting place instead." When Tegan saw that meant nothing to Jax, she explained, "It's a statue of a dog in Central Park, near East Sixty-seventh Street. Tommy or I will be waiting there."

Jax nodded and made no comment about dog statues and smelling talents, although it crossed his mind.

Suddenly Thomas pushed Jax aside and dived into the Rockefeller Center garden. A moment later, he emerged, dragging a boy pinned under his arm. "Look what I got."

"Dorian," Jax growled. "What're you doing?"

"Dad told me to follow you and find out who you were meeting." Dorian tugged at Thomas's forearm.

Jax groaned. He didn't think he'd been that obvious. "Let him go, Thomas."

Thomas did, reluctantly, and Dorian brushed himself off with injured dignity. His eyes darted around the little group. "I guess you must be Tegan," he said to her. Jax groaned again.

"What does he mean?" Tegan demanded.

"Never mind that," Jax said. "What're we going to do?" Mrs. Crandall seemed just as aghast at Dorian's sudden appearance as Jax was. *Is our side going to start kidnapping kids now?*

Dorian looked back and forth between the Donovan twins. He gasped and pointed at Thomas. "You're the boy who picked Dad's pocket at the bus station. And you"—the finger moved to Tegan—"you bumped into Jax in the doorway. Which means"—he whirled on Jax—"you have his keys. Oh wow, you have *Dad's keys!*"

Thomas slammed a fist into the palm of his other hand. "This is going to get ugly."

Dorian, for some reason, was grinning. "No, this is perfect! But you can't let Billy leave with them now, or you'll give it all away, and we'll never be able to find that girl."

"What?" exclaimed Mrs. Crandall. Jax blinked in confusion.

"*This* is why you didn't run away with Billy last night," Dorian said, his eyes alight. "Even though you had the keys. You couldn't get *her* out last night, but we can do it tonight."

"You know your family's keeping a girl prisoner in your building?" Jax asked, horrified to find out Dorian was an accomplice to it.

"I heard my dad talking about it," Dorian said. "I haven't seen her for myself."

"Why would you help me?"

Dorian faltered. "Because . . . uh, because . . . the only thing necessary for the triumph of evil is that good men should do nothing?"

He said it like it was a question, like he wasn't sure, but Mrs. Crandall took a step backward, her expression changing.

"I did nothing when Albert Ganner broke Billy's arm," Dorian admitted. He turned to Billy. "It's a good thing you don't remember. It was *hours* before we could get you to Mom."

Billy gulped.

"And I've done nothing while Dad tortures my sister. I . . . I can't stand it anymore . . . and I don't think I can stop it by myself." Dorian seemed to shrink a couple inches. "I need your help," he whispered.

"He's telling the truth," Mrs. Crandall said, but Jax didn't need her talent to know that.

Twenty minutes later, Jax, Billy, and Dorian sat on a wall overlooking the band and ate ice cream, while Uncle Finn and Aunt Marian watched from nearby.

"What'd you tell your dad?" Jax asked Dorian.

"That your girlfriend followed you to New York because she was worried about you."

Jax nodded but still felt obligated to say, "She's not,

you know. I made that up."

Dorian shrugged. "If you say so."

On the plaza, Lesley danced to the music, spangled bracelets glittering on her arms, her dark hair loose and bouncing on her shoulders. She didn't look like someone subjected to experiments, alternately ignored and tormented by her father.

"Do you think she'd run away with us?" Billy asked. "I mean, this is her home."

"My dad did it," Jax said. "If Uncle Finn is going to try blood magic on Lesley, we'll *make* her come." Thinking whose blood Dorian said Uncle Finn wanted to use made Jax's own blood boil.

"I know she won't want to leave. But if the nightmares and the sleepwalking keep going, and Dad won't leave her alone . . ." Dorian looked at Jax. "Would your guardian take her in?"

"Absolutely."

"You're that sure without asking him?"

Jax tried to imagine Riley turning away a fourteen-year-old girl in trouble and couldn't picture it. Of course, this girl was related to people who'd killed Riley's own family—and who might still want to kill *him*. In spite of that, Jax said with confidence, "I'm sure."

It was two thirty by Jax's Grunsday watch when Uncle Finn decided to go home. Jax was starting to worry the whole night would get away from them.

"Not a problem," Dorian assured him. "Trust me."

Aunt Marian pried her daughter away from the music under protest—at least until Lesley caught her father's eye. Then she scrambled to do as she was told. Uncle Finn flagged down a blue pedicab, and they climbed aboard. The cyclist pedaled down the sidewalk, diverging onto the road when there was space between the stopped cars. Billy leaned over the side to look at the stationary vehicles, fascinated.

They were delivered to the Dulac apartment building. Jax yawned, then shook himself vigorously. He doubted there was any time to be wasted sleeping tonight. As he stepped out of the pedicab, an urgent tug in his heart caused him to stop and look down the street.

At the end of the block, a motorcycle idled softly. The rider was anonymously dressed in a black leather biker's jacket and jeans, wearing a helmet with the visor down, but Jax recognized the bike.

Dang it, Riley. What part of "hang tight and wait to hear from me" didn't you understand? He must have jumped on his bike at 12:01 and ridden ninety miles an hour to get here this fast. But it was the irresistible pull drawing Jax's attention to the motorcycle that alarmed Jax most—because he had no such bond with Riley.

Then the passenger on the bike shifted position, peeking out from behind the driver. She was dressed in a too-large jacket and also wore a helmet, visor down. There wasn't a strand of blond hair visible, but there didn't need to be. Jax knew her with every cell in his body.

Crap! Why did he bring her here? But Jax knew why. Evangeline's sister and vassal were here. She'd refused to be left behind.

Jax cut his hand sharply across the air in a *back off* gesture, then looked up to find his uncle watching him. Uncle Finn changed direction and walked briskly toward the motorcycle.

The rider gunned the engine and took off, weaving between the cars, passing the Ambroses, and disappearing around a corner. Uncle Finn turned to Jax, eyebrows raised, but Jax didn't look at the departing bike. He yawned deliberately and headed, zombielike, for the door of the apartment building as if he had nothing but sleep on his mind. But his heart thumped madly.

The two people the Dulacs wanted were now within their reach.

This was not part of Jax's plan.

Why didn't anybody ever listen to him?

23

"WHY CAN'T I COME?" Billy demanded. Jax shushed him. Dorian's bedroom door was closed, but Uncle Finn and Aunt Marian were nearby.

Dorian said, "Because I have a way to get to the basement without anyone knowing, but you won't be able to use it. I'm not even sure Jax can."

"You mean the brownie hole? I can." Jax didn't know why he'd been able to enter one when Balin and A.J. said no humans could, but he was betting Dorian did.

"How do you . . ." Dorian's face showed the same amazement as when he realized Jax had acquired his father's keys. It gave Jax an ego boost, impressing his cousin.

"What are brownie holes, and why can't I use them?" Billy asked.

"The holes are entrances to invisible tunnels made by magical animals called brownies," Dorian said.

"They sort of look like rats except bigger and with no tails," Jax added, holding up his hands to estimate the size. "They've got faces like pug dogs and fingers like monkeys, and they can jump right through walls." He knew this sounded ridiculous, but Billy was listening intently and nodding, believing every word.

"Brownies burrow through time and space," Dorian clarified. "Our clan scientist has been experimenting with them for years, trying to figure out if people can travel the way they can."

"Locking them up in cages," Jax grumbled.

"You sound like Lesley and her animal rights stuff." Then Dorian's eyes got wide. "*You're* the one who let them out!"

"You bet I did!"

"They weren't being hurt."

"They wanted out." Jax remembered the one shaking the bars of its cage in its little fists.

"If they can jump through walls, how do you keep them in cages?" Billy asked.

"Wards," said Dorian. "Symbols that prevent them from using their magic. Dr. Morder releases the brownies a few at a time with blood samples from certain families strapped to their bodies. The blood is enhanced with a spell giving members of that family partial access to the tunnels." Dorian pressed his ear against the bedroom door. Uncle Finn seemed to be talking on a phone, although Jax knew it couldn't be a phone on Grunsday. It had to be a radio. "If Jax found the tunnels and got into them, it's because he's an Ambrose, and our blood was granted access."

"Are brownie tunnels everywhere?" Billy asked. "Or just in this building?"

"You can find them anywhere brownies go," said Dorian. "But we have more than our fair share—thanks to Jax's dad."

"What?" Jax scowled. *Now* what was his dad being blamed for?

"When your dad was a kid, he had a pet brownie living here. Dr. Morder thinks Stink is responsible for all the tunnels in this building except the one in the basement. That one was made by the brownies he releases. They run away from the lab, outside, and into the park."

"Back up a little," Jax said. "You said Dr. Morder's spell gives partial access to the tunnels. What do you mean by *partial*? I got through okay."

"The tunnels all have dead ends," Dorian said. "The one that goes to the park is the longest, but even it just stops dead. The brownies somehow continue on to wherever they're going, but we can't follow."

Jax didn't understand that, but Billy apparently did. "You mean, the brownies go into warp speed like the Starship *Enterprise* and *poof*, they vanish from here and appear somewhere else?"

Dorian looked startled. "Maybe. I thought the brownies moved the tunnels, but your idea makes more sense. Like hyperspace and the *Millennium Falcon*."

"Skip the sci-fi convention," Jax interrupted. "Can we use the tunnels to rescue Addie?"

"*She* can't use them. Only a few families in the Dulac clan have access to the tunnels," Dorian said. "*You and I* can use them to avoid the guards and Dad's keys to get her out of wherever they're holding her, but we'll have to find a way to smuggle her out of the building without the tunnels."

"You're going to be in big trouble when this is over," Billy said to Dorian.

Oddly, Dorian's face lit up. "Yeah, I will."

"Are your parents in bed yet?" Jax checked his Grunsday watch. "We're wasting time."

Dorian smirked. "No we're not. Didn't you hear what I said about burrowing through time?"

Jax didn't like leaving Billy in the apartment, but Dorian insisted it was safer than having him caught wandering the building. "We'd have to leave him behind here anyway," Dorian said when they reached the third floor. He stuck his head out of the elevator and motioned Jax to follow him.

Halfway down the hall, Dorian stepped through the

wall, and Jax did likewise. Inside the tunnel, Dorian stuck his hand out awkwardly. "We'd better hold hands," he said. "I've never tried this with another person, and I'm not sure we'll end up together if we're not touching."

According to Dorian, the brownie tunnel not only existed outside of time, it could move them backward or forward in real-world time. "It has limits," Dorian had explained on the elevator. "I've never moved more than a couple hours."

Jax clasped Dorian's hand, which was clammy. He couldn't tell if his cousin was scared or superexcited. His eyes were glassy, and his hair was rumpled. Aunt Marian would've reached for the nearest comb. "I think I moved in time last night," Jax said. "I got back in only eight minutes, but I'd been gone at least an hour. I don't know how I did it, though."

"The trick is to concentrate on *when* you want to be," Dorian explained. "I'm going to try to get us back to when we were still at Rockefeller Center." He led Jax to a squishy hole in the floor, and Jax realized why they'd gotten off on the third floor instead of taking the elevator to the basement. His expression must have given his thoughts away, because Dorian said, "It's like going down a water slide. Except with no water."

A pretty tall water slide, thought Jax. The tunnel was made out of some weird fabric in time. Could it rip? Throw them out against a solid wall? Drop them to their deaths?

But Dorian had done it before, so Jax took a deep breath and slid in when his cousin did. He tightened his grip on Dorian's hand, expecting them to be wrenched apart by the fall, but instead of falling, they sort of oozed down the tunnel. It was like sliding through sausage casing. Or intestines. And then Jax wished he hadn't thought of that.

The tunnel contracted around him briefly and squirted him out in a heap beside Dorian. "That was disgusting." Jax let go of Dorian's hand and brushed himself off.

Dorian stood, then grabbed Jax's arm and helped him up. "You'd better hang on to me. We might get separated in time otherwise."

"When are we?" Jax looked around. They were standing in a storage room he recognized from last night's trip. It was beyond Balin's cell and near the outer wall of the building.

"We aren't anywhere yet. I mean, *anywhen*. Not while we're in the tunnel."

"So if this time shift works," Jax said, as Dorian led them back toward the center of the basement, "could we go up to the lobby and watch ourselves come into the building?"

"No. I've tried on purpose to run into myself, but I can't. It's probably against the rules to see yourself."

"Whose rules?" Jax demanded. Now they were passing Balin's cell.

Dorian noticed Jax looking into the room and said, "This isn't where they're keeping her. They've got a different prisoner in here."

"I know." Maybe it was a bad idea for Jax to give away what he knew, but he'd never had a cousin to impress before. "Angus Balin."

"How do you know that?" Dorian gasped.

"Ran into him last night. He said your dad's been grilling him about my liege lady."

Dorian looked ashamed. "You have to keep her away from Aunt Ursula, Jax. She's planning something bad for both Emrys girls."

"She's probably planning to kill them," Jax predicted grimly. "If the Emrys line dies out, the eighth day will cease to exist and so will all the Kin trapped inside it. Including the bad ones who just broke out of prison."

"Yeah, Dad said Aunt Ursula liked the timing of it. I didn't understand what he meant until I heard you and your friends talking about the Llyrs. But it still doesn't make sense. We get *our* magic from the eighth day," Dorian said. "I can't imagine Aunt Ursula giving up the advantage we have from the extra day—or our talents. Without the eighth day, we'd be cut off from . . ."

Dorian stopped talking, and the two boys stared at each other. They were standing in an alternate timeline very similar to the eighth day, and they could *feel* the magical potential buzzing through them. "Oh," said Dorian.

"Only members of your clan can get in here, right?" Jax said. "She wants to destroy the eighth day, kill every member of the Kin race, and turn all Transitioners into Normals."

"Except for the ones she lets into the tunnels. Dad said that any Transitioners who wanted to regain what they'd lost would have to come to us." Dorian looked horrified. "She'd have to be sure. I mean, *really, really sure* the tunnels replenish our magic like the eighth day does."

"That's probably the only reason Addie's still alive. The experiments aren't done yet." Jax tugged Dorian on. The tunnel was now passing through the corridor. Next would be the furnace room and then the lab.

But Dorian stopped him. "This is as close as we can get to where I think they're keeping her. The other end of the basement is mostly utility rooms—furnaces, water heaters, batteries for the solar panels, that kind of stuff. Over here are smaller rooms used by the clan families for storage. Any one of them would make a good cell. We can use the keys to check them out, but we're going to have to step into real time. And there are guards."

"Okay." Jax whipped his dagger out of its sheath and balanced it on the palm of his hand. He muttered a verse Melinda had taught him and closed his eyes.

"Uh, what are you doing?" asked Dorian.

Jax cracked an eye open. "Using my talent. What are you doing?"

"Watching you talk to yourself. How is that using your talent?"

"I need to know if there's anyone in the corridor before we step out."

"Who're you going to interrogate to find that out?" Dorian ran his hand along the wall of the tunnel, searching for the way out.

Jax had already found the exit, but he stepped in front of it. Something told him it wasn't safe to leave the tunnel. "I'm using my talent for information. The *Ambrose* talent for information."

"We're inquisitors. We get our information from *people*. Weren't you trained at all? You can't pull information out of thin air." Dorian spotted the exit and pushed Jax out of his way. "Let me look." He used his fingers to pry open the gap and pressed his eye to it.

"But I *can* get information without interrogating someone. I mean, I can do that too—"

"I don't see anybody out there. Let's go."

"Wait a minute." Jax didn't feel like it was safe, but Dorian pulled him into the corridor. Jax glanced at his wristwatch. It had stopped in the tunnel and was just now starting again. There was no way to tell what time it was to everybody else. "Now I'll need three watches," he complained. "One for the tunnels, one for Grunsday, and one for all the other days."

"No time-measuring device works in the tunnels,"

Dorian told him. "We'd better get moving. No matter what time it is, there'll be a guard passing by soon." He fumbled through the ring of keys and jammed one into the nearest door.

Jax glanced over his shoulder. Balin's cell was just down the hall. If they ran into someone, it might help to have a big, angry killer with them. But it would also give their intentions away. "What will they do if they catch us?" Jax asked.

Dorian peeked into the first room and apparently saw nothing of interest. "For sure we won't remember any of this." He moved to the next door but glanced at Jax. "What Gran said about Dulacs never using their talent on family? That was a lie. I have something to give you when we get back to the apartment. A journal that belonged to your dad."

Jax froze. "My dad kept a journal? You mean like a diary?"

"More like a log of the truth. So he could tell when they changed his memory."

A chill ran up and down Jax's spine. *When* they changed his memory, not *if*.

This is why he left. Oh, crap, this is why Dad left them. Jax opened his mouth to ask more questions, but something down the corridor drew his attention. Had he heard footsteps? No, it was the same feeling he'd had when he'd realized Evangeline was outside this building earlier tonight. "This way," he said. "Addie's farther down."

"What makes you think so? Your *talent for information*?"

"My bond." Jax marched off and left Dorian to follow. His cousin could make fun of him all he wanted. Jax was an Emrys vassal, and there was an Emrys down here. The pull wasn't as strong as it was with Evangeline, and it felt muffled. *Wards,* he thought—wards that would block Evangeline's scrying spell and the Donovans' scent sensitivity.

The corridor made an almost complete circuit through the basement in the shape of a squared-off *U*—or more accurately, a *G*. The elevator and Addie's cell were on opposite ends of the building, with her room beyond a set of fire stairs. Jax knew for certain they'd found it when he saw the warding symbol painted above the door. He rattled the doorknob and held out his hand to Dorian. "Quick! Give me the keys!" He'd free Addie and then Balin. They'd take the stairs, and Balin could overpower any guard who might be there. Billy, well, he'd have to come back for Billy.

Dorian tossed him the keys, but the knob turned by itself, and the door opened. Jax looked up into the face of a tall man in a lab coat with piercing blue eyes—Kin eyes. His complexion was pale, but his hair was a very un-Kin jet black and pulled into a ponytail.

Jax peered around him. "Addie?" he yelled.

Somebody moved in the semidarkness, reacting to his

shout. Someone with blond hair. The man pulled the door shut, cutting off Jax's glimpse of the room's occupant. "What are you doing here?" he asked coldly. "Dorian? Why did you bring him down here?"

"Dad said . . . um . . ." Dorian's voice faded away as he groped for a lie that would explain their presence in the basement in the middle of the night with a ring of keys.

Jax's hopes sank. *That was a FAIL, Dorian.*

"Dr. Morder!" a man called from behind Dorian. "Everything all right?"

"I don't think so," the man in the lab coat replied. "These boys need to be taken upstairs to see Ursula."

Nope. Jax was not going to visit Ursula and get his memory wiped. He launched himself *toward* the security man. With a dead end behind him, it was the only way out.

The guard held out both arms like a linebacker. Jax barreled straight for the guy, then rolled himself into a ball at the last second and hit him in the knees. The man staggered but grabbed a fistful of T-shirt. Jax rolled to his feet, and his momentum pulled him free.

He knew he'd never outrun this guy on the stairs, and there was probably another guard above. His best chance was the brownie hole. It was invisible, but Jax remembered its position in the corridor. He'd dive into it and—

Jax yelped as a weight crashed into him from behind. His knees hit the concrete *hard*, and his chin next. The force jarred his teeth together.

"Kid," said a voice in his ear, "I have a Taser. Don't make me use it."

Jax went limp. He'd been Tasered before and had no desire to experience it again.

Dr. Morder marched Dorian around the corner with one hand on the collar of his shirt. The other hand, slim and pale, held a radio. "You may have just seen them go up in the elevator," he was saying in an unhurried voice, "but they are here *now*. Yes, that's *exactly* what it means. Please let Ursula know to expect them." He paused. "No, don't alert Finn Ambrose. Ursula will call him when she wants him."

The look of fear on Dorian's face let Jax know that, as much as he distrusted Uncle Finn, they were going to be worse off meeting Ursula Dulac without his protection.

24

NO ONE BOTHERED TO hold Dorian on the elevator, although Albert Ganner and one of his brothers both kept their hands on Jax. Dorian was expected to stand in the corner, obedient and quiet, because that was what he'd always been.

Obedient and quiet.

Jax, meanwhile, kept trying to throw off the grip of his guards. He glared at them and wiped his bloody chin with the back of his hand. Dorian couldn't believe the way he'd run straight for Albert, trying to knock him down like a bowling pin. It had been stupid. Completely stupid and pointless and brave.

And I just stood there.

Aunt Ursula was waiting for them when the elevator arrived at the penthouse. Her son Daniel stood beside her, and behind them, Sloane. No one would've guessed they'd all been roused from their beds, and Sloane—dressed in a short skirt and a glittery top with her hair pinned up—probably hadn't been. If Dorian knew his cousin, she'd just come back from clubbing. Not dancing in the plaza at Rockefeller like Lesley, but schmoozing with other Very Important Transitioners at a private club.

What did you do? Sloane mouthed at Dorian.

Aunt Ursula cast a cold look at her errant nephews. "What were they up to, Ganner?"

"Dr. Morder said they were trying to get into the room with . . . uh . . . our guest. They had these." Albert Ganner held up Dad's keys.

"Not your guest," said Jax. "Your prisoner. The girl you have locked up in your nasty old cellar. The same place I'm guessing you wanted to put my liege lady."

"How did you know she was there?" Aunt Ursula glanced at Dorian.

"*He* didn't tell me," Jax said. "I'm an Emrys vassal. I felt her presence." Aunt Ursula scrutinized Jax, then looked back at Dorian. "I *made* him help me," Jax added loudly. "I said I'd beat him up if he didn't."

Dorian swallowed. Was Jax trying to protect him?

"Bring them in here." Aunt Ursula turned and led the way down the hall. The Ganners had to haul Jax bodily into Ursula's office, his feet dragging behind him.

"You old bat," Jax shouted at Aunt Ursula. "I'm not afraid of you."

Dorian had no doubt now. Jax was trying to draw all her

anger toward himself and away from Dorian.

"I've been patient with you," Aunt Ursula said. "But you are distressingly like your father." She addressed the Ganners. "Hold him still." She laid her hands on his head.

Jax fought.

It sickened Dorian, seeing how hard his cousin fought. At first Jax stiffened, like he was trying to resist her mentally. Then he panicked. His body thrashed as he tried to get away from her hands. He kicked wildly. Albert and his brother shifted their positions, pinning Jax's arms and legs. Daniel moved in to help.

This was worse, way worse, than watching Sloane manipulate Billy's parents into believing their son was going off to golf camp when he was really passed out in the back of Dad's car with the bone protruding from his arm. It was worse than erasing the entire memory from Billy's mind.

Because Jax knew what was happening to him and was fighting it with all his strength.

"Sloane!" Aunt Ursula called sharply.

Sloane went to assist her grandmother. She laid her hand on Jax's head, and when her strength was added to the attack, he stopped kicking and went limp in their hands.

When Dad showed up, he looked annoyed to be kept from his bed. But at his first glimpse of Dorian, he stumbled over his own feet and glanced over his shoulder in a double take.

Dorian realized his father had left their apartment completely certain that all three boys were there.

We probably were, Dorian thought, remembering his father's voice on the radio before he and Jax snuck out.

Dad's eyes passed over Dorian to Jax, sitting on a sofa next to Sloane with an ice pack on his chin. "What's going on?" he asked, his eyes darting between Jax and Dorian and his aunt.

"The boys have been on an adventure," Aunt Ursula said.

Jax looked up. "Sorry, Uncle Finn. We shouldn't have, but when Dorian told me about the brownie tunnels, I couldn't resist."

Dad licked his lips nervously. "Aunt Ursula, we agreed—"

"We tried it your way, Finn, and nearly had a disaster on our hands." She tossed him his keys. He caught them and stared at them, flabbergasted. "Jax is seeing things our way now." Aunt Ursula smoothed Jax's wavy hair. "Aren't you?"

Jax didn't pull his head away or glare at her or anything he would normally have done. "I'm sorry I caused so much trouble," he said. "I didn't trust you when I first came, but that's because Riley lied to me."

"We understand," Aunt Ursula reassured him.

"He didn't want me to know I had a decent family I could be living with instead of him," Jax said. "And *she* didn't want to lose her *vassal.*" He spat out the word like it meant the same as *slave.*

"You realize how dangerous it is for her to be running

around loose," Aunt Ursula said.

Jax dropped the ice bag into his lap. "You bet I do! I was there when the world nearly ended. We were *that* close!" He held up his thumb and finger a quarter inch apart. "Can you get me free of her? And Riley? He's got custody papers, but he must've forced Dad to sign them."

"Yes, Jax," Dad said. "Of course, we'll get your custody away from him. It's what we've wanted all along. But you've got to help us with your liege lady first." Dorian stared at the floor. Dad had said he didn't want this, but he was going to use it anyway, now that it had happened.

"I want out of my bond," Jax said. "She forced me into it."

"Do you know where she is?" Aunt Ursula asked.

"She's here, and so is Riley!" Jax said triumphantly. "I saw them earlier."

Dad grunted. "On the motorcycle. I thought so."

"Yeah, the motorcycle," Jax repeated bitterly. "Riley loves that thing almost as much as—" He faltered as if trying to remember how he'd planned to end that sentence. What did Riley love more than his motorcycle?

Sloane picked up the ice bag, put it in his hand, and guided his hand back to his chin.

"Loves that motorcycle more than anything," Jax finished.

"Do you have a way to contact them?" Dad asked.

"Yeah."

Dorian cringed as Jax blabbed the twins' meeting place, helpfully providing descriptions of them and ratting them out for stealing his uncle's keys and wallet. "Sorry about that," Jax added with a sheepish grin. "Like I said, I didn't know any better back then."

Dad gave him a false, forced smile. "It's all right, Jax. At least you know where your loyalties lie now."

Jax's face fell. "Still with her. I don't like it, but I'm bound to her. I can't—"

"What about *him*?" Sloane asked. "Pendragon or Pendare or whatever he calls himself."

"Him? I have no bond with him." Jax bared his teeth. "I hate him. Always have. Tell me what you want me to do."

Dad hauled Dorian into the elevator by the back of his shirt. "I don't know what's gotten into you," he growled. "But I'll deal with you in the morning."

"You mean give me my lesson on loyalty?" Dorian surprised himself with the tone of his voice, but he was shaken. Aunt Ursula's parting words to them had been: *Dorian needs a lesson on loyalty.* The *or else* had been implied. "Are you going to let Aunt Ursula change me into a different person too?" Dorian was sure the only reason he'd escaped tonight was because Jax had drawn all the fire, making Dorian look innocent so he would be spared.

"Don't be ridiculous. Jax isn't a different person."

"Isn't he? She made him hate his friends."

Dad stabbed the elevator button for the fifth floor. "His

friends are, in fact, a rival clan lord and a very dangerous, high-ranking Kin lady."

"You mean a *girl*. Like the girl you have locked up in the basement." Dorian had never talked back to his father like this before. *I sound like Jax.* For a wild moment, Dorian wondered if his aunt had changed him after all and he didn't remember it. But she would never have made him more like Jax!

"I won't even ask how you know that," his father snapped. "But the *girl* you're talking about almost killed me and several of your clansmen during her capture. She and three Kin kids traveling in a luxury Hummer—none of them older than fifteen—nearly defeated us. And that was the week before Kin with an American aircraft attacked Oeth-Anoeth in Wales and released the Llyrs and Arawens. I don't think that's a coincidence."

"But it's convenient for Aunt Ursula's plan, right? It gives her an excuse to eliminate the eighth day and all the Kin while cornering the market on magic with our tunnels."

Dad had given up showing any surprise over what Dorian knew. "Perhaps you've forgotten why the Llyrs and the Arawens were imprisoned in the first place," Dad said as the elevator stopped on their floor. He opened the cage door. "I thought you were smarter than that. Those Kin will be bent on warfare, and outside Oeth-Anoeth they're free to exercise their full powers. Life as we know it on this planet could be over if they aren't stopped. *That's* why the girl is locked up in our basement. *That's* why the other one needs to be in our custody too."

Llyr was a power of darkness in Welsh mythology—a god of the wind and the sea. For those who knew better, the Llyrs were a family of Kin with magic controlling the weather, formidable enough to be remembered as gods and ambitious enough to want to *be* gods. And the Arawens—they had power over death itself.

Dad steered him into their apartment. Dorian didn't fight. He let himself be directed through the living room and down the hallway. Dad yanked the bedroom door open and pushed him in. The door slammed closed, and a key turned in the lock.

Billy sat up in the bottom bunk, just a dim shape in the dark. "What happened?" he demanded. "Where's Jax?"

Dorian stared at him, his brain mired in the question of whether ending the life of two girls and destroying the eighth day was better than seeing the world enslaved by Kin lords. "Jax is gone," he said.

25

THE PATH THROUGH CENTRAL PARK was deserted at midmorning on Grunsday, even though there were more Transitioners in New York than Jax could ever have guessed. He suspected there was a lot of stuff about the eighth day Riley had never told him—or lied about.

His head hurt, and not just from slamming his chin on a concrete floor. After his adventure in the basement last night, Aunt Ursula let Jax get a couple hours' sleep in the penthouse before sending him on this mission. But he still felt dog tired. He hadn't slept much the past two nights— the past *three* nights, actually, although at the moment he couldn't recall what he'd been doing on all of them. But tonight he could sleep like a stone.

In his new home.

With his family.

There'd be no more cramped little house for Jax, with nothing to eat in the broken-down refrigerator and Riley forgetting to pay the gas bill . . .

Oh wait, Riley didn't live in that house anymore. He'd forgotten that. But it didn't matter. Jax was going to live with Uncle Finn and Aunt Marian from now on.

The Grunsday sunlight filtered through the trees, casting a mottled pink pattern on the path. He passed under a bridge and spotted the statue of the Alaskan sled dog perched on a large rock. He slowed his pace, looking left and right—and then up. Those awful Donovans had to be around here somewhere, maybe waiting to jump on him from the bridge.

At the sound of a shoe scraping on pavement, he froze, and then somebody appeared from behind the Balto statue.

Not a Donovan. Riley.

Jax grinned. He couldn't help it. *Jackpot.*

Riley grinned back. "Jax, you idiot. Are you all right?"

"Yeah, I'm fine." His own smile wavered. Was he supposed to be glad to see Riley?

"I should smack you upside the head." Riley reached for him, and Jax flinched, expecting the promised smack. Instead Riley tipped Jax's head back to look at his chin. "What happened?"

"Nothing. I fell. It was dumb."

"Look at me," Riley ordered. It was a command. Jax had to meet his eyes.

But he didn't have to be happy about it. "I don't have

time to gaze into your eyes, Riley. Knock it off."

Riley laughed and let go of him. "You seem okay to me."

Jax stepped backward, thinking quickly. "Look, I can pretend I got lost in the park for a minute, but any longer than that and they'll come searching for me." He had a prepared script, but he'd expected to deliver it to the twins. He needed to alter it—and stall. The Ganners were watching, and if he'd met the Donovans, they would've kept their distance. But Aunt Ursula had planned for this possibility. If Riley or Evangeline showed up, the watchers were supposed to take action.

Of course, if the twins scented the Ganners approaching . . . "Where are the Donovans?"

"Tegan's making a survey of the area, and Thomas went to grab some hot dogs." Riley ran a hand through his hair. "Jax, why didn't you wait for us? Evangeline was upset you came after Billy on your own. Did you think it was going to matter to us, who you were?"

"Where is Evangeline?" Jax asked, feigning concern. "Is she okay?"

"She's safe. Is Billy in the park with you? I'll get A.J., and we'll snatch him."

"What about Evangeline's sister?"

"Leave that to me. I sent Arnie and Gloria to make nice with Sheila Morgan. No matter how mad she is at me, she won't like the Dulacs holding an Emrys heir. Once

I've got you and Billy out of here, *I'll* handle extracting Addie."

"I already have a plan for getting her out," Jax said. "If you just listen, I'll tell you." He put distance between them, as if he were pacing. The Ganners had a talent for aim, but Jax didn't want to get in the way of a good shot.

"Okay, so tell me," said Riley. "Evangeline doesn't want you doing anything risky."

Dare he ask again? Was it too obvious? Jax turned away from Riley and put his hand on the honor blade sheathed at his side. "Where *is* Evangeline?" he asked.

"In the zoo with A.J.," Riley replied promptly. "What's your plan?"

Jax raised his right hand to his forehead in a salute. He'd gotten what he needed.

Take him.

At the same moment, Riley caught on. His voice changed as he realized Jax had used his talent on him. "Jax?"

The buzzing sound was no louder than a mosquito. Riley slapped his neck, and his hand came away with a dart between his fingers. He looked at it, then at Jax.

"Riley, you suck." Jax delivered the code phrase for *all is well*, which Riley had forgotten to get out of him. "*And* you're a sucker."

"Jax," Riley said hazily, making a grab for him. But Jax dodged, just as the second dart hit Riley in the chest where his leather biker's jacket was unzipped. He went down on one knee. "Don't—"

Jax braced himself to fight off a command. But Riley's voice didn't carry even a hint of magic. Maybe he was too weak to call on his talent, but it was almost like he was pleading. "Not Evangeline," he whispered, looking up at Jax. "Don't—"

"Jax! Hey—Riley?"

Jax spun around. Thomas stood ten yards down the path, a hot dog in one hand and his mouth full of what was probably another. He gaped at Riley, who keeled over into the grass. Then Thomas whirled and started running.

Jax took off after him. In a sprint between him and Thomas, he would normally have bet on Thomas. But maybe the hot dogs slowed him down, because Jax caught him under the bridge and leaped onto his back. They went down in a tangle of arms and legs. Thomas twisted beneath Jax and clouted him in the head with the fist that held the hot dog.

"Resting objects stay in motion," Thomas hollered, kneeing Jax in the stomach, "unless unbalanced actors force them!"

That sounded familiar, although it made no sense, and Jax had no idea why Thomas was shouting it at him. But he hung on, even when Thomas dragged himself to his feet. "Objects at rest stay at rest," Thomas tried again, "and other objects—oh heck!"

The dart hit him in the back of the neck, inches from Jax's head. Thomas yanked it out immediately, but it had already delivered its drug. He was only half the size of Riley, and it didn't take a second dart to put him facedown in the dirt.

Jax stood up and brushed bits of hot-dog bun out of his hair, then glared at Albert Ganner, who was running toward him. Two other men headed for Riley, lying motionless beside the statue.

"That was pretty close to my face," Jax complained.

"We never miss," Albert assured him. "Now, where are we headed?"

Jax opened his mouth to tell him . . . and stopped. "There's a problem."

"I can't betray her," Jax explained to Aunt Ursula. "I'm her vassal."

His great-aunt was very patient. She sat at her desk in her office in front of a large picture window overlooking Central Park and the pinkish eighth-day sky beyond. "You're not betraying your liege, Jax. She needs to be in protective custody."

"Yeah, but if *she* would view it as a betrayal, I can't do it. I tried!"

Jax *had* tried. But he'd been unable to tell the Ganners where she was. The words literally wouldn't leave his mouth. He couldn't write the name of the place. He couldn't lead them there or walk there on his own and let them follow. The compulsion of his oath wouldn't allow it.

He'd repeated everything else Riley said, including how the Crandalls were appealing to the Morgan clan. Aunt Ursula waved away that information. "I'm not afraid of Sheila Morgan."

Sloane sighed. "Maybe Uncle Finn and I should pay a visit to Pendragon."

"Not for a while," said Ganner. "We had to double-dose him because I thought he was going to hurt Jax. He'll be out cold for hours."

Jax sat up in alarm. "How can Uncle Finn question him? If you let him talk, he'll command you."

"Don't worry," said Sloane. "We have our methods." She reached out to pat him, but Jax moved his arm out of reach. Sloane was always touching him, and it bugged him. Plus Jax could've sworn her touch made his head hurt worse.

It had to be his imagination. And lack of sleep.

"What about the other boy?" Aunt Ursula asked.

The Ganners had complained they were running out of space for prisoners in the basement, so Thomas, who posed little threat, had been locked into a bathroom in the Dulac penthouse. "He'll wake up sooner than Pendragon," Ganner promised.

"He's dumber than a box of rocks, though," Jax warned them.

"All he needs to know is her location," Aunt Ursula said.

"Which will change, if she suspects we've captured her allies," Sloane said. "Grandmother, we're going to have to rely on Jax to bring her to us."

Jax rubbed his aching head with his hand. "I'm telling you, I can't go to her!"

"Not if you bring Albert with you." Sloane reached into the suede jacket she was wearing and removed her honor blade. "But if I swear that the Ganners will stay here, you can rejoin your liege and convince her to come to us willingly."

"How am I supposed to do that?"

Aunt Ursula smiled. "Tell her we have Pendragon, and we'll kill him if she doesn't cooperate. Does she care for him at all?"

Jax searched his memory, which was strangely murky. Something about a kiss on a pyramid . . . "Yeah, I think she does," he said. "But I don't know if I can lie to her, and besides, one of the Crandalls is a truth teller." A trickle of alarm ran down his spine. "It *is* a lie, right?" He didn't care about Riley. Riley was a jerk. But Jax was opposed to murder, even for jerks.

"Of course, it's a lie," Sloane said reassuringly. "So tell

her we have him, and let her imagine what we might do to him. That's better anyway."

There were no animals in the Central Park Zoo on Grunsday.

Jax almost felt sorry for Evangeline, hiding in a zoo without any animals, because he knew how much she longed to see one. He remembered wanting to bring her a cat—before such ordinary concerns got left behind in an effort to save the world.

Back when he liked her.

It was eerie, passing the empty sea-lion exhibit. The leftover smell of animals still hung about the place. *The animals are gone, but their smell is still here. Weird.*

"Jax?"

He felt her presence and turned toward her even before she came running out of the bushes and palm trees behind the sea-lion pool. The bond of vassalhood felt like a noose around his neck as she threw her arms around him. Halfheartedly, he gave her a quick hug back, but his eyes were on A.J., who also stepped out of the shrubbery. Jax had always thought A.J. was a big useless lump, but he looked a lot more menacing with a rifle slung over his shoulder.

"Are you all right?" Evangeline unwound her arms

from him. "Did they hurt you?"

"Why would they?" Jax said, stepping backward. "They're my family."

"Where's Riley?" A.J. demanded.

His mouth too dry to answer, Jax pointed behind him—toward the Dulac building, which was in the same direction as the Balto statue. Let that serve as an answer, till he figured out how to break the news without A.J. shooting him.

"I was so worried about you." Evangeline's startlingly blue eyes searched his face.

"I don't know why you were worried. They're *family*," he repeated.

"They kidnapped your friend," A.J. said.

"They didn't kidnap him. He's their guest."

Evangeline frowned. "But they're *Dulacs*, Jax."

"My grandmother is a Dulac," Jax said. "So that makes me one too. Maybe we're not as bad as you think."

A.J. muttered something about *murderers* under his breath, but Evangeline spoke over him. "My sister. Is she there? As a guest? Willingly?"

Yes, he wanted to say. His lips wouldn't form the word. As he feared, he couldn't lie to her. "I haven't met her yet, but you can see her today. All you have to do is come back with me."

"What?" exclaimed A.J.

Evangeline nodded, and for a moment Jax felt a thrill

of relief, that it was going to be that easy. But then she said, "Why would I do that?" and Jax understood the nod wasn't agreement. It was confirmation of something in her mind.

"So you can be with your sister," Jax said.

"What's the other reason?"

She knew. Jax didn't know how, but she did. His eyes slid uneasily toward A.J. before he answered. "Because they have Riley, and my aunt says if you want to see him again, you have to turn yourself over to her."

A.J. swore loudly, and Evangeline pressed her fingers to her lips. "Jax," she whispered. "What have they done to you?"

26

"THEY HAVEN'T DONE ANYTHING to me," Jax protested, but he was drowned out by A.J.'s yelling.

"I *told* Riley! I told him not to go!"

Evangeline shook her head tearfully. "He was so sure he'd be able to tell."

"Tell what?" Jax growled.

"Where were the Donovans? Weren't they supposed to be able to sniff it out?" A.J. stared at Jax like he'd sprouted three heads.

"Thomas is with Riley, and they're fine for now." Jax felt a twinge of guilt at that barely true statement. When he'd last seen them, both boys had been stone-cold unconscious.

Evangeline gasped. "They have Thomas too?"

"They'll kill Riley." A.J. groaned. "If they haven't already." He lifted his head and stared off into the distance, as if trying to sense whether the bond to his liege still existed.

"No, they won't." Evangeline grabbed A.J.'s arm. "They want *me*. If Jax can't deliver me, Riley will be their only other means to get to me."

"Look," Jax said angrily to Evangeline. "Do you care about your sister or not? Because if *I* had a sister—or a brother—nothing would stop me from going to them. I thought I didn't have any close family left, but turns out I did. Not a brother or sister, but cousins and an uncle and grandparents who wanted me. Riley knew and didn't tell me . . ."

"He *didn't* know," protested Evangeline.

"He dragged me away from my mother's family and didn't take care of me," Jax said bitterly. "He didn't buy groceries! He left me alone when I had my first Grunsday—never explained anything to me—and I thought it was the zombie apocalypse! He left me again, and I was kidnapped by a bank robber. He left me *again*, and the Balins got me . . ."

"None of that is true," A.J. snapped.

"It's all true," Evangeline said. "But it's *twisted*. Jax, he came for you when you were in danger."

"No, he came for *you*. He sent Miller Owens to torture *me*."

A.J. lifted his fists. Evangeline stepped between

them, and A.J. stopped. "Miller died saving your life!" he growled over her head.

Jax faltered. It was something he didn't like to remember, but it was *true*, and somehow, it didn't match everything else he remembered about that day. "Stop changing the subject. I want to go back to my family, and if Evangeline cared about hers, we'd be there already."

"They used their magic on you," Evangeline said. "Think, Jax! Aren't there gaps in your memory, things that don't match up? They can't have changed everything so fast." She reached for him, trying to put a hand on his shoulder, but he flinched away.

"Crap. He's not even Jax anymore," A.J. said to Evangeline.

Jax's skin rose in goose bumps. "You can't fool me like you did before. But I'm still *me*."

"Is it permanent?" Evangeline asked A.J. "Can't we do anything?" Then, in horror: "Can they do this to Riley too?"

A.J. ran both hands through his sloppy blond hair. "It's not safe here. Who knows what Jax told 'em? Riley would want me to get you someplace safe, then come back for him."

"What about Jax?" Evangeline asked, her voice breaking.

"Release me," Jax said. "I don't want to be your vassal

anymore. I'm sick of tagging along behind you and Riley like a dog. Let me go." Jax's head hurt so badly, it felt like it was going to split open. Maybe if he rid himself of this terrible bond, the pain would go away. And then he could turn her over to Aunt Ursula.

"You should do it," A.J. said in a low voice. "He might be able to track you, otherwise."

"I can't abandon him," she whispered, as if Jax wasn't right there, listening.

"He's a lost cause," A.J. hissed. "And I hope like heck that Riley isn't, that he's strong enough to fight them, but even if he's not, the most important thing is to keep *you* away from them. You know that, Evangeline."

Her whole body seemed to crumple in defeat, and she pressed both hands over her eyes. "Kneel," she said to Jax.

He dropped to his knees on the path. She uncovered her eyes and took his face in her hands. "Jaxon Aubrey," she whispered, tears on her cheeks. "Is this really what you want?"

"Ambrose," he corrected. "And yes."

She sniffed. "You swore to me as Aubrey."

"Jax Aubrey!"

Jax pulled out of Evangeline's hands, hearing his name shouted from another direction.

Tegan Donovan marched down the path from the zoo

239

entrance, her hands clenched into fists. "Objects at rest stay at rest," she yelled, breaking into a run, "while objects in motion stay in motion unless acted upon by an external or unbalanced force!"

Then she slugged Jax so hard in the face, she knocked him over.

He rolled in the grass, moaning. "Ow! Ow! Weren't you listening?" He thrashed around and sat up. "Smitty just said you didn't have to hit me!"

But Smitty hadn't *just* said it. He'd said it two days ago. Dimly, Jax knew that.

Tegan had insisted Jax meet her father's friend Smitty as soon as their bus pulled into New York City—and definitely before he contacted his uncle to arrange a swap for Billy.

So on Tuesday morning, at a fast-food restaurant near the Port Authority bus station, Jax showed his mark to a tall, lanky Transitioner with a bulging Adam's apple, who gave Jax only a flash of his own mark before sinking into a chair at their table. "What can I do for the Donovans this time?" he asked. Jax tried to meet his eyes, but Smitty's irises bounced around like Ping-Pong balls.

Tegan pointed a thumb at Jax. "Our friend is meeting the Dulacs later today. We need a way to make sure he stays himself."

Smitty's zigzagging eyes rested briefly on Jax. "Best way to do that is *not* meet the Dulacs."

"Let's suppose he can't get out of it."

Jax grunted in exasperation. "How can this guy help?"

Jax's disapproval caught Smitty's attention. His eyes locked on Jax like a guided missile.

"Smitty's a memory manipulator," Tegan said. "Kind of like Riley's friend Miller and the Dulacs."

"Not like the Dulacs," Smitty muttered. "Nothing like them."

Tegan waved down his protest. "His specialty is planting things in your memory that get activated by a trigger," she told Jax. "He's pretty awesome."

Thomas grinned. "There's this woman we used to work with who turned on us. Now, every time she tries to snitch on us to the police, she barks like a dog instead of saying our name! Seriously. She thinks *Donovan* but says *bow wow*!"

Tegan addressed Smitty. "I know you can't block the Dulacs. But can you *outsmart* them? C'mon. There's gotta be something you can do."

Smitty's fingers danced on the table like he was playing piano. "A total reset might work," he said after a few bars. "Erase him back to this morning. But that's a pretty big plant. It'll only work once. No do-overs."

"What's he talking about?" Jax demanded.

"Shush." Tegan punched him in the arm and focused

on Smitty. "Yeah, bring him back to this morning. But he'd have to remember what happened in between. Can you do that?"

The piano recital switched to a drum solo. "That's trickier."

"But can you do it?"

"Your dad'll owe me big-time."

"What are we talking about?" Jax rubbed his arm.

"Smitty can plant a memory manipulation that will send your mind back to this point when you hear the trigger. But we're going to need you to remember what happened in between or you might land yourself right back in trouble."

"It'll have to be encapsulated," Smitty said. "It won't be real clear. You'll remember it like a really vivid dream." His index fingers bounced down the table, finishing off a drum solo.

"But any changes made by the Dulacs . . ." Tegan prompted him.

"Will be part of the dream," Smitty finished. "Total reset."

Tegan turned toward Jax. "We need a verbal trigger, something only you and me and Tommy might say."

"Do you remember what Miss Cassidy used to recite every week?" Jax fumbled for the beginning of their science teacher's favorite physical law. "An object at rest stays at rest . . ."

"While an object in motion stays in motion." Tegan's eyes lit up.

"Unless acted upon by an external or unbalanced force." They finished in unison and grinned at each other.

Thomas looked confused. "Say what now?"

Smitty leaned across the table and gripped Jax's head. "Total reset, triggered by that sentence," he said. "Got it."

"And a smack in the face," added Tegan.

"What? No! I don't need to be smacked in the face," Jax protested. "Do I?"

Smitty smiled for the first time. "Only if Tegan thinks it's called for."

"He said I could if it was called for." Tegan shook the hand she'd hit him with. "Where's Tommy?"

Jax held his aching cheek in one hand and looked around, disoriented. The last thing he remembered clearly was leaning across the restaurant table and letting Smitty do who-knows-what to his head. Now he was sitting in the grass in the middle of an empty zoo with Evangeline crouched beside him. Her face was blotchy and wet with tears.

"What's the matter?" he asked in alarm. "What happened?"

"Jax?" Evangeline whispered. "Is it you?"

"What'd you do to him?" A.J. asked.

"I knew a guy with a memory-manipulation talent," Tegan said. "We set this up before he met the Dulacs. He's as stupid as ever, but at least he's back the way he was. Now, *what happened to my brother?*"

Jax looked up at Tegan. It was fuzzy—just as Smitty had warned him—and he had to swim through disjointed images of the past two days. Dorian. Uncle Finn. Ursula Dulac. Billy's arm. His brain conjured a memory of gleefully signaling the Ganners to shoot Riley with a tranquilizer. Jax felt sick. *I betrayed Riley and loved doing it.* "Thomas couldn't remember the trigger," he whispered.

Then every nerve in his body came alive, and he launched himself at Evangeline, knocking her flat on the ground. A dart embedded itself in a tree trunk over their heads. "Take cover!" he shouted.

Tegan took off running between the trees and bushes, but A.J. staggered, plucking a dart out of his shirt sleeve. "Grazed me," he said, ducking behind a palm tree and unslinging the rifle. He shook his head, trying to clear it, and put the rifle up to his shoulder. "Get her out of here, Jax. I'll cover you."

Evangeline scrambled up and ran after Tegan, but Jax hesitated. "A.J., some of those people are my relatives." He couldn't believe he was saying this, but his muddled memories dragged at his limbs like lead weights. "Please—"

A.J. sagged against the tree and blinked, fighting the tranquilizer. "I'm just gonna distract 'em. I've never killed anybody in my life, and I don't really want to start."

Jax dodged sideways, and another dart whizzed by, missing him. *Sloane Dulac swore the Ganners wouldn't follow me.* He remembered her oath, but he had no idea why his altered self had been so easily fooled by it. Sloane had obviously been free to send other vassals instead, trailing far enough behind Jax that he didn't know they were there—and allowing him to approach Evangeline without violating his oath.

Lucky for him, these vassals didn't have the Ganners' magical aim.

"Jax!" hissed A.J. "Go!"

Jax glanced at A.J., whom he'd never liked, never respected, and for the first time saw why he was Riley's best friend.

Then he ran.

27

JAX CRASHED THROUGH THE decorative plants and onto a path that curved into the wilder areas of the zoo. He caught up with the girls in front of a pavilion overlooking one of the exhibits just as they came running back his way. "We're cut off!" Tegan gasped. Jax skidded to a halt, realizing the enemy must have spread out strategically before revealing themselves.

"Follow me." Tegan left the path and clambered up a tree. "*Up* is the last place anyone looks!"

Jax cupped his hands for Evangeline to step in, and Evangeline followed awkwardly in Tegan's wake—up the tree and onto the roof of the pavilion. Jax scrambled after her and lay flat beside the girls.

No sooner were they out of sight than they heard footsteps on the path below—footsteps that passed the exhibit without pausing. Jax sighed with relief, but Evangeline's face was pinched with worry. She flinched at the sound of gunfire in the distance. "A.J.," she whispered.

"A.J.'s doing the shooting," Jax assured her. "The other guys just have tranquilizer guns." At least he hoped so.

Tegan slid down the roof—not toward the walking path, but toward the exhibit. "We can't stay here."

"You said they never look up," Jax objected.

"I said they look up *last*," Tegan corrected. "We need to hide someplace they think it's impossible for us to be."

The adjacent exhibit was surrounded by a chain link fence. A metal netting covered the entire enclosure and was bolted on one end to the eaves of the pavilion. Visitors entering the pavilion could observe the animals through glass windows. *Must be birds in here,* Jax thought, wriggling down to sit on the edge of the roof next to Tegan. Evangeline joined them, and Tegan demonstrated where they should place their feet on the steel net below. They kicked in unison. Five or six hard kicks dislodged a wooden plank with the net still attached. This created a narrow gap between the net and the pavilion, which Tegan widened by bracing it open with her legs.

Evangeline slid through the hole and into the yard beneath the netting. Jax wiggled through next and landed beside Evangeline. Above them, Tegan squeezed as much of her body through the gap as she could while still bracing the opening with her feet and hanging on to the roof with her hands.

"Catch her," Evangeline urged Jax. "Or she'll break her neck."

Before Jax could do more than awkwardly hold out his arms, Tegan let go. She dropped and landed on her feet, and the loose plank fell back where it belonged, weighed down by the steel net. Tegan looked triumphantly at Evangeline. Then they heard voices and all three of them dived deeper into the animal enclosure for cover, lying flat in the grass between rocks and trees.

"What about in there?" a new voice asked.

"They can't get into the snow leopards' cage. It's fenced in over the top."

Leopards? Jax turned his head to stare at Tegan, but he waited until the men moved away before whispering. "Are you crazy? You made us climb in with leopards?"

"They aren't here today, dummy," Tegan whispered back.

Evangeline lifted her head up from behind a clump of grass and glared at Tegan. "Why didn't you tell us you had a fix for Jax?" she snapped. "You let us worry for nothing."

"You didn't tell them?" Jax asked incredulously.

"It would only work once," Tegan said. "The fewer people who knew, the safer you were."

"You should have told *me*," Evangeline hissed.

"I don't owe you anything. *I'm* not your vassal." Tegan put her head down and wouldn't look at either of them.

Jax exhaled in aggravation. Yes, Tegan had been clever, getting Smitty to manipulate his memory, but Jax couldn't believe she hadn't let his friends in on the plan. If she had, maybe Riley and Thomas wouldn't be in the hands of the Dulacs right now. He didn't know why Tegan was so secretive and dishonest—or why she disliked Evangeline. If he didn't know better, he'd think she was jealous because Jax and his liege were such good friends. But that was impossible. Tegan thought Jax was a jerk and said so all the time.

More than an hour elapsed, and it was getting late in the afternoon. At one point, they heard alarmed shouting, and Jax had the impression someone might have been hurt. *Not A.J.,* he told himself. *Or they'd be happy, not upset.*

Men passed by their hiding spot several times, and by their conversation they seemed frustrated and puzzled over how their quarry had gotten out of the zoo. Some of them paused to peer into the leopard exhibit, but most didn't bother because the netting still appeared to be nailed in place. One man eventually hollered to check the roof of the pavilion, proving that *up* was indeed the last place they looked.

Jax had to credit Tegan for brains. *Shame she's so mean.*

Eventually, silence descended over the zoo. Tegan got

up, walked the perimeter of the enclosure, sniffing, and decided it was safe to leave. Nimbly, she climbed the outside of the pavilion, digging her fingers and toes into the wooden siding between the observation windows. Once she reached the roof, however, she encountered a problem. From the inside, using her hands, the net was too heavy to lift. "Do you want me to come up?" Jax called.

"No, get me something to prop it open. Break off some tree branches—sturdy ones."

"Hurry," Evangeline urged.

"Chill, Blondie," Tegan said. "The leopards won't be back till midnight, and you'll be gone by then. Only Jax and I can get eaten."

"I'm worried about Riley and A.J.," Evangeline retorted. "And Thomas."

"Nice of you to add him to the list." Tegan took a thick branch handed up to her by Jax and shoved it between the broken plank and the building. "I know he's not a high priority for you."

"Higher than you," muttered Evangeline, stomping a low limb off a nearby tree.

Tegan used the branches to pry open the gap between the net and the pavilion. Once it was wide enough, she slithered through onto the roof, where she again braced the gap open with her legs. Jax boosted Evangeline, and Tegan offered her a hand from above. At least the girls confined themselves to verbal jabs, Jax thought with relief, and worked together when they needed to.

Reluctantly, they decided not to look for A.J. The Dulac clansmen had spent well over an hour searching the zoo. Either A.J. had been captured, or he'd escaped, or he was hiding in a place as good as theirs—possibly passed out cold from the tranq dart. So, instead, while the pink sky darkened toward purple, Tegan led them through the park toward the Dulac building. "We can't take Evangeline there," Jax protested.

"Then this is where we separate," Tegan grunted. "'Cause I'm going for Tommy."

"And I'm not abandoning Riley and Billy," Jax said. "But the best thing is for me to go back and pretend I'm still on their side. I'll lie about what happened in the zoo."

"They'll only believe that if you turn me in," Evangeline said. "And that's what you're going to do."

"Are you crazy?" Jax felt like he had to ask that question way too often.

"They have four hostages. Five if they caught A.J." Evangeline trudged down the path. "We can bargain for them to give up Thomas and Billy. I ought to be worth that much to them."

"Then why didn't we surrender at the zoo!" Jax

exclaimed in exasperation.

"I won't go in unconscious, like a wild animal. I'll walk in under my own power and by my own choice. With someone they think has turned against me—but hasn't."

"Shhh!" Tegan grabbed Evangeline and Jax and dragged them off the path. Then she darted toward something on the ground about thirty yards away. Some*body* on the ground.

Tegan poked the motionless figure with the toe of her shoe before bending to take a closer look. Then she beckoned them over. Jax didn't recognize the man, but by his mark he was a Ganner. "He's part of the Dulac security force," Jax said.

"He's not dead." Tegan rolled him over to search him. "Just asleep."

Evangeline looked around. "Did he get shot accidentally by one of his own men?"

"I don't see any dart." Tegan pocketed his wallet. "And it smells like a spell to me."

The Dulac building was across the street, and this guy might have been on watch duty. But he was a fair distance into the park. Had he been lured away from his post—or was *this* his post? Why would they post a guard on a random park path? Jax pulled out his honor blade to focus and enhance his talent. A memory nagged at him, something Dorian had said. *The tunnel that goes to the park is the longest.* Jax walked back and forth until he sensed what he was looking for. Then he flipped the dagger into its sheath and reached his hand into a brownie hole. *Wow, if anything in my head had turned out to really be just a dream, I would've bet on this part.*

He was gratified to see both Evangeline and Tegan staring at his apparently severed arm with identically stunned expressions.

It took Jax a few minutes to explain—at least what he remembered—and he knew he wasn't making much sense. Tegan refused to accept that she couldn't use the tunnel, so Jax stepped inside and reached out to take her hand. But the tunnel didn't exist for Tegan. Jax's disembodied hand dragged her around empty air, but he couldn't pull her inside.

Jax stepped back into the park to consider the situation. "I can sneak into the building this way," he said to Evangeline. He didn't like the idea of leaving her, but turning her over to the Dulacs was unacceptable—and so was abandoning Riley and Thomas, not to mention Addie and Billy. He eyed the sleeping Ganner man. Something weird was going on. Weirder than usual, even. "You and Tegan are going to have to hide someplace in the park. You can't stay near this building." Jax looked uneasily at Tegan, wanting to ask, *Can I trust you with Evangeline's safety?* and knowing he'd offend her if he did.

Instead of replying to his suggestion, Evangeline, who'd watched Tegan's attempts to enter without saying a word, darted forward, slipped past Jax, and disappeared into the brownie hole.

Tegan howled in outrage. "How come she can get in and not me?"

Jax was just as flabbergasted. "I—I don't know." Maybe he was remembering it wrong? No, he was *certain* that Dorian said only a handful of Dulac vassals had access to these tunnels.

"Never mind." Tegan scowled. "I'll find my own way into the building if I have to."

Jax hesitated. If the look in Tegan's eyes was any clue, Jax was close to getting punched in the face again. "I'll get Thomas out," he promised.

Then he slid into the brownie hole after his liege.

28

DORIAN THOUGHT HE MIGHT snap if he had to endure close quarters with Billy Ramirez much longer. In between complaining that the eighth day wasn't as much fun as he'd thought it would be, Billy had spent the bulk of the day pawing through every drawer in Dorian's room, rummaging in his closet, and peering under the beds. "What are you looking for?" Dorian demanded.

"Resources," Billy replied.

They were under house arrest, locked into Dorian's bedroom in disgrace.

That morning, Dorian had been required to present himself to his father and "explain his actions." The command was followed so quickly by an angry tirade, Dorian never had a chance to explain anything. Dad finished up by telling Dorian how lucky they were that Aunt Ursula wasn't angrier with him.

"Because she would've changed my memory?" Dorian asked.

"Dorian, we don't—" Dad amended his words. "We don't *usually* use the Dulac talent on family. In Jax's case, it was unfortunate, but necessary."

"Dad, I can't figure something out." Dorian paused and then, thinking about Jax and how brave he'd been, took the plunge. "Do you *really not* know what happened to Uncle Rayne?"

Dad's face turned beet red. "How would you know anything about Rayne?"

Dorian said nothing, already regretting the question.

"What do you know about my brother?" Dad's voice reverberated with magic. Dorian swayed in surprise. It took a supreme effort of will to keep his mouth shut. Dad reached for his honor blade. *"What do you know about Rayne—and how?"*

"Aunt Ursula made him do something terrible, then changed his memory. I read it in a journal I found in Gran and Gramps's apartment." Dorian blinked against the sting of tears. His father had *interrogated* him.

Next Dad had marched Dorian into the bedroom, giving him no choice but to hand over the journal. If he hadn't, Dad would have unleashed his magic again, and Dorian couldn't bear the humiliation, especially in front of the very curious Billy. The color drained from Dad's face when he saw Rayne's message on the last page of the journal, and he left the room without another word, locking the boys in behind him.

Mom let them out for lunch and a bathroom visit. Lesley

refused to look at Dorian, which he thought was stinky considering how many times he'd stuck his neck out for her. Billy tried to ingratiate himself with Mom by helping her set the table, although that didn't prevent her from locking him back up with Dorian afterward. Lesley, too, was locked into her room, even though she protested she hadn't done anything.

Hours passed. They didn't see Jax all day, and Dorian was left to imagine all the terrible things Aunt Ursula and Dad might be making him do. Billy searched Dorian's bedroom for "resources" while Dorian gritted his teeth and tried not to lose it. "Aren't there any brownie holes in *your* apartment?" Billy bugged him.

"Dad remodeled any room where he found one, which destroys them. Once people could pass through them, he didn't like having them in our home." Aunt Ursula had done the same thing, although Dorian happened to know she'd missed one in a room she never used. Too bad they weren't locked in the penthouse instead of here.

When Billy finally gave up searching and settled into his bunk to read, Dorian sighed. Not with relief. With resignation. *It's out of my hands now. They got Jax, just like they got my father and my mother and everybody else in this clan. Just like they'll get me, eventually.*

Late in the afternoon, Mom knocked at the door. "Dorian? Albert Ganner needs me to treat an injured man, and your father is . . ."

She paused, as if trying to decide between the truth and

something more acceptable. "With Jax?" Dorian asked.

"Dealing with a situation for Aunt Ursula," his mother finished vaguely. "You three are going to stay here. I'll be back as soon as I can." Dorian didn't bother answering.

She'd only been gone about five minutes when Billy sat up with a grin. "It's about time. I was beginning to think we'd never get out of here!"

"Think again," Dorian said dully. "The door's still locked."

Billy rolled off the bottom bunk, threw up the bed skirt, and hauled out a box that rattled and clanked. "Did you forget about this?" The box held a fire ladder. A five-story fire ladder.

Several years back, his mom had gone on a safety kick, bugging Dad about the elevator key and the one stairwell. "What if the stairs are blocked? What if our children end up trapped in a fire?" To satisfy her, Dad bought a collapsible ladder for every bedroom. Dorian hadn't exactly forgotten about it, but he didn't see how it could help them. "If we climb out the window, someone will see us!"

"Plus we'll be on the outside of the building, which won't help Addie." Then Billy grinned. "What do you do with your trash?"

Dorian's mouth fell open. "There's a chute, but—"

"Just like in *Star Wars*! They rescued a damsel in distress too."

"And almost got crushed by a trash compactor."

That gave Billy a moment's pause. "Does this building have a compactor?"

"Yes!" Dorian said firmly. Then it was his turn to pause. "But . . . it won't be working today. They turn off a lot of stuff on the eighth day to conserve power." Billy's grin returned. "We're still locked in the room, though," Dorian reminded him.

Billy hiked up his shirt, revealing a screwdriver tucked into the waistband of his pants.

"Where'd you get that?"

Billy knelt by the door. "From a drawer in your kitchen."

No wonder he'd been so helpful at lunch! "Are you going to pick the lock?"

"Not exactly." Billy inserted the screwdriver into the head of one of the screws that bolted the entire metal plate with the handle and the locking mechanism to the wooden door.

Dorian felt really, really dumb.

Billy reassembled the outside door plate, so it would look intact at first glance. "There were flashlights in that drawer too," said Billy. "Go get 'em."

"Flashlights?"

"Do you have lights in the garbage chute?" Dorian dashed off to the kitchen. When he returned, Billy was talking to Lesley through the keyhole in her door. "I can get you out."

"Go away," Lesley hissed.

"Les," Dorian said. "I'm sorry you got in trouble too. Maybe you should come."

"Leave me out of this, Dorian. You're the son and the heir and the one with the talent. No matter how mad they get, they're not going to mess with you too bad."

He hesitated, feeling guilty and protective, but Billy nudged him on. They lugged the ladder out of the apartment and to the garbage chute at the end of the corridor. Billy pulled down the door, and Dorian wedged the ladder in, hooking the top of it to the door and unrolling the rest. It clattered its way down the dark chute.

"The door will close if no one's holding it," Dorian pointed out.

Billy shut the door and tested the hooks. "I think we're good." He opened the chute again, clambered onto the door, and started backing down. "This is so cool."

Dorian followed, his heart pounding. The instant his weight was off the door, it began to close. "Hang on!" he shouted. For one stomach-dropping second the ladder was falling; then it jerked to a halt when the hooks caught in the door. Dorian clung tightly to the rungs. "You okay?" he called.

Billy almost blinded Dorian, shining his flashlight at him from below. "Yeah, I was expecting that."

Of course you were. Dorian had seriously underestimated Jax's friend.

Dorian kept his elbows tucked against his sides as he backed down. The chute was barely the width of the ladder.

And it smelled. Rank and nasty.

"Dorian," Billy called. "We got a problem." Dorian looked between his feet. Billy was shining the flashlight down the chute. "The ladder's too short."

"It can't be," said Dorian. "It's a five-story ladder. Dad tested it."

"Yeah, but we're going to the basement." Billy leaned back enough for Dorian to see the ladder dangling several feet above a mound of garbage bags. How many feet? In the dark and from this angle, Dorian couldn't tell.

"Oh well," said Billy. "Geronimo."

Geronimo? "No, don't!" exclaimed Dorian. He pointed his flashlight down, but the ladder beneath him was empty. A scream echoed up through the chute. "Billy!"

"I'm okay!" Billy yelled. Then he moaned. "Banged my arm on the way down. Gosh, I wish your mom were here."

Dorian balanced on the bottom rung. "I'll come down to help, but I'm afraid I'll land on you." His light finally caught Billy in its beam, curled in a ball and half buried in trash bags.

"Let me get out of the way." Billy rolled like a toddler in a disgusting version of a ball pit.

"Are you insanely brave or just plain crazy?" Dorian called down.

"Is there a difference?" Billy shot back. "Okay. Clear."

Dorian gulped, then jumped. The garbage cushioned his landing, but not completely. Sharp objects jabbed him. Bags broke beneath him, squishing messily into his fingers and hair.

Guided by Billy's flashlight, he wriggled out of the garbage bin, onto the concrete floor, and shuddered like a dog, trying to throw off the ick.

Billy cast his light around the room, holding his injured arm close to his side. "Is that the outside door?" He illuminated a large, roll-up door that was padlocked closed.

"Yeah, and that one goes to the rest of the basement." Dorian shone his light on the opposite wall.

"Is that how we're getting out?"

"Not unless we want to run into the guards."

"So what's your plan?"

My plan? You got us down here, and now it's my plan? But Dorian realized he did have a plan. "Still got that screwdriver?" Billy handed it over. "Okay," said Dorian. "Brownies might be smarter than rats, but they love trash just as much. If there's not a brownie hole in this room somewhere, I'll eat a bag of garbage."

"You can get out that way, but what about me?"

"You, Mr. Resourceful, are going to find a way to bust that padlock loose. And I'm finally going to make the brownie holes take me where I want to go. I'll get myself into the room where they've got Addie locked up." Dorian held up the screwdriver. "And then we'll see if they've got the same kind of door locks down here."

29

DORIAN SEARCHED FOR MANY fruitless minutes and eventually had to climb back into the garbage bin before he found what he was looking for: a puckered opening in the air above the trash. "It figures," he said. "They probably dive in like it's a swimming pool. Wish me luck."

Billy had found a copper pipe joiner and was trying to bust the lock. "Luck."

Dorian pushed into the brownie hole and ended up standing in midair above the trash bin. Outside of time, Billy was no longer visible. Dorian felt the tingle of magical potential and drew it into himself like a lungful of air. This tunnel didn't connect with the other one in the basement. But he had to believe it could take him there. *If brownies can do it, I can do it.*

He visualized the location of the room that held the Emrys girl. *I want to go to that prison cell. The room with the girl.* In his previous attempts to move through space, Dorian had willed the tunnel to extend itself. But if Billy was right and shifting location was like hyperspeed, it wasn't the tunnel that needed to move; it was Dorian. The tunnels were similar to airplane runways, used only for traveling short distances.

Dorian imagined a ship hurtling through space and vanishing in a blur of stars. *I'm going to the room with the Emrys girl. The room. The girl. The prisoner.* He started moving forward, walking at first, then breaking into a run, wobbling crazily on the uneven, squishy surface. Suddenly the fabric of the tunnel burst open like a torn grocery bag, and Dorian tumbled into a tiny, dimly lit storage room—startling the heck out of the guy who was in there.

He was bent into a *W* on the floor, bound with his hands behind his back. Dorian had caught him in the act of trying to force his hands past his rear end so he could get them around his legs, which were also tightly tied. Perhaps he would've succeeded if his leather biker jacket hadn't been so bulky. When the guy stared up at Dorian through disheveled reddish-brown hair, Dorian saw that he was also gagged.

Biker jacket. And gagged. "You gotta be Pendragon." Dorian reached for his dagger. When the guy squirmed away from him, he said, "No, it's okay. I'm going to cut you loose."

The honor blade wasn't as sharp as it could've been, but he'd never used it to *cut* anything before. The prisoner's hands finally came free, and Dorian would've cut the gag off next, but the guy ripped it off himself. Spitting out whatever they'd wadded up inside his mouth, he said in a hoarse voice, "Give me your blade and stand against the far wall."

No thanks, Dorian wanted to say. Instead, he passed over his dagger and plastered himself against the wall.

Okay, that was a handy talent to have, and it pretty much confirmed the guy's identity.

Pendragon glanced at the crest on the blade, then sawed at the ropes around his ankles. "You must be an Ambrose."

"I'm Jax's cousin Dorian."

"Where's Jax?"

"I don't know." With shame he added, "They changed him."

Pendragon looked up through his long hair. "I know," he said. "How'd you get in here?"

"Brownie hole."

"People can't use brownie holes, last I heard."

"Some families in this clan can," Dorian said. "It's a long story."

"Can I get out that way?"

"Not without a brownie, a vial of your blood, and a spell only our spell caster knows."

"That's a *no* then." The final strands of the rope broke, and Pendragon stood up. "Next question. Why'd you come in here and cut me loose?"

"I wasn't aiming for here. I was trying to get to where they're holding Addie Emrys." Dorian had ended up in a room with a prisoner, but he'd specified a girl, and he'd pictured the location of the room. What had gone wrong?

Her room is warded! The tunnels can't go there. They sent me to the next closest thing.

"You didn't really answer my question," Pendragon pointed out.

Dorian gave the most honest answer he had. "I don't want to be a Dulac vassal."

Pendragon handed Dorian's dagger back, hilt first. "You're free to move. And your blade's dull. You should take care of that."

Dorian fell away from the wall as though demagnetized. "Okay. Let's get you out of here." He fished the screwdriver out of his pocket, turned toward the door, and froze.

No screws. Apparently the basement locks were important enough for an upgrade.

"Are you planning to dig your way out with a screwdriver?" asked Pendragon.

Dorian sucked in his breath. Before his eyes, the door handle jiggled, and he heard a key scrape in the lock. Whirling around, he flung himself toward the brownie hole. He'd given Pendragon a fighting chance—more than a chance, with that voice of command. No one could blame Dorian for not wanting to be caught in the cell.

But the brownie hole was gone. Dorian reached up, waving his hands through empty air. He hadn't expected to get *stranded* at the other end of his jump!

The door cracked open, and Billy stuck his head inside.

"Oh hey, Riley. You weren't the damsel in distress I was look-ing for."

"Billy?" Dorian gasped. "How'd you—"

Billy held up a ring of keys. "Found the keys on this guy," Billy said, pointing. Pendragon yanked the door open and stepped around Billy into the corridor.

Dorian followed, dumbfounded. Pendragon knelt beside a fallen man, checking for a pulse. "What'd you do to him?" Dorian asked. If Billy said he was a black belt in karate, Dorian would not have been surprised at this point.

"Nothing. There's another guy just like him down the hall. That padlock wasn't coming off. So I peeked out the other door and saw somebody lying on the ground. And I thought—"

"Drag him inside," Pendragon interrupted. "I'll get the other one."

Dorian's mind raced as they dragged the guards into the cell. Men didn't fall unconscious for no reason. Pendragon hadn't done it. Billy hadn't. *Who else* was down here?

Billy looked up at Pendragon with a grin. "I'm so psyched to be part of this."

"You are one weird kid." Pendragon turned to Dorian. "You said Addie was here?"

"Yeah. Follow me."

If they could have tunneled through the walls like brown-ies, she was actually quite close. But because they had to go around by way of the corridor, she was at the farthest point from them. And they didn't make it halfway before Dad, Aunt Ursula, and Sloane turned the corner that led to the elevator. It crossed Dorian's mind, as he came to a sudden, horrified stop, that maybe Addie Emrys wasn't even real. She was just a mirage he was never going to reach.

"Dorian!" Dad roared when he spotted his son where he shouldn't be *again*. And then, when he saw who was with Dorian, Dad pulled out a gun from his suit jacket.

Dorian's knees almost folded beneath him. He'd never seen his dad with a gun before.

"Freeze, Pendragon!" Dad yelled.

"Drop the gun," Pendragon commanded.

Dad almost did. Dorian saw him fumble it. Then Aunt Ursula grabbed his shoulder, and Dad recovered himself, tightening his grip. "Dorian!" Sloane exclaimed. "Get over here!"

Dorian backed up, moving closer to Pendragon and Billy. Choosing his side.

"Drop the gun," Pendragon said again.

Dad fought the command. "Unhand my son!" he shouted back.

Pendragon looked at Dorian. "Him? I don't have any hands on him. *Ambrose, drop the gun!*"

Adding the name magnified the magic. Dad nearly lost all will to hold it, but then he looked at Dorian and put a second hand up to hold the gun steady. "Dorian, try to come to us. He's got you under compulsion."

"No, he doesn't, Dad."

"You're not going to shoot me, Ambrose," Pendragon said. "Put the gun down."

Aunt Ursula gripped Dad's arm and leaned toward him. "If you can't shoot him, distract him. Shoot the Latino boy."

Dad's aim swung toward Billy.

"Dad!" screamed Dorian.

His father shuddered, and Dorian wasn't sure what would've happened next if a couple hundred brownies hadn't poured out of the wall behind them.

30

JAX GAVE EVANGELINE a moment to marvel at the brownie tunnel. She ran her hands along the silky, translucent walls and peered out at the park. Tegan might've still been standing where they left her, but if she was, they couldn't see her. "It's another timeline?" Evangeline asked.

"It's *outside of time*, according to my cousin Dorian." Jax took Evangeline's hand. "We need to move together, or we might get separated."

"How does it work?"

"I wasn't totally clear on it before, and I'm even less sure now. The past two days are pretty fuzzy." Jax remembered hurrying through the tunnel on the night he discovered it, wanting to return to the Ambrose apartment before anyone noticed his absence. He hadn't *asked* to return eight minutes after he left. He just wanted to avoid being caught.

"They said Riley would be unconscious for hours," Jax recalled, "and they couldn't question him until he woke up. We can't carry him, so we've got to focus on arriving after he can walk, but before the Dulacs get to him." He led Evangeline out of the park and onto Central Park West. He was so busy concentrating—*Get us to a time when we can help Riley*—he only belatedly noticed how Evangeline's fingers tightened convulsively around his.

He looked back. She was chewing on her bottom lip and blinking back tears. "I'm sorry," he mumbled. He'd gotten Riley shot up with tranquilizers. What if they'd been bullets instead?

"You were under the influence of magic. I don't blame you for what happened." She wiped her eyes with the back of her free hand.

"*He* will, though," Jax said glumly. "He's not going to forgive me for this." Betraying Riley felt like a nightmare, except Jax wasn't going to wake up and realize it hadn't really happened. This *had* happened.

"Don't be silly." Evangeline squeezed Jax's hand again, this time to comfort him. "Why do you think he insisted on waiting for you at the dog statue, even though A.J. begged him to let the Donovans check you out first? Jax, you said you didn't have a brother, but you *do*, in a way."

At first Jax didn't know what she meant. Then he remembered what he'd said to her under the Dulac manipulation. *If I had a sister—or a brother—nothing would stop me from going to them.* And here he was, leading his liege lady into their enemy's stronghold to rescue Riley.

Central Park West was eerily empty of all the cars that Jax had seen stuck there when he crossed this street earlier on Grunsday. Jax started to point out this oddity of the brownie tunnel to Evangeline—and then froze.

Someone was walking through the tunnel toward them from the direction of the park. "C'mon!" Jax yanked Evangeline forward.

She glanced backward. "Who's that?"

"A Dulac vassal. Maybe he hasn't seen us." That was wishful thinking. If they could see him, he could see them. Jax started running. But the Dulac scientist, the Transitioner with the black ponytail and the Kin-blue eyes, quickened his pace, catching up with them so quickly, Jax had to stop and put himself between the guy and Evangeline.

The man spoke directly to Evangeline. "You must be Jax's liege, the sister of Adelina Emrys. How lucky for both of us that I encountered you here." He raised his hand to show his tattoo. "But perhaps it's not luck. It's fate. Events are being manipulated by a force greater than any of us."

"I don't recognize your mark," said Evangeline, "but I see your family is branched off from the Mordred line. That doesn't commend you to me." Her voice had taken on the haughty tone she used with adversaries, but her hand was pumping Jax's urgently, telegraphing a message: *danger, danger, danger.*

"My name is Morder, and I'm no enemy of yours."

"That's a lie," Jax said. "He's one of the people holding your sister prisoner."

Morder shook his head. "I'm the one who gave Adelina's blood access to the brownie tunnels so I could help her escape. You would not be able to pass through here otherwise."

"Don't believe him!" Jax exclaimed. "He's a Dulac vassal."

"There are ways around a loyalty oath, if you know the right spells," Morder countered.

"They must be dark spells," Evangeline said with a frown, taking a step backward. "Loyalty oaths don't break easily."

"Dark and light is a matter of perspective." He smiled, and Jax thought his smile was as creepy as his ponytail. "You are very young," he said to Evangeline, "and probably not trained to reach your full potential. Come with me. I'm on my way to rescue your sister."

"You're rescuing her out of the goodness of your heart?" That seemed unlikely. Jax reached for his honor blade. "What are you planning to do with her?"

"No need for your magic, Jax," Morder said. "I'll speak freely. I've risked much, defying my liege lady, because I oppose her plan to kill the Emrys heirs and destroy the eighth day and the entire Kin race." Casually, Morder reached inside the pocket of his lab coat to remove a pouch as he addressed Evangeline. "Your sister provided me with the means to contact people invested in your family's cause. I've just come from meeting with them, and they are eagerly awaiting my return with Adelina. They will be even more pleased to find themselves reunited with *both* Emrys heirs."

"*Reunited?* You must be talking about the conspirators in my father's plan to overturn the Eighth-Day Spell," Evangeline said coolly. "I have no interest in meeting them and no interest in their plot."

"Don't be foolish." Morder slipped his fingers into the pouch and withdrew a pinch of powder. "The spell that binds the Kin in the eighth day *must* be properly counter-manded before Ursula destroys the timeline. Our people are too vulnerable, with only the lives of two Emrys heirs standing between us and annihilation."

"*Our* people?" Evangeline repeated. "You may have some Kin blood in you, but you're a Transitioner. If you think the Llyrs or the Arawens would ever consider you their equal—"

Jax's eyes were on Morder's hands and the pouch of powder, and he remembered the guard lying unconscious in the park by the tunnel entrance. "Watch out! He's got a sleep spell." Jax pushed Evangeline away and braced himself to block Morder from reaching her. Jax didn't know if the guy was a double agent or a triple agent, but he was bad news all around.

Dr. Morder raised his hand and started muttering a spell, only to be interrupted by a high-pitched shriek— then a chorus of shrieks. Morder looked over his shoulder. A brown mass surged toward them like an ocean wave breaking on the shore. Seconds later, a herd of brownies filled the tunnel from side to side.

Evangeline clutched Jax in alarm, but the brownies swarmed around them and kept going. Morder wasn't so lucky. Squirrel-sized brownies clambered up his pants legs, clung to his arms, and leaped onto his shoulders. He batted them away, but they bit him with their sharp teeth and yanked on his ponytail with their nimble little fingers.

Jax backed up. The brownies were attacking Morder, but they didn't touch Jax and Evangeline except to brush past on their way to the Dulac building. *Why are they going there?*

One brownie with a white-tufted head leaped out of the seething mass and landed on Jax's shoulder. Evangeline screamed, but Jax reared back his head to stare at it. This was the same brownie Jax had let out of the cage, the big one who'd shaken the bars and looked at him expectantly. Now it grabbed Jax's shirt in its little fist and stuck its flat face into his, chattering in agitation.

"What is it?" The swarm of brownies was stamped-ing toward a place they ought to avoid. Jax peered at their point of origin just as a huge mass shimmered at the extreme end of the tunnel. Something big was coming behind the brownies—so big the tunnel had to stretch to accommodate it. If Jax didn't know better, he'd say it looked like a . . .

"The brownies are running from something!" Evangeline exclaimed.

But at that moment, the brownies all stopped, stood up on their hind legs, looked back, and let out a high-pitched screech in unison. The dark shape at the end of the tunnel barreled forward as if drawn by the noise, and the brownies started running again.

"No!" gasped Jax. "They're *leading* something. Oh crap!" As much as Jax disliked animal experimentation, he bet the animals hated it more.

It was payback time, and the Dulacs were in for a nasty surprise.

Morder seemed to realize what was going on at the same moment. With a last swipe at the brownies clinging to him, he turned ninety degrees, lunged forward, and vanished.

Jax felt for an exit where Morder had disappeared, and there wasn't one. *Dang! How'd he do that?* Was this the "hyperspeed" Dorian and Billy had been yammering about? Whatever it was, Morder obviously knew how to use this tunnel better than Jax did. With no other choice, Jax grabbed Evangeline's hand and dragged her toward the building. The brownie on his shoulder chattered unhappily, ears flat against its head. It gestured at the walls of the tunnel. "Yeah, well I don't know how to do what he did," Jax yelled. "And besides, my friends are inside!"

The tunnel shuddered and convulsed. Jax stumbled and went down on one knee. He glanced over his shoulder—and someone outside the tunnel caught his eye.

A girl stood among the trees on the sidewalk in front of Central Park.

Jax shouldn't have been able to see anyone outside the tunnel, but there she was. Dark hair whipped around her face, obscuring her features. She wore something like a short white dress, her legs bare, and when she raised her hands to the air, crows circled her head. *Crows?*

"Do you see that?" he yelled at Evangeline. *Riley, you were wrong . . .*

Evangeline hauled him to his feet. "Yes, I see it! Come on!" But her eyes were on the terrible gift the brownies were bringing to the Dulacs. Jax grabbed Evangeline's hand and dashed through the outside wall of the apartment building with her in tow.

Forget the Morrigan, if that's what she was.

Who needed a girl with crows to foretell destruction and chaos when a dragon was rampaging toward them?

31

THE TUNNEL WOUND ITS way through the basement, twisting and turning. Jax and Evangeline struggled to keep pace with the brownies, running as best they could on the spongy floor and stumbling against the walls when they couldn't turn fast enough. Finally, they pushed through the hole into the Dulacs' laboratory—and back into real time. *What* time, Jax had no idea. He'd completely lost track. Even discounting his internal confusion, the tunnels were capable of depositing them anywhere: morning, afternoon, or evening. He only knew it was still Grunsday because Evangeline didn't vanish.

The white-headed brownie jumped off Jax's shoulder, scurried through the lab, and popped through the wall on the other side. Jax took the more conventional route, opened the lab door, and looked outside.

The hallway teemed with brownies. Several yards to the right, Ursula and Sloane Dulac were besieged, just as

Morder had been. Ursula picked the creatures off her body by the scruffs of their furry necks and flung them against the cinderblock walls, while Sloane flailed her arms over her head, squealing like any girl with rodents in her hair. Farther down the corridor Jax saw Dorian, also under attack, and Billy, who wasn't, but who was trying to beat them off Dorian.

And Riley was wrestling Uncle Finn in a brownie-free patch of floor for control of a gun.

"Riley!" Evangeline cried as soon as she saw him. That was a mistake. At the sound of her voice, Riley looked up, and Uncle Finn used the distraction to kick Riley backward and scramble to his feet with the gun in hand.

But as soon as he was free of Riley, the brownies swarmed him. One bit his hand, and he dropped the weapon. The white-headed brownie snatched up the gun and scampered away.

The sound of falling bricks and breaking glass came from the lab. Jax glanced back. The wall that used to contain the brownie hole was now a gaping hole into the furnace room. He scanned the corridor full of people he cared about—and some he didn't—and screamed at them all. "Run! Everybody run!" He pulled Evangeline down the hall to the left.

The brownies lifted their heads and screeched in unison, just like they had before. The monster that had followed them through the tunnel turned toward the sound. Then the brownies all poured through a wall like a river, vanishing in seconds.

Riley must've spotted what was coming, because he started cursing and ran toward Jax and Evangeline, clearing the lab entrance just in time. He grabbed one of them in each hand without breaking pace. The three of them rounded the nearest corner together, then skidded to a stop and looked back from a safe vantage point. Uncle Finn and the others—Billy, Dorian, and the Dulac women—hadn't reacted quickly enough to get past the door of the laboratory and were now trapped on the dead-end side of the corridor, their escape route cut off by the emerging creature.

The head ventured out first—a head nearly as big as Jax's whole body—breaching the doorway and surveying the corridor on the end of a sinuous neck. Sloane screamed, and just like the high-pitched shriek of the brownies, the sound seemed to attract the creature. When its body didn't fit through the door, it reared back and battered its way through.

"What *is* that?" Riley gasped.

"I think it's a dragon," Jax whispered.

"It's a wyvern," Evangeline said.

"They're extinct!" protested Riley.

"Not to mention make-believe," Jax added.

"You," Riley said gruffly, hauling Jax closer by a handful of shirt. "You sound like Jax, but you're not really him.

Evangeline, they've turned him."

"No! I'm fixed," Jax protested. "Tegan knew a guy with a talent—"

He was interrupted by a crash. The creature unfurled a pair of wings, wiping out a section of the wall between the lab and the corridor. Its tail, barbed on the end and curled like a scorpion's, cracked a hole in the warding symbol painted at the back of the lab.

Riley looked Jax directly in the eyes. "Whatever they've done to you, you're still bound by your oath. Get Evangeline out of here before that thing knocks out a load-bearing wall and buries us all." He let go of Jax and drew the honor blade Evangeline wore at her side. "Let me borrow this back. They took mine."

Jax felt the sting of Riley using the voice of command on him, but he grabbed Evangeline's arm obediently and started tugging her down the corridor. "What about Billy?"

"I'm going for him now." Riley ran back the way they'd come.

"Wait!" Evangeline cried. "You don't even know what you're up against!"

Jax pulled on Evangeline. "C'mon. There's stairs this way."

Evangeline shook off his grip. "Riley can't fight a wyvern alone, and what about my sister and Thomas? I'm not leaving any of our people behind."

Jax took her arm again, compelled to make her leave. "Riley ordered me."

Evangeline wrapped her fingers around the tattoo on his left wrist. "And I'm your liege. I'm countermanding him."

The feeling of compulsion left him, like water draining from a sink. *Wow, does Riley know she can do that?*

"I'm going to help Riley." Evangeline marched back around the corner. She muttered a spell under her breath and clenched her fists. Jax put a hand on his honor blade and followed her. She was his liege, and besides, she was right. He didn't want to leave Riley to fight a monster alone in the lair of his mortal enemies. Taking a deep breath, Jax forced himself to get a good look at what they were facing.

The wyvern had the head of a giant lizard, with a long snout and eyes on the sides of its head. A flexible neck thickened into a body mounted on two powerful legs, like a rooster on steroids. Wings too short for flying sprouted above its legs, and leathery scales armored all of its body except the head, which was covered in sleek, gray feathers. It had shaken loose from the rubble of the laboratory wall and was orienting itself in its new environment, cocking its head to survey the five tasty morsels bottled up in a dead-end corridor.

Jax's dagger was no weapon for this kind of monster. But what else could he use? Cinderblock fragments? This place was sadly lacking in wyvern-fighting materials. It seemed that Riley reached the same conclusion, because he sheathed his blade and darted into the ruined lab.

Meanwhile, trapped on the other side of the beast, Uncle Finn opened a door and waved Sloane and Ursula inside. "Stay in here until I tell you to come out," he said. Then he called back over his shoulder, "Boys, use that door behind you."

The wyvern hunkered down, its head low and its tail arching over its body. It made a keening sound, and automatically Jax looked up. Billy, too, stopped just inside the doorway of a room at the end of the corridor and turned to stare, while Dorian stood transfixed in front of the creature, his face blank.

"Don't look at its eyes!" Evangeline shouted, turning her face away. "It has magic! Don't let it trick you into looking at it!"

The warning came too late for Dorian, who stared into the wyvern's eye, unblinking.

"Dorian!" Jax yelled. "Move!"

Evangeline threw out one of her hands, splaying her fingers wide, but the wyvern scuttled forward, and her spell missed. A ball of blue fire fizzled uselessly against a cinderblock wall.

The wyvern's tail darted over its own head and toward the helpless boy.

Uncle Finn barreled into his son, throwing him out of the way. The barbed tail of the beast slashed across

Uncle Finn's forearm, knocking him to the floor before curling upward for a second strike. At that moment, a ball of fire from Evangeline's other hand nailed the wyvern's head. The creature roared in anger, its tail uncurving as it tried to shift its body in the narrow corridor to face a new enemy.

Riley emerged from the wreckage of the lab, gripping a cage in his left hand and a long rod in his right. "I told you to get her out of here!" he yelled at Jax.

"We're not leaving you!" Jax hollered back.

At the end of the corridor, Dorian shook his head dazedly while Billy pulled him to his feet. Uncle Finn lay on the floor, writhing in pain and gripping his torn arm.

"Avoid its eyes!" Evangeline called to Riley. "It'll call to you and hypnotize you. And I think the tail is poisonous!"

"Of course it is," grumbled Riley, holding the cage up like a shield. "Why not?" As the wyvern turned, he whipped the rod around, knocking the tail away. The end of the rod crackled, sparking with electricity, but it bounced off the armored creature harmlessly.

The thing Riley held was a cattle prod. Jax wondered why there'd been a cattle prod in the lab, and then it dawned on him. No wonder the brownies were *ticked*.

The wyvern continued its slow turn, no longer having the space or momentum to knock walls out of its way. It let loose its keening call again. Jax couldn't help looking up in response, but the wyvern wasn't aiming its predator eye at him. It was after Riley, who struggled to keep his face averted.

This is useless, Jax thought. They couldn't look directly at its head, and every other part of it was armored with scales. Uncle Finn was down. Sloane and Ursula were hiding, and what could they do anyway? Change its memory? Evangeline's fireballs and Riley's cattle prod only annoyed it. Jax could run from it if he wanted to—and so could Riley and Evangeline—*if* they were willing to abandon Billy and Dorian.

What can I do?

"Keys!" he shouted. "Billy, does Uncle Finn have keys on him?"

"I have keys!" Billy yelled back.

A set of keys skidded across the cement floor, between the wyvern's legs, and smack into the cinderblock rubble. Jax snatched them up and ran away from the monster.

"Find Thomas and Addie and get them out of here!" Evangeline shouted after him.

But that wasn't Jax's plan at all. He had somebody else in mind.

Somebody big and strong and deadly—and immune to magic.

32

JAX PELTED TOWARD ANGUS Balin's cell. Above him, the ceiling shook violently, and the lights flickered. *That's it. The building's coming down.* He covered his head as he ran, like he could hold off twenty stories with his arms. But all that happened was the ceiling lights on the far end of the corridor exploded into glass shards, and footsteps pounded overhead.

Something was going on upstairs. Maybe the brownies were taking their revenge one story at a time, and after dropping off a wyvern in the basement, they'd delivered Big Foot to the ground floor. Jax thrust a key into the lock on Balin's door, shoved his way in, and found Balin standing in the middle of his cell, looking just as menacing and hostile as ever.

Jax didn't waste words. "There's a wyvern in the basement. You gotta help me."

"You're kidding," Balin said in a flat tone.

"Do I look like I'm kidding?" At that moment, the wyvern let loose its magical cry again, and even with solid walls between them, Jax whirled around to look in its direction. Balin frowned, his forehead hunching into ridges.

"You swore an oath you'd help me get my friends out of here if I could get you out too," Jax reminded him. "And there's a *wyvern* in the way!" Riley couldn't reach Billy with that monster blocking the corridor, and Evangeline wouldn't leave without Riley. He needed the wyvern neutralized and Balin's muscle to get his friends out of here before the Dulac security force arrived and captured them all.

Balin turned back, into the cell. For a moment Jax thought he was going to say he preferred to stay a prisoner. But Balin overturned the mattress on his cot, revealing a wooden crossbar that had been wrenched from the bed frame and broken into two jagged pieces. Balin took up one in each hand. Jax realized that if anyone besides him had opened this door, they might've received a splintery surprise.

Balin glanced longingly at the stairs at the end of the hall but stalked left instead. Jax started to follow, then paused. Between him and the stairs, a red wooden box hung on the wall. Jax dashed over and threw open its glass door. The coiled fire hose didn't interest him, but the fire extinguisher did. When he pulled out the canister, he found a small axe hanging behind it. *Aha!* With a decent weapon in each hand, Jax sprinted to catch up with Balin.

Back in the other corridor, Evangeline stood on a pile of rubble, peering anxiously into the laboratory. Jax guessed from her worried expression and the wyvern's repeated head butts into the ruined lab that Riley was tucked into a corner where the beast couldn't reach him. Jax couldn't see Billy or Dorian anywhere, and Uncle Finn was gone too.

"Evangeline!" Jax called. She jerked in his direction, and when she spotted Balin, she gasped. "It's okay!" Jax assured her. "He's on our side!" *Sort of.*

Balin stared in disbelief at the creature. Half its body was in the lab, and its deadly tail waved wildly in the corridor. He grimaced at Jax. "Only you could cause me this much trouble."

The wyvern keened again. Evangeline threw both hands over her eyes and yelled at the top of her lungs, "Don't look, Riley! Don't look!"

Jax, meanwhile, stared helplessly at the beast even though he wasn't its chosen prey. He didn't know if the wyvern was ridiculously strong or if he was just weak, but Jax couldn't fight the compulsion to look at it.

The tail whipped around, and Balin ducked it emotionlessly. "Has it got magic in its call?" he wanted to know, like a deaf man asking about music.

"Yes, and if you look in its eyes, it hypnotizes you."

Balin snorted, unimpressed. "And it's completely armored?"

"Not the head."

"Then I need to get to the head." Balin surveyed the beast, looking for the least dangerous way to reach its vulnerable spot.

"Riley?" Evangeline called out worriedly.

"Still here!" he hollered from somewhere inside the lab. "Why are *you*? I told you, Evangeline, *get out!*"

The voice of command made Jax want to bolt for an exit even though it wasn't directed at him. But Evangeline braced herself against the wall. "Stop making me waste my strength fighting you!" she shouted. "I'm not leaving!"

The wyvern's tail whipped around again, reminding Jax of a very irritated cat. He ducked underneath it and ran toward Evangeline. "What's Riley doing in there?"

"He tried to lure it back into the hole it came from. But either it can't leave that way—or it won't—or he couldn't find the right place." She whispered her magic words under her breath again, clenching and unclenching her hands. But her face was streaked with sweat from the effort. Producing the fireballs was exhausting her, and they weren't very effective anyway. Riley was right. She ought to get out of here.

"Where are Billy and Dorian?" he asked.

"They dragged the wounded man into the room at the end of the hall."

With the wyvern's attention on Riley in the lab, Jax could reach Billy and get him out of here, but he'd have to abandon Dorian with his poisoned, possibly dying father. Jax felt a twinge of guilt at the thought. He couldn't. "That man's my uncle. Can you help him?"

Evangeline spared Jax a glance of regret. "I'm not a healer."

Running away without all his friends was not an option. Jax considered the situation. Balin needed to reach the wyvern's head, but it would be easier if they could entice the creature out of the lab. Jax scanned the corridor and spotted something he could use.

"Stand back," he told Evangeline. He shoved the axe through the belt of his dagger sheath, ripped out the safety tab on the fire extinguisher, and fired at a plastic smoke alarm in the ceiling. The device registered the foam as smoke and went off with an ear-piercing shriek.

The wyvern began to back up and turn around. Jax pushed Evangeline out of its path but couldn't dodge a body blow from the wyvern's wing. The breath left his chest in a *whoosh*, and the next thing he knew, he was lying flat on his back, gasping for air.

The wyvern smashed its head against the ceiling, silencing the alarm and cracking the concrete all around. A fissure ran into the room where Uncle Finn had hidden the Dulacs. Sloane screamed, and the beast drove its head toward the sound, caving in the door.

If Sloane screams again, she's dead, Jax thought, climbing to his feet. But she didn't. Either she'd finally realized her voice was attracting the wyvern, or Aunt Ursula had muffled her into silence. The wyvern drew back its head and surveyed the corridor with first one eye and then the other, looking for suitable prey.

And there stood Balin, staring up at the beast unafraid. The wyvern dropped its head, bringing its right eye and hypnotic gaze level with the man. Its tail arched for a strike.

Balin slammed a stake into the wyvern's eye.

The creature screamed and wrenched its head up. The tail thrashed from side to side. Jax crouched, watching it pass overhead. It was segmented, just like a scorpion's tail.

While the beast was wailing and shaking its injured head, Sloane peeked out and apparently decided this was a good time for an escape. "Now, Grandmother!" She shot across the corridor into what was left of the laboratory, pulling Ursula by the hand.

The wyvern broke off screeching and attempted its siren call. Jax clenched his teeth but couldn't stop himself from looking up. The punctured eye was bleeding, its hypnotic power gone. The head whipped around, seeking prey with the functioning left eye.

Every muscle in Jax's body seized up. His mind raced, but he couldn't so much as twitch a finger. The eye, as large as his whole head, fixed on him with rage and pain, its pupil a black bottomless hole for Jax to fall into.

Then a meaty hand covered his face and shoved him backward.

"Sing all you like," Balin shouted at the wyvern. "Doesn't bother me!"

Jax's muscles went limp like cooked spaghetti.

"Jax, you idiot! Get out of the way!" Riley yelled, emerging from the lab. When he saw Balin, he recoiled, swearing loudly.

"I feel the same way about you." Balin tossed his second wooden stake to Riley. "Trade you for the cattle prod. You beat off the tail and leave the head for me."

Riley threw Balin the electric prod. The wyvern snapped at Balin, who whacked its snout and snatched up the other stake from the floor. The monster retreated a few paces. "Smell the blood on it, do you?" Balin taunted. "C'mon, bring that other eye down here!"

Instead, the tail snaked around, passing through the space where the laboratory wall had been and coming at Balin sideways. Riley batted it away with the stake. Instantly, the wyvern swept a wing back, knocking Riley into the air and six feet across the lab. He landed on his back among the wreckage of broken tables and smashed glass.

Across the room, Sloane was investigating the hole made by the wyvern when it burst through the brownie hole and into the lab. "The entrance to the tunnel's gone, but we can still get out this way." She climbed through the wall and into the adjacent furnace room. "Grandmother, hurry!" But Ursula was watching the battle with calculating eyes and didn't seem as interested in escaping the mayhem as her granddaughter.

Jax wasn't happy about the idea of Sloane getting away to fetch reinforcements, but he didn't see how he could stop her, and he still had no intention of abandoning Billy and Dorian. He removed the axe from his belt. If the monster's tail came by him again, he had an idea.

Balin held up the cattle prod and whistled through his teeth, calling the wyvern. But the beast was learning. Feinting with its head, it turned sideways at the last second, bashing Balin with a wing. It swung its head into the lab just as Riley rose to his feet, weaponless.

And Ursula, seeing her chance, strode forward and kicked Riley in the small of his back, catching him unawares and sending him to his knees. His hands smacked the floor, and when he looked up—he faced the unblinking eye of the wyvern.

The tail curled into strike position, out of Jax's reach. "Riley!" Jax yelled. Evangeline hurled a fireball at the wyvern's head. She might as well have thrown the cinderblock dust.

Riley couldn't move, but out of the ground, a stream of brown fur erupted like a geyser. Two dozen brownies enveloped Ursula Dulac, swarming up her body and shrieking like a teakettle on full boil. The wyvern's head snapped toward the sound, breaking eye contact with Riley. The tail reoriented and lashed forward. Just before the barb struck home, the brownies leaped off Ursula, leaving her to take the blow alone.

It cut straight through her abdomen.

"Grandmother!" Sloane screamed, running back into the lab as Ursula fell. The wyvern's tail whipped backward out of the dying woman, slapping the concrete wall next to Jax's head and launching forward again toward its new noisy target.

Riley was too dazed to make it completely off the ground, but he dived forward and hit Sloane in the knees. She fell, butt first, and the barb sliced the air over her head.

The tail whipped backward again, and this time Jax was ready when it hit the wall in the same spot. His axe caught the tail between two segments, severing the barb. Jax didn't think the wyvern felt the blow. It struck again, trying to pin Riley and Sloane to the floor, but it had nothing to hit them with except a stump.

Balin leaped onto the wyvern's back and ran down its snake-like neck. He raised the bloody stake and jammed it into the base of the wyvern's skull where the armor ended and the feathers began. The beast collapsed but kept snapping at its prey. Sloane scooted backward while Riley kicked its snout away from them. Balin leaned on the stake with all his weight. The debarbed tail hit the ground next to Jax, and the massive body slumped to the floor.

Jax looked across the monster at Evangeline, who covered her mouth with her hand and gave a shuddering sigh of relief.

Balin jumped off the corpse and, before anybody could react, grabbed Sloane and Riley by their shirts and hauled them off the ground. "Dulac and Pendragon," he snarled. "Lucky me. Neither of you is covered in my oath to Aubrey." He shifted his grip to their throats and slammed their heads against the wall beneath the cracked warding symbol.

Jax's mouth fell open. He hadn't thought to include Riley in his deal with Balin.

33

SLOANE'S KNEES GAVE WAY, and her eyes rolled up into her head. Riley tried to peel Balin's hand away from his throat. He still seemed dazed from the wyvern's stare—or maybe the head blow.

"Stop it, Balin!" Jax yelled, climbing over the wyvern's body. "I didn't expect him to be here, but he's covered in the oath!"

"No, he's not," growled Balin.

"Let him go!" Evangeline, too, was trying to clamber over the wyvern blockage.

"Count yourself lucky, Emrys," Balin said between clenched teeth. "I swore not to harm anyone in Aubrey's clan—otherwise you'd be next."

Evangeline started muttering and clenching her fists, and Jax knew she was working on her fireball spell again, despite how exhausted she looked. "Wait!" he said, holding up a hand to signal her to stop. He didn't want her threatening Balin.

In spite of his menacing tone, Balin hadn't done anything to Riley except knock him around, and if he'd really meant to harm him, he could have. Jax remembered Mrs. Crandall saying that an oath demanded obedience in ways one didn't always expect. "You're bluffing, Balin," Jax guessed. "He's my guardian by law and magic; that makes him part of my clan, and you know it."

With a sneer, Balin shoved Riley away from him. "She's not, though." He held Sloane pinned to the wall. "Maybe I'll snap her neck, just to make up for missing out on Pendragon."

Sloane's eyelids fluttered. She licked her lips, leaving a smear of blood. "Safe passage," she murmured.

"What's that?" Balin pulled her closer, cocking an ear.

"I can grant you safe passage out of here," Sloane said in a hoarse voice. "Otherwise my clansmen will kill you before you can get out of this building."

When it looked as if Balin was going to let her go, Jax called out, "Wait a minute, Balin. Hang on to her." He took a step closer and asked Sloane, "What about *my* friends? Do they get safe passage?"

Sloane glared at Jax through narrowed eyes, Balin's hand still around her throat. "If your friends leave today without any hostile action against my clan, they have safe passage." She placed her right hand over her heart, tightening her hand on the fabric of her suede jacket where they could see the shape of her dagger. "I swear it on my bloodline, as leader of the Dulacs."

"Okay," said Jax, and Balin released her. She steadied herself with a hand against the wall. Her eyes swept the room, and her face crumpled when she saw her grandmother's body shoved out of the way like a piece of garbage.

Riley rubbed the back of his head, eyeing Balin resentfully, but he spoke to Sloane. "Where was your useless clan when we had a wyvern to fight?"

She wiped her eyes. "I don't know. Grandmother couldn't raise anyone on her radio."

A voice spoke behind them all. "Is it dead?"

They turned. Dorian stood in the corridor, looking small and pale.

"Yes," said Evangeline. "It's okay. You can come out."

Dorian blinked at them. "Can—somebody help my dad—please?"

He led them into a large room with a trash compactor and a huge stinking bin of garbage. Finn Ambrose lay on the floor, shaking uncontrollably.

Billy sat beside him, looking every bit as pale as Dorian and shaking almost as much as Uncle Finn. "I thought a tourniquet might help, and then I opened the wound with Dorian's knife, to let the poison out as much as I could.

But I only read about this in books. I don't know if it was the right thing to do." He stared up at them with worried eyes.

Jax saw that Billy had removed Uncle Finn's belt and buckled it tightly around the injured arm. And yes, from all the blood on the floor, it was obvious Billy had opened the wound.

Evangeline was the first to react. "You did the right thing. Maybe saved his life." She swooped in and pulled him to his feet and away from the gore. "You're Billy, right? I'm Evangeline."

Billy looked at her, and his eyes got big. He leaned into her arm with a goofy smile.

"My mom's a healer," Dorian said. "We have to get him to Mom. Will you help?" He turned to Riley as if he were half scared to hear the answer. *"Please?"*

"For you, Dorian, yeah." Riley bent over and slung Uncle Finn's uninjured arm around his shoulder. "C'mon, Ambrose."

Uncle Finn couldn't stand, and it didn't look like Balin was going to offer any assistance, so Jax stepped in on the other side, even though that was the messy side.

"Bring him to the elevator," said Sloane. "You have to go up with me, or you're liable to be shot on sight."

Riley half dragged Uncle Finn out of the garbage room. "Did you thank the kid for saving your life, Ambrose?" he asked in the quiet tone he used when he was really angry.

"You know. The kid you were going to shoot."

What? Jax looked up at his uncle.

Uncle Finn could barely hold his eyes open, but he managed a resentful glare at Riley. "You have no idea how hard I was *resisting* being manipulated into shooting him."

Once they'd carried Finn over the dead wyvern's tail, Evangeline looked at Jax expectantly. "Jax?"

Of course! "Dorian, can you get your dad? I have to help Evangeline."

Dorian nodded and took Jax's place. "Are you—back to yourself?" he whispered.

Jax grinned. "Yes, I am." He grabbed Evangeline's hand and helped her climb over the bulk of the monster's corpse and into the laboratory.

Jax didn't realize Billy was tagging along until he said, "Is it damsel-in-distress time?"

"Yup."

"Can I go in first? Maybe she'll say, *Aren't you a little short to be a stormtrooper?* That would be so cool."

"I doubt she's seen the movie, Billy."

Addie was being held in a room adjacent to the laboratory. That symbol painted on the wall, the one cracked by the wyvern, had been a ward on the outside of her room, not on the inside of the lab, Jax realized.

Jax led Evangeline through the hole in the wall to the furnace room. As Sloane had said, there was no longer a way to get into the brownie tunnel from here. Jax guessed the tunnel itself still existed, but this particular entrance had been destroyed along with the laboratory wall.

They exited from the furnace room into the opposite corridor, just across from Balin's open cell door. Jax rifled through the ring of keys, and by the time they turned the final corner, he was sure he had the right one. He stuck it into the lock as soon as they reached the door with the warding symbol above it. "Uh . . ." He looked at Evangeline. "Can she do the fireball thing too?"

Evangeline pounded on the door. "Addie? It's Evangeline! Addie?"

Jax turned the key and opened the door.

Through a haze of dust, Jax had an impression of pink and black. The hair on his arms rose with the tickle of lingering static electricity. He looked around the room—and then straight up.

Addie's cell was empty, and there was a hole blasted right through the ceiling.

34

JAX CIRCLED THE ROOM in disbelief. Evangeline stopped in the center and stared at the walls. This wasn't a bare cell like Balin's. Someone had tried to make it comfortable for a girl, and Jax's bet was on Aunt Marian. There was a pink comforter on the bed, a fluffy rug on the concrete floor, puzzle books, and a hairbrush.

"Wow." Billy held up a corner of the comforter. "Did she hate Hello Kitty or what?"

A black Sharpie had been used to X out the eyes on all the bow-topped kitties. Jax could hardly blame Addie. Only Aunt Marian would think a Hello Kitty comforter would make up for being locked in a dungeon and tapped for blood samples.

There was graffiti on the walls, too, scrawled with the same black Sharpie: symbols and letters Jax didn't recognize. Evangeline moved from wall to wall, reading them. "What does it say?" he asked.

"Curses mostly, directed at the Dulacs in general and your uncle in particular."

Jax grunted. Addie probably had good reason to hate Uncle Finn, since he was the one so eager to experiment with her blood.

But Evangeline looked puzzled and disturbed. "This is more than Addie being obnoxious. The writing corresponds to the location of the wards on the other side of the walls. They're not just swear words. They're magical *curses*—spells—meant to weaken the wards on this room. It's a combination of what I do with my spells and what A.J. does with his artwork. I wonder where Addie learned how to do this."

"Maybe at the Carroways'? It was a way station for refugees, right?"

"What kind of Kin did they have passing through there?" Evangeline's brow was furrowed. "Curses skirt the dark edge of magic, like Morder subverting his loyalty oath to the Dulacs. Jax, your uncle *did* get gravely injured and this cell *was* broken into. The curses worked."

Jax looked up at the hole in the ceiling. A freckled face stared down at him, surrounded by a halo of orange hair. Jax gasped. Tegan *told* him she'd find a way into the building! "Did you do this?" He wouldn't put it past her to have explosives on hand.

"Me?" exclaimed Tegan. "It was Kin that did it! There were Kin all over the park after you left, and some creepy guy with a ponytail. They walked in here with lightning and wind and . . . urp . . ." She disappeared from view. Jax heard scuffling.

"Tegan?" he yelled.

"Got her!" a man hollered. Then somebody else stood at the edge of the hole, looking down. It took Jax a moment to search his memory for the name. Albert Ganner.

"Jax!" Ganner's hand twitched upward with a weapon in it. "Don't move!"

"Talk to Sloane!" Jax called out. "She knows we're here."

"The radios don't work," Ganner said. "We can't reach Ursula."

And you're not going to. "Sloane went up on the elevator," Jax said. "With my uncle, who's hurt pretty bad. Uh, can you point that gun somewhere else?"

"One of my men was injured chasing you in the zoo today, Jax. A Pendragon vassal bashed him in the head with the butt of a rifle. And now you turn up with *her* right after we've been attacked." Ganner looked at Evangeline.

"You wanted me to bring her here," Jax reminded him.

Footsteps clattered in the hallway outside, and suddenly the room was filled with heavily armed men who would've been useful ten minutes ago. *It figures.* Jax put his hands up and let himself be prodded out of the room.

The nearby stairs led to an exit on the first floor—a heavy nondescript door that normally opened into an alley, but that was instead lying on the ground, blown off its hinges. There were scorch marks on the walls and bodies laid out on the floor. A smoking hole in one wall led to the place where the floor had been blasted open above Addie's cell. Tegan was in the custody of a man who had her arm twisted so far behind her back she had to stand on her toes.

"Ease up on her," Jax said angrily. "Are you afraid of a girl?"

"She tried to steal my gun," the guy replied.

"Let the girl go," called Sloane, striding down the hall with Riley on her heels.

The men whirled, guns raised. "Freeze!" Ganner yelled.

Riley put his hands up. Sloane waved at Ganner impatiently. "Put your guns down. We have a truce."

"You're under his compulsion, Sloane," said Ganner.

"I'm not under his compulsion; I'm in his debt," Sloane snapped. "Owing him has made me irritable, but if you shoot him, you'll put me in breach of my oath as head of this clan, and then I'll really be ticked."

"I won't be thrilled either," Riley muttered.

The guns started to come down. Jax watched realization dawn on their faces one by one. "Ursula . . . ?" Ganner said hoarsely.

"Grandmother is dead," Sloane said. Jax noticed the grief on Sloane's face was gone. He supposed she needed to assert her new authority, but it seemed cold even for a Dulac. "Where were you when we needed you?" she demanded of her security chief.

"We were under attack." Ganner's hand shook as he holstered his weapon.

Sloane looked around at the devastation. "You lost, I see."

"What happened to my sister?" Evangeline asked.

When Ganner hesitated, Sloane snapped her fingers. "Answer her."

"It was the Llyrs," he said. "They took us by surprise, coming in through the alley. They seemed to know exactly where they were going. They targeted this room, blasted open the floor, and abducted the girl."

"Not abducted," piped up Tegan. "She went willingly. I was watching from across the street. She knew them— greeted one of them by name."

Evangeline and Jax exchanged glances. What kind of friends *had* Addie made at the Carroway house?

"You're *sure* it was Llyrs?" Sloane asked.

"Six men are dead by electrocution," Ganner said grimly. "Our radios are fried. Lights burst as they passed by. The wall and floor here were blown away. Do you know of any other Kin who can throw bolts of lightning and raise small tornadoes?"

Sloane indicated the hole in the floor. "Not even a Llyr

should've been able to break in there with magic. That cell was warded."

"One of the wards was cracked by the wyvern," Jax said. He didn't mention that Addie had also weakened it with her curses.

"Did he say *wyvern*?" whispered one of the security men.

"Ganner?" somebody called up from below.

Ganner kicked debris aside and leaned over the gaping pit. "Report?"

"We lost Ursula," said the man.

"I know." Ganner swallowed hard, and Jax marveled that anyone could feel sorrow over that horrible old woman.

"We need Luis Morder down here right away. A creature came through these tunnels that hasn't existed since Niviane's day—and Sloane says the *brownies* brought it here. Did Morder know this was possible?"

"Morder's dead," Ganner said grimly. "He was one of the first victims of the Llyrs."

Jax sucked in his breath and leaned close to Evangeline. "Why? I thought he was on their side."

"That type of Kin hate Transitioners," Evangeline murmured. "It wouldn't matter that he was a half-breed. Once they didn't need him anymore, they killed him. I tried to warn him."

Sloane zeroed in on their whispering and fixed

Evangeline with an accusing glare. "Your sister is colluding with Llyrs. Do you know what that means?"

"Forget her sister," Tegan spoke up loudly. "Where's my brother?"

"He's upstairs. We have more important concerns right now," Sloane said.

"Not to *me*, Dulac," Riley said. "My friends are my priority."

Sloane glared at Riley. "My grandmother is dead, and my clan is in crisis. But fine. You and your allies are invited into my home under our truce. I'll release your *friend*, and we'll discuss what to do now that the Llyrs have an Emrys heir."

Jax marveled at how anybody could speak with such self-righteous indignation about releasing her prisoners. As they walked around to the front of the building, Riley grabbed Jax by the arm. "I don't trust her. When we get near the front door, take Evangeline, make like Balin did, and get the heck out of here."

Evangeline wrapped her fingers around Riley's hand. "Stop commanding my vassal to act against my will. It's bad manners." Jax felt the compulsion of Riley's command dissipate before it could really take hold.

Riley sputtered, smothering the beginnings of several bad-mannered words.

Sloane glanced over her shoulder. "Do you *really* want to send her and Jax into the street when Llyrs are out there?

Better you stay together. Of course, the street urchin and the Normal are welcome to wait in the lobby."

The street urchin and the Normal. Tegan and Billy. Not invited to the penthouse.

Riley snapped back at her, "If it's better to stay together, then we'll *all* stay together. Thanks anyway."

They crowded onto the elevator with Sloane and Ganner. Jax was shoved up against Tegan, and he wondered how she could still smell like tangerines when he smelled like sweat and wyvern blood and possibly leopard droppings.

But more than that, he couldn't shake the feeling that accompanying Sloane to the penthouse was a mistake.

"The boy's over here," Sloane said, turning left when the elevator stopped at the penthouse. But Tegan marched the other way and threw open the door to Ursula's office.

Inside, Thomas had his ear pressed against a safe in the wall while his fingers played with the dial. "Oh, hey, everybody," he said, glancing over his shoulder without any surprise. He turned back to the safe. "I could really use a drill."

"Amateur," said Tegan. But Jax saw the relief on her face.

"Get away from there!" Sloane exclaimed.

Thomas threw up both hands and sidled away, but when he saw Jax, he looked alarmed. "Uh, forces of nature . . ."

"Shut up, Tommy," Tegan said. "Jax is fixed."

Sloane looked at Jax, probably wondering how her magic had been reversed. "I'm sorry, Jax. It wasn't my idea."

"You helped, though," Jax replied, unmoved by the apology.

"I obeyed my clan leader," Sloane said. "But the current situation supersedes any rivalry between Transitioner clans." That comment was addressed to Riley.

"Rivalry?" His voice was deadly quiet. "Your grandmother had my entire family killed."

"She may have," Sloane conceded. "I wouldn't know. But we should be more worried about the future than the past. The Llyrs have an Emrys heir."

"I'll get her back," Riley said.

"What? You and these kids against the Llyrs?"

"We saved *you*, didn't we?"

"Why did you?" Sloane asked. "Chivalry? Hero complex?"

Jax thought she'd nailed it pretty accurately, but Riley stared her down. "Strategy. I knew we needed you alive to get out of there."

Sloane smiled. "Strategy is why you have to cooperate with me now."

Albert Ganner interrupted then, clearing his throat in the doorway. "Sloane, Sheila Morgan is here, demanding to see you regarding Pendragon."

"Now, Ganner? Really?"

"His vassals have reported he's being held here against his will. I can deny it, but Sheila will draw her own conclusion."

A rescue party, Jax figured. *A little late.* Or maybe not. They weren't out of Dulac custody yet. Outside the huge picture windows, New York City was a blur of leftover light in a deep purple Grunsday sky. *What time is it?* Jax wondered, looking around for a working clock.

"Send her up, then," Sloane said with a wave of her hand.

"And I couldn't stop this bunch from coming, even though *he* ought to be in an infirmary bed." Ganner moved aside to make room for Uncle Finn—not exactly on his feet, but not dying either. He had an arm over the shoulder of a security man, and Aunt Marian had her arm around his waist, but he walked in partly under his own power. Dorian scurried in behind them, but Lesley was nowhere to be seen. Jax wondered if her parents had forgotten to unlock her door, or if she was still staying in her room, out of all the action, by choice.

"Finn!" exclaimed Sloane.

"I owe you my oath of allegiance," he gasped in a raspy voice.

"It can wait," Sloane said when he tried to pull out his honor blade and go down on his knees right there.

"But I need a boon from you, about Jax . . ." Finn looked at his nephew.

Jax swallowed past the sudden lump in his throat. He couldn't stand Uncle Finn. But he was *really* glad to see him alive.

"I haven't forgotten Jax," Sloane promised, helping Aunt Marian ease Finn into a chair.

"What about Jax?" Riley demanded.

Sloane straightened up. "You're free to go, Pendragon. And although I'd rather Emrys remain here, in our safe-keeping, I swore an oath that she has safe passage to leave. But Jax stays. He's an Ambrose and a member of my clan. You can't have him."

35

"YOU SWORE I COULD go!" Jax exclaimed.

"I said your friends could go," Sloane corrected him. "Not you."

"I'm not leaving Jax behind," Riley protested. "I came here to get him."

"We're his family." Uncle Finn's voice was weak. "Jax belongs with us."

"If you were a decent family, maybe." Riley glared at the bunch of them. "But you're kidnappers and murderers. I wouldn't leave a dog with you."

"Watch your mouth, young man," Aunt Marian snapped.

"His father left him in my care," Riley said.

"He's my vassal," Evangeline said to Sloane. "My claim to him is greater than yours."

"Jax is thirteen and too young to be a vassal. By rights,

you should release him. Or," Sloane added sweetly, "you could stay with us too."

"What a dirty trick!" Jax scowled at his cousin.

"You're safer with us," Uncle Finn said, "now that the Llyrs are free and in this country."

"Really? Are you sure? You guys didn't even know Dr. Morder was a traitor. He brought the Llyrs here, and he was going to smuggle Addie out to them." Jax's accusation met with stunned silence. Sloane and Uncle Finn looked at each other in surprise. "Let's get out of here," Jax said to Riley and Evangeline. "They can't stop me."

"Pendragon," Sloane called out, "if you leave this apartment with my clansman, a minor child and my cousin, I'll consider it a hostile act. And then I'm not bound by my oath."

Riley's eyes darted around the room, marking everyone's positions: Billy and the twins, Evangeline . . . Albert Ganner, who'd moved to stand in front of the only door . . . the men stationed in the hallway near the elevator . . .

It'd been a trap all along, Jax realized. Riley's fingers twitched toward his honor blade. He could use the voice of command, but they were in the penthouse, with twenty floors of enemies between them and the street. Jax looked at Evangeline, who'd taken his hand and was staring at his mark with her brow furrowed. He squeezed her hand, then gave it to Riley. "Get everybody out of here. I'll stay. Nobody else is getting hurt tonight because of me."

Uncle Finn spoke up. "Jax, nobody wants to hurt your friends. We only want you."

Jax glared at his uncle. "Really? Because when you had me, all you did was try to get me to hand over Riley and Evangeline."

"I won't leave without Jax," Billy protested. But Riley jerked his head toward the door, and the twins grabbed Billy, pulling him in that direction.

Riley faced Jax, looking stricken. "It's my choice," Jax whispered to him. "I came here knowing this was a possibility. Keep Evangeline safe. And find Addie before they do."

Riley squeezed his shoulder. "This isn't over," he promised, tugging Evangeline toward the door. But Jax knew it probably *was* over. Smitty's fix was a one-shot deal. By morning, Jax could be completely brainwashed. He shuddered at the memory of what they'd made of him last night—a creepy *Bad Jax* who hadn't even known he'd been manipulated.

If my friends are safe, he reminded himself, *it doesn't matter what happens to me.*

Evangeline, however, refused to move. "Wait a minute. Jax, let me see—"

"Sloane." Ganner glanced over his shoulder. "Sheila Morgan has arrived."

Sloane looked as if she was enjoying herself. "Let her in."

Like her daughter, Sheila Morgan was petite with black hair. She wore a red leather jacket over leggings and boots, and although there were no weapons visible, Jax bet she carried a few concealed. But while Deidre always seemed to be on the verge of laughter, this woman's face looked like it might crack if she smiled. Jax doubted she'd be calling him "cutie."

"Good evening, Sheila," said Sloane. "What can I do for you?"

"I'm told condolences are in order," replied the Morgan clan leader. "It's unfortunate when someone as young as you is catapulted into a role of such responsibility."

Despite his grim circumstances, Jax had to smother a smile. On the surface, her words could've been an expression of sorrow for Ursula's death, but taken literally, they didn't have to be. Sloane's expression soured. "Thank you for your concern," she said stiffly. "But this has all so newly happened. I'm afraid you've found me unprepared for condolence calls."

Sheila Morgan pointedly eyed all the occupants of the room. "These people aren't here to comfort you? Then I assume they're here on business, and my visit is justified. I've come to inform you that Riley Pendragon is in breach of contract with my daughter, Deidre. If you were thinking about entering into your own contract with him, my clan would consider you a party to the breach, and all previous agreements between your clan and ours would be null and void."

Evangeline gasped as she finally figured out Riley's former relationship with Deidre.

Sloane crossed her arms. "I see. You didn't dare walk in here and accuse me of holding him captive, so you're accusing me of trying to arrange a marriage with him instead?"

"Well, are you?" Sheila demanded.

"Am I holding him captive or planning to marry him?"

"Either."

Jax had never realized how much Riley's lineage made him the Transitioner equivalent of *The Bachelor*. For his part, Riley was looking back and forth between Sheila Morgan and Sloane Dulac as if one were a man-eating shark and the other a man-eating tiger.

"Neither one," Sloane said finally. "Pendragon is turning over custody of my cousin, Jax. And then you're welcome to him."

"But we're not leaving without Jax." Evangeline glared at Riley. "Are we?"

"Sheila," Sloane said. "I call on you as a neutral witness. They're abducting my clansman. Any action I take is justified."

"He's not your clansman," Evangeline replied. "He would be if he was an Ambrose, but he's not." She took Jax's arm, making him hold up the wrist with the tattoo, then turned to Dorian. "Would you show me your mark?"

Dorian's mouth fell open. He held up his left hand.

Aunt Marian clucked in annoyance. "Yes, we know Jax's mark isn't right. It was an act of vandalism, if you ask me. But he's an Ambrose."

"My father told me," Evangeline said, taking Dorian's arm, "that ninety-nine times out of a hundred, if you alter a mark, you'll either ruin any chance of the person developing his talent—or it'll make no difference at all. But once in a hundred times, if the artisan is extremely talented and the change has significance, a branch-off line is created." She held Dorian's wrist and Jax's next to each other and turned to Sheila Morgan. "Sloane called on you as a witness, and so do I. Jax is an Aubrey. The very *first* Aubrey."

Deidre's mother frowned, examining the two tattoos. "Who marked you?" she asked Jax.

"A.J. Crandall," Jax said. He saw Riley cringe.

Sheila's eyebrow twitched. "The Crandalls have never struck me as particularly gifted. And the only difference between these marks is the type of bird."

"It's a significant change," Evangeline insisted. "A falcon is a hunter's bird, trained and tethered to its master. An American bald eagle is a symbol of freedom."

"I resent that implication," Uncle Finn muttered, but Dorian gasped and looked at Jax—and then drooped. Because he had a falcon.

"He's always been stronger than he should've been," Riley put in. "That's typical for a new bloodline, isn't it?"

Sheila mulled it over, and Jax wondered how much her decision was going to be influenced by how angry she was with Riley. "If the boy is the beginning of a new line, his talent will be different, too. Is it?"

"No," Uncle Finn said. "He's an inquisitor, just like his father."

"Yes, it is," Dorian spoke up. "Jax told me he can pull information out of the air. He doesn't need to interrogate anyone."

Jax *had* said that, but he remembered Dorian ridiculing him for it.

"Don't butt into things you don't understand, Dorian," Aunt Marian said. "Jax's talent is the same as yours."

"*Can* you get information without interrogating someone?" Sheila asked Jax. "That would be a significant change."

Jax glanced around. Uncle Finn shook his head, and Sloane crossed her arms with a smirk. The Donovans slunk closer to him, sniffing, but they only looked puzzled. Billy gave him two thumbs up, but what did he know? Riley's face was totally blank.

Jax fixed his eyes on Evangeline, who nodded her faith in him.

"Yes," he said. "I can."

"Prove it," Sloane replied promptly.

Well, he'd expected that. Jax sucked in his breath and drew out the honor blade his father had made for him, balancing it in the palm of his left hand. But its hilt was engraved with the Ambrose mark, and insecurity overwhelmed him. Maybe he couldn't do this. Maybe he'd just imagined that his talent worked this way, and he really was an Ambrose. His memory still seemed muddled, and he didn't feel sure of anything.

Who am I?

Jax closed his eyes and imagined himself back at Melinda's duplex house, filled with children's toys, sweet-smelling candles, and old encyclopedias. The place where he'd first pulled answers out of thin air. *I need information— something I can't possibly know through other means—something Sloane doesn't want me to know—something impressive.*

When he opened his eyes, he was standing in front of Ursula's safe. He sheathed his dagger and fingered the dial, feeling the ridges in the knob. There was no point pressing his ear to the safe door like Thomas; he'd never hear the tumblers clicking into place. He was going to have to depend on talent alone. Jax turned the dial until the buzzing in his brain told him to stop. Twelve. Now the other way. Seventeen. Reverse it again. Nine. Again. Four.

Jax yanked on the handle and heard Sloane gasp as the safe door swung open. Inside were papers and CDs and some floppy disks that probably held Ursula's old secrets. But Jax was only interested in the object lying on top of the pile. Triumphantly, he pulled it out.

Excalibur.

"You *were* going to give this back to Riley, right, Sloane?" Jax asked.

"Of course." Sloane crossed the room and smacked the safe closed with her hand.

"Can *you* interrogate a safe, Ambrose?" Sheila asked. The stunned look on Uncle Finn's face was answer enough. She turned to Sloane. "A branch-off line has no obligation to you. He can choose his allegiance or have none at all." Then she raised an eyebrow at Jax. "I don't know exactly how to classify you, boy, but you're definitely more than an inquisitor."

Jax's mouth dropped open. *You're something new.* That was what the Kin woman at the Carroway house had said to him.

"Jax." Uncle Finn wiped sweat from his face with his good arm. "I know we didn't get off on the right foot."

Jax snapped out of his shock. "Ya think?"

"But you're my brother's son. I want to give you a home." Uncle Finn indicated Riley and Evangeline. "These people aren't your family."

"You used me. They came for me. There's no contest." Jax offered Excalibur to Riley, hilt first. "Here you go, bro. It's just a rusted piece of junk, but I know you're attached to it."

"Jax, you idiot." Riley accepted the dagger, then wrapped his arm around Jax's neck in something that was kind of a noogie, but mostly a hug. Jax would have appreciated it more if he hadn't glimpsed Sloane's face.

She didn't look upset. She looked smug.

"What time is it?" Jax yelled, thrashing his way free of Riley's embrace. Riley yanked the sleeve of his jacket up and cursed. It was one minute to midnight.

Sloane smiled at Evangeline. "Looks like you're going to be my guest this week."

Even if they ran like heck for the elevator, there was no way they could get Evangeline down from the penthouse in one minute. All this time—talking and arguing, fighting for Jax—Sloane had been stalling. Her sworn oath guaranteed Jax's friends safe passage *today*. Not tomorrow. And not next week if Evangeline was trapped in this building between Grunsdays.

Had Sloane planned this when making her oath? Even with Balin's hand around her throat? Jax turned to Evangeline, aghast. If his and Dorian's suspicions about the brownie tunnels were right, Sloane had absolutely no reason to keep her alive.

"I can get her out."

The voice startled everyone. Aunt Marian reacted first. "Dorian, stay out of this!"

But Dorian grabbed Evangeline's hand. "Come with me."

36

DORIAN KNEW THERE WAS still a brownie hole in the Dulac penthouse, one overlooked by Aunt Ursula in her remodeling because only Maria, the maid, ever used the pantry.

Brownies liked pantries almost as much as garbage bins.

As he dragged the Kin girl through the Dulac penthouse to reach the hole in time, Dorian wondered how much he was going to regret this. It was one thing to sneak around behind everyone's back. It was another thing to betray the leader of his clan in front of her very eyes.

In front of his father's eyes too.

Dad saved me. He almost died doing it.

But when his father had needed him, Dorian had frozen. He'd stood there like a rock in the garbage room while Dad writhed on the ground in agony. It was Billy who acted in time to save him—whipping off Dad's belt and tying it on the right pressure points, cutting open the wound and draining the poison. He'd almost passed out afterward, but he'd *done* it.

Dorian had done nothing.

But he was acting now.

He wasn't even sure the Emrys girl could enter the brownie hole. He only knew she and Jax had appeared from the lab between the stampede of brownies and the wyvern. Jax *must* have brought her in through the tunnel. Dorian also recalled his father complaining about the empty vials of Emrys blood—the ones he'd hoped would cure Lesley. Dr. Morder had claimed Addie's blood had disappeared during the seven-day timeline, but if Morder was a traitor like Jax said, maybe he'd lied to Dad. How else would he smuggle Addie out of the building except by sending her blood through the tunnels?

In spite of what he'd reasoned out, it was only after Dorian plunged through the brownie hole in the pantry wall, and Evangeline slipped in behind him, that he was sure.

Phew!

Then he looked up at her. She was a little taller than Dorian and probably pretty—to someone who liked Kin, which Dorian didn't. Mom and Dad had taught him that the Kin were practically a different species, and although he now questioned everything they'd ever told him, Dorian still thought Evangeline was way too pale for a normal girl.

"You're safe," he said, letting go of her hand. "We're outside of time."

She stared at the shelves and cabinets of the penthouse pantry. "What do we do now? Can you move us backward half an hour and get me to the elevator?"

"We'll have to leave the penthouse too. If there's any chance we might run into ourselves, the brownie magic won't allow us to shift into the past. I do have a way to get you out, but you'll have to trust me."

"I do." She said it as if it should be obvious.

Dorian frowned. She *shouldn't* trust him. "Even though I'm a falcon?"

She pushed her long silvery hair behind one ear. "You don't have to be a falcon. You have a choice, no matter what's on your mark. I trust you because I'm *here* right now, instead of facing Sloane Dulac a week from now, not know-ing what happened to my friends."

Dorian squatted down and showed her the puckered hole in the floor. "This is the way out. It either takes us to a tunnel on another floor—or all the way down. We won't know for sure until we try, but as long as we're moving away from this spot, I can shift us in time and get you to a safe place before you disappear."

"What if we fall twenty stories?"

"It'll be more of a slide." Dorian had never dropped from this height, but he didn't see any other way to get her off this floor.

Unexpectedly, she gave him a shy smile. "Will it be like a roller coaster?"

"No." He stared at her. "Not really."

She sat down beside him. "That's okay. I won't know the difference."

He took her hand again, and they slid into the hole. He expected her to scream when they dropped.

Instead she laughed. All the way down.

Dorian had no idea what time it was when they finally pushed out of the tunnel and into Central Park. It had taken three total drops and a couple of sideways tunnels to find a way to street level. He didn't dare attempt a "hyperspeed" jump with her in tow, because when he'd tried it earlier, he'd ended up stuck in Pendragon's cell. Taking a longer route didn't matter as long as Dorian willed the tunnel to give Evangeline Emrys the time she needed.

Cars were frozen in the street when they followed the park path back to the sidewalk, the street lamps blurred and dim. "Still Grunsday," Evangeline said sadly, as if she'd been hoping he could take her to Thursday.

"Hey! Who's that?" One of their security men started running toward them.

"It's Dorian Ambrose!" he shouted back. "On orders from Sloane. This girl has safe passage on her oath!"

The guy stopped and reached for his radio to consult his superiors. Dorian knew Sloane had given that order earlier and he hoped she hadn't countermanded it. If it was still late on the night of the eighth day—and it must be—then Dorian hadn't betrayed Sloane yet.

He looked up at the building, trying to pinpoint the penthouse windows. *I'm probably still up there, watching Jax open the safe.* In all the times Dorian had used the tunnels to shift himself in time, he knew that—theoretically—there were two of him living through the same moment. *Wouldn't it be cool to see myself?* But as he'd told both Jax and Evangeline, the brownie magic didn't seem to allow that.

A block down the street, a dark SUV jumped the curb and drove toward them on the sidewalk. The security guy reached for his gun, and Dorian surprised himself by jumping in front of Evangeline. But she said, "No, it's all right. This is my ride."

The vehicle stopped, and the woman who'd been at Rockefeller Center with the twins threw open one of the back doors. "Get in, quick!" The girl climbed into the car.

The security guy grabbed Dorian's arm. "You're sure Sloane okayed this? I can't reach anyone. Half our radios are out of commission."

"Yup," said Dorian. "Sloane said she could go."

"Dorian, come here!" Evangeline beckoned him over to the car. "I owe you," she said.

"You don't." He hadn't done it to put her in his debt.

"Then let's say I *want* to do you a favor." She smiled at him, and Dorian decided that maybe she was pretty after all. "Everyone needs a favor sometime, right?"

Dorian considered Lesley. The lab was destroyed, Dr. Morder was dead, and there was no more Emrys blood to experiment with. That would hold up any further efforts to "fix" his sister, but if Dad persisted . . . "I might," he admitted.

"You have only to ask. This is my promise." Then she kissed him on the cheek and vanished into thin air, leaving him blushing with his head stuck inside the car.

Surrounded by three large and angry-looking Pendragon vassals.

"Where are Riley and Jax?" growled the man who'd yelled at Dad on the video call.

"Coming," Dorian said, and hoped it was true.

It was an uncomfortable wait, with the three people in the car and the one security guy on the sidewalk glaring suspiciously at each other. Dorian assured everybody that everything was just fine, even though he had no idea. The late-night traffic of Normals drove around them, ignoring the SUV parked on the sidewalk.

Finally, a group of people spilled out the front door of the apartment building. Dorian figured they must have headed for the elevator right after he disappeared into the brownie hole with Evangeline. Pendragon was in the lead exiting the building, breaking into a run with Jax right behind him. The youngest of the vassals got out of the car to meet them.

"A.J., do you have her?" Pendragon shouted.

"Yes! We got her!"

Pendragon slowed and called back over his shoulder.

"Thanks for the hospitality, Dulac!" Dorian saw Sloane making long-legged strides down the sidewalk, trying to catch up to Pendragon without the indignity of running. "From the tranquilizer darts to the dungeon guest room and the wyvern—it's been a real pleasure."

"This is not over," Sloane snapped. "My people will go after the Llyrs, and anyone who gets in the way trying to rescue a little Kin girl is liable to end up dead."

"Noted," Pendragon said.

Sloane spotted Dorian. If she could have pulverized him with laser vision, she would have. "Dorian, get over here."

For a second, Dorian thought about climbing into the car with the Pendragon clan and begging for sanctuary. Instead he slunk forward to face his doom.

Jax stopped him. "Dorian—thank you. I don't know what we would've done if you hadn't jumped in like that. I messed up."

Dorian didn't see how Jax had messed up. "I just wanted to do something right."

"You were awesome." Jax glanced at Sloane. "But what's going to happen to you now?"

Pendragon swung around and stuck his finger in Sloane's face. "Don't you dare take this out on Dorian."

Sloane slapped his hand away. "Are you telling me how to discipline members of my own clan?"

The guard surged forward to defend his liege lady, but Pendragon shouted, "Back off!" and the guy stepped backward, obeying the voice of command. Sloane looked outraged, but she didn't flinch when Pendragon leaned over her threateningly. "If his parents want to ground him and take away his Xbox, I don't care. But if you get into his head, I'll take that as a personal affront. And then you'll see how much damage one lone Pendragon can do."

"You won't be alone, Riley," Jax promised.

The big blond vassal, A.J., put in his two cents. "Evangeline says she owes this kid. That's good enough for me."

"We'll know if you mess with him," Thomas Donovan added. He slung an arm around Dorian's neck and pulled him close, sniffing his head.

His sister did the same, taking her turn sniffing Dorian—which was weird but not unpleasant—then whispered into his ear. "I'll get you the name of the guy who fixed Jax. Tell him Tegan sent you."

Dorian looked up at Sloane through eyes filled with tears. He could tell she was furious, and he was pretty sure the blurry shape coming down the sidewalk was Mom. Dorian was in deep, deep, *deep* trouble, but his cousin Jax was proud of him, and his family's enemies were poised to defend him.

He felt brave.

Mom got hold of his ear, but she couldn't wipe the grin off his face.

37

JAX SLUMPED IN EXHAUSTION against the rear bumper of the Land Rover, watching Aunt Marian drag Dorian home in disgrace and Sloane stalk back to her devoted vassals. Evangeline was safe; they had Billy back, and they could leave.

Riley made no move to get into the car, though. He waited for Sheila Morgan, who was striding toward them from the Dulac building, her bootheels clicking briskly on the sidewalk. She had her phone out and was flicking through screens. Her expression was grim.

"Thank you for coming, Sheila," Riley said. "If you hadn't been there as a witness, Sloane Dulac would've ordered us all shot at 12:01—with tranquilizers, if she was feeling generous. And they would never have let Jax go, especially with the talent he has."

"I bet Sloane's sorry she invoked me as a witness now. It won't be quite as easy to snatch him back from you

331

after I declared him a branch-off." Sheila put her hands on her hips and looked up at Riley. "But I didn't come here entirely for your sake. I thought Ursula having an Emrys heir in her clutches was a bad idea."

"You were right," Jax piped up. "Wait until you hear what she was planning to do with them."

Sheila scrutinized Jax with narrowed eyes. "Young man, between your talent for pulling a rabbit out of a hat and your unfortunate family ties, I suspect you're a font of information. I look forward to hearing everything you can tell me about the Dulacs, but it'll have to wait for a less critical moment." She looked at her phone again.

"What do you know about the Llyrs?" Riley asked.

"They've disappeared, gone into hiding." Sheila frowned, swiping her finger across the screen. She seemed to be scanning incoming texts. "We have multiple teams searching the area, dispatched as soon as we heard what was happening at the Dulac building. We still missed them." She looked up. "But they have to be close. They can't have gotten far before the eighth day ended. We'll track them down by their vehicles if nothing else."

"They've got Evangeline's sister with them," Riley told her. "They took her from the Dulacs."

"That's an unfortunate development." Sheila Morgan seemed to have a gift for understatement. *Unfortunate* hardly covered the danger Addie could be in. Not only was she in the hands of Kin who could raise lightning and tornadoes, they probably wanted to use her to counter the Eighth-Day Spell. Jax remembered how Myrddin Wylit had threatened and tortured Evangeline, trying to force her to destroy the seven-day timeline. "Did the Llyrs kill Ursula?" Sheila asked. "Her vassals wouldn't say."

Riley ran a hand through his hair. "No, Ursula was killed by a wyvern delivered to her building by a horde of brownies." Sheila narrowed her eyes and looked at Jax, who nodded vigorously. "And as bizarre as that sounds," Riley went on, "what's even stranger is this happened at the same time the Llyrs attacked. I can't believe Llyrs are using brownies as a weapon—that seems *beneath* them—but it's too big a coincidence."

"Maybe it's not a coincidence." Jax remembered what Dr. Morder had said about accidentally meeting Evangeline in the brownie tunnel. *Events are being manipulated by a force greater than any of us.* "It's the Morrigan," he blurted out. "She's arranging things to happen the way she wants them, for maximum destruction. I *saw* her, right when the wyvern arrived, which must have been when the Llyrs showed up too."

Everyone stared at him. Riley turned to Tegan. "Are you *sure* his head is fixed?"

"Maybe not," Tegan admitted.

Jax looked at Sheila Morgan. "*You* believe me, don't you? Deidre said her men saw the Morrigan in Mexico."

Sheila hesitated. "It doesn't matter what I believe," she

said after a moment. "The Llyrs are the people I need to find. Which is what I should be working on right now." She turned to leave, and Riley held out a hand to stop her.

"About Deidre—" Sheila shot Riley an angry look, but he finished anyway. "*She* broke off the engagement. I would have kept my word."

"I think my daughter wanted more from you than just *your word*," Sheila replied tersely.

"Our families have been allies a long time," Riley pressed.

"But you're the only member of your family left." Sheila looked him up and down. "Deidre says you're claiming your seat at the Table. Let's see if you can fill your father's shoes. *Then* I'll consider whether our alliance is worth continuing." She walked away briskly, and everyone got out of her way—A.J. and Billy and the Donovan twins. Mrs. Crandall, leaning out of the Land Rover, watched her leave with a worried expression.

Jax, however, was watching Riley's face and could see that the idea of filling his father's shoes intimidated him more than the wyvern had. "Just be yourself," Jax said impulsively. "You can do it."

"You didn't know him," Riley replied.

"At least *your* dad was someone to look up to." Jax's dad had made a living at selling secrets and spent half his life hiding from his relatives. And even though Jax knew *why* now, he had a hundred more questions he wanted to ask his dad—and couldn't.

"Don't sell your father short. He must've done something right." Riley slung an arm around Jax's shoulders and steered him toward the Land Rover. "Look how *you* turned out."

The Donovans insisted on being left in the park where Mr. Crandall stopped to pick up Riley's motorcycle. Mrs. Crandall didn't approve. "We can take you all the way home. We have to drive Billy anyway. I have no idea where your father's gone, and I don't want to leave you here."

Tegan shrugged. "We can take care of ourselves."

"We'll hire a limo to take us home when we're ready," said Thomas, handing a wad of cash to his sister. "Do you think there's any pawn shops open all night?" He pulled jewelry out of his pants pockets—pearls and diamonds and gold bracelets. Obviously Ursula's safe had been the *last* thing Thomas tackled, after he was finished ransacking the rest of the Dulac penthouse.

Mrs. Crandall sucked in her breath, then clamped her lips shut and got back in the car. There was no doubt in Jax's mind that the twins would've been in a world of trouble if Mrs. Crandall had her way with them.

Jax faced Tegan awkwardly. Her help had been

invaluable. But she was also a big pain in the rear end. Not knowing what else to do, he stuck his hand out, offering to shake.

Tegan looked at his hand. "Well, I suppose you deserve a cut." She peeled a couple fifties off the wad of bills and stuffed them into his palm.

"Gee, thanks." He felt a little insulted. Tegan gave him a fleeting grin, then dashed off into Central Park. Jax had no idea why Thomas winked at him before disappearing after her.

Riley let Billy ride on the back of his motorcycle, following the Land Rover to a motel outside the city. Billy looked like he was having the time of his life, which made Jax feel a little sick because he was pretty sure what was going to happen next. His suspicions were confirmed when Billy walked into the motel room behind Riley, bouncing on his toes, and neither Riley nor A.J. would look at Billy or meet his eyes. Mr. and Mrs. Crandall, who had the adjoining room, came to the door with grim faces.

Riley addressed Jax quietly while A.J. opened up a bucket of fried chicken from KFC. "You know what I have to do, right?"

"Yeah, I know."

"It's for his own good. Things are going to get dangerous from here on out."

"I said I know, Riley. Just . . ." Jax glanced at his

friend, who was happily stuffing his mouth with chicken. "Explain it to him."

"He won't remember afterward."

"He deserves an explanation anyway."

Riley nodded solemnly. "Hey, Billy—come here a minute."

He sat Billy down and explained it all: the importance of Evangeline and her sister for keeping the Eighth-Day Spell in place, and the fact that a group of dangerous Kin now had a way to interfere with the spell. Then he bluntly described how his own family had died—and Jax's dad too—although he didn't know what Balin had said about Jax's father deliberately driving into the river, and Jax didn't correct him. That was something Jax couldn't deal with right now.

Billy's face grew pale. "But who would come after me? I don't know anything important."

"You know us," Riley said. "That was enough to get you kidnapped in the first place. You don't want your family in danger, do you?"

"No." Billy swallowed. "But you just said the whole world's in danger from these Kin lords."

"You're a security risk," Mr. Crandall put in. "It's nothing personal, boy."

Billy looked up at Riley. "What're you going to do?"

"I'm going to order you to forget everything that happened this week. Some commands I make wear off in time, but if I order you to forget something, that memory is gone for good. And I can't make up new stuff for you to believe, like the Dulacs can. You're going to be dropped off at home with injuries and a big hole in your memory—and there's probably going to be a big stink about it and maybe the police, and I'm sorry about that."

"But"—Billy looked at Jax—"what good does that do, if—"

"I'm going to order you to forget you were ever friends with Jax," Riley went on. "You might remember him from school, but not anything personal about him. You'll forget what you know about the Donovans. And Jax is never going to contact you again." He shot a look at Jax. "Which is what I told him in the first place, and if he'd listened, maybe you wouldn't have been involved at all."

"But this is the best thing that ever happened to me!" Billy's eyes were getting glassy. "I've never done anything like this before—nothing important—nothing—"

"Heroic," Riley finished for him. "I know. And you did tonight. You were a hero. You saved the life of a man who came close to shooting you. You're the kind of person I'd like to have at my back."

"I'm not going to remember it, though." Billy leaned over and stared at the floor.

Jax looked around. Mr. Crandall was stone faced, but Mrs. Crandall shifted her weight uncomfortably. A.J. tossed an uneaten chicken leg back in the bucket like he'd lost his appetite. Jax appealed to Riley. "Is there no other way?" Hijacking Billy's memory would make them no better than Dulacs.

"He's a security risk," Mr. Crandall repeated. "It's the correct thing to do."

The correct thing to do. Those were the words Mrs. Crandall had used when talking about sending Jax back to Delaware. *How come the correct thing always sucks?* Jax turned to Riley and asked in an undertone, "Are you going to wipe my memory when you dump me back with Naomi? Is that the correct thing too?"

Riley looked startled. "What makes you think I'm gonna to do that?" Jax tilted his head toward Mrs. Crandall. Riley followed the gesture and put two and two together. "Jax, I have to do what I can to help track down the Llyrs—and Evangeline's sister. I don't know where I'll be going in the next few weeks or months. And you're going to need a safe place to stay and go to school in the fall. But *dumping* you is out of the question. You're stuck with me as your guardian till you're eighteen." His eyes bounced back and forth between Jax and Billy a few times. Then he grinned, as if he'd just had an idea. "Okay, Billy," he said, "you leave me no choice."

"I understand," Billy mumbled.

"I'm gonna have to make you my vassal."

Billy's head came up. "What?"

"If you're my vassal, you and everyone in your

household are entitled to my protection. It doesn't guarantee my enemies won't bother you, but at least it ought to make them think twice before starting a war with the Pendragon clan." Riley drew his blade. "C'mere. And kneel down."

Billy gaped at Jax, who grinned and waved Billy to go ahead. Jax realized that Riley was killing two birds with one stone—protecting Billy and setting up a safe place where Jax could live while attending school. Mr. Crandall groaned loudly, but his wife smacked his arm, and A.J. said, "Chill out, Dad."

"I'll lend you Excalibur." Riley offered it hilt first across his forearm when Billy sank to his knees on the motel carpet.

"Is it really?" Billy handled the blade like it might break into pieces. "It belonged to King Arthur? The real King Arthur?"

"Yeah, it did." Riley showed him how to balance the dagger on his palm. "Repeat after me: I, Billy Ramirez, swear on my bloodline—"

"I, Guillermo Ramirez Junior, swear on my bloodline and on the blade of King Arthur," Billy blurted out, interrupting him, "my loyalty to Riley Pendragon and his entire clan as his vassal and servant."

Riley looked a little startled. "Well, okay then." He put a hand on Billy's forehead. "I accept you. I take you into my protection, and I order and require your loyalty."

Mr. Crandall huffed in the corner. "Is a vassal bond with a Normal even valid?" he asked his wife. "The boy has no magic to bind him to that oath. It's meaningless."

Jax didn't know what other Transitioners would say, but he thought Mr. Crandall was wrong. Riley had the power of command, and that oath wasn't meaningless to Billy.

Grinning from ear to ear, Billy turned Excalibur over and over in his hands before offering it, with proper form, back to his liege lord. "This is so cool."

ACKNOWLEDGMENTS

IT TAKES A TEAM of people to create a book, and I'm lucky to have such an awesome group of people who played their part in the creation of *The Inquisitor's Mark*. I want to thank my agent, Sara Crowe, who saw potential in my eighth-day world right from the start; my amazing editors, Alexandra Cooper and Alyssa Miele; and the design department at HarperCollins, who did such a beautiful job on both books.

I can't forget my family, Bob, Gabbey, and Gina, who supported me along the way—whether that meant creating a diagram with silverware on a restaurant table so I could choreograph a wyvern battle or taking a day trip to New York City. We may be the only family ever visiting the Central Park Zoo more interested in photographing the roof of the observation pavilion than the beautiful snow leopards.

My wonderful critique partners, Krystalyn Drown and Marcy Hatch, each contributed to the development of this story, as did my beta readers, Lenny Lee, Katie Mills, Susan Kaye Quinn, Melissa Sarno, Mary Waibel, and Maria Ann Witt; my coworkers, Tina Bennett, Kelley Crist, and Matt Krykew; and three former students who gave me feedback, Laura, Javi, and Brayden.

Finally, I can't forget the amazing students in my 2013–2014 reading classes, the best cheerleaders a writer could ever have: Nik, Edson, Evelyn, Julian, Ava, Jasmine, Annie, Jack C., Kimberly, Omar, Brisa, Brandon, Belinda, Yareli, Aidan, Michael, Dylan, Jenny S., Tori, Liliana, Jenny B., Jacqui, Kate, Emma, Reece, Marley, Max, Jacob, J.J., Jimmy, Ethan, Rachel, Michelle, Erik, Chloe, Jackie, Lucy, Lauren, Sophia, Maggie, Matt, Joey, Caleb, Victoria, Ricky, Caitlyn, and Jack T.

To catch a sneak peek of the next action-packed
book in the Eighth Day series, just turn the page!

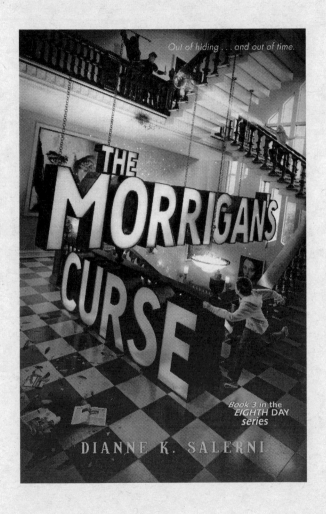

Out of hiding . . . and out of time.

THE MORRIGAN'S CURSE

Book 3 in the
EIGHTH DAY
series

DIANNE K. SALERNI

1

NORMALLY, ADDIE EMRYS DIDN'T like heights, but in this case, the view was worth it. Leaning on the wooden railing of a second-floor balcony, she watched waves crash against rocks on the shore below, blasting themselves into wild sprays of foam. Addie had never seen an ocean before today. Lakes, yes. Her Transitioner foster parents had taken her to lakes, but even Lake Champlain was a puddle compared to this.

She found herself mesmerized by the motion of the water. In Addie's experience, natural bodies of water were always caught in the moment between two Normal days. Trapped within a single second that stretched over twenty-four hours, lakes lapped listlessly like water in a bathtub, streams lay as still as ponds, and waterfalls dripped like leaky faucets.

The waves she was watching now were abnormal for the eighth day and roused by wind, which was also new to her. Addie raised her face, exulting in the cool air that brushed against her cheeks and rustled her long ponytail. This was *weather*.

Only magic could create weather on the eighth day, and for the last fifteen hundred years, the weather-working Llyrs had been confined to the bowels of Oeth-Anoeth, an ancient Welsh fortress that suppressed magical talents. Two days ago, an armed military force had broken into that fortress, releasing the only surviving descendants of the half dozen Kin families originally imprisoned there.

Two Llyrs. One Arawen.

Now free of their physical and magical constraints, the Llyrs were creating the first eighth-day weather since their ancestors had been captured centuries ago. Addie was on her way to watch them work their magic in person, but she had stopped here for a moment to enjoy this panoramic view: the vast ocean, the thin line of land in the distance that marked the coast of Maine, and the endless sky where dark clouds now swelled.

Droplets of water struck her skin, but the sudden prickle of gooseflesh on her arms had nothing to do with the cold sea spray. Someone was trying to spy on her through a scrying spell again. Whoever it was, he was persistent. Turning around, Addie stared at the white stucco exterior of the house and imagined herself surrounded on all sides by walls like that one, hidden from view.

The scryer could have been someone from her foster

home, but Addie doubted it. More likely, it was the Dulacs, a ruthless Transitioner clan who'd imprisoned Addie and from whom she'd escaped only yesterday. Unfortunately she'd left plenty of herself behind that could be used for scrying: Hair. Bitten-off fingernail scraps. Blood.

I am invisible behind my wall. Addie concentrated on her pulse, the rhythm of her blood rushing through her veins—the blood of an Emrys carrying the Eighth Day Spell through time. After a few seconds, her goosebumps subsided.

"Again?" asked a voice from behind her. She turned to find Kel Mathonwy watching her from inside the glass balcony doors. "I didn't want to break your concentration," he said. The wind rustled his silvery hair, and he smoothed his side-swept bangs back into place, copying the famous style of a Normal pop star whose music neither Kel nor Addie had ever heard.

"They've given up. For now." Addie smiled at her old friend. Well, really, her *new* friend, who she'd known briefly a long time ago, back when *his* father had worked with *her* father on a daring and rebellious plan to countermand the Eighth Day Spell. As children, she and Kel had played games in the woods behind her house, in spite of her sister trying to keep them apart.

Meeting Kel again a few days ago had been more than a coincidence. Addie thought it was a sign that she was destined to follow in her father's footsteps. Getting captured by Dulacs immediately afterward had interrupted that destiny, but only until Kel came for her with the most astounding rescue party imaginable.

"You should tell my father that someone's been scrying for you," Kel said, holding the glass door open for her. "And stay in the house, where you're warded." Kel's father had a knack for protective wards, which were tricky to master.

"There's no reason to. I have a blocking spell."

"You're going to exhaust yourself, casting a defensive spell over and over."

"No," Addie said confidently. "I won't." She flashed Kel a grin.

"Come on. You don't want to miss the show, do you?" Kel led the way downstairs and through his house. *His mansion,* Addie corrected herself, admiring the spacious rooms with white carpets, suede furniture, and floor-to-ceiling windows facing the sea. Bookshelves were filled with classics as well as recent bestsellers. Newspapers and magazines were stacked on end tables, and expensive artwork adorned the walls. During Addie's years at the way station run by her foster parents, she'd seen fugitive Kin pass through homeless and destitute. None of them had used their extended lives to amass such wealth by Normal means the way Kel's father, Madoc Mathonwy, had.

Of course, it helped that the Mathonwy magical talent was *prosperity.*

She and Kel exited through the ground floor by way of patio doors and hurried along the path to the airplane hangar. On the tarmac, a group of people were watching three figures at the end of the runway. Kel's father stood among the larger group, calmly smoking a cigarette and looking smug. It was Madoc's long-term planning and wealth that had brought this cabal of powerful Kin together. Addie supposed he had every right to be pleased with himself.

With him were members of the Aeron clan—the muscle behind Madoc's brain. The Aerons were gifted with a talent for invoking havoc and mayhem. The day prior to Addie's rescue from the Dulacs, the Aerons had manned military aircraft purchased by Kel's father to break the Llyrs out of Oeth-Anoeth in Wales. In the gloom of the gathering dark clouds, their faces seemed ghostly and devilish. The Aerons made a habit of adorning their faces with fearsome tattoos to celebrate their achievements, and all those present had earned new ones for their role in the triumphant assault on the medieval Welsh fortress.

At the end of the runway, Bran Llyr, leader of the most famous family imprisoned in Oeth-Anoeth, faced the sea and shouted ancient words into the wind. In one hand he held a staff, and his long, straight white hair flew behind his head like a flag. Beside him, his son, Griffyn, muttered his own spells, his brow compressed in concentration. Griffyn was eighteen or nineteen years old, and he, too, had long hair, although his was braided like a medieval warrior's. The final member of the trio was a girl, as tall as Griffyn and almost as broad across the shoulders. Ysabel Arawen wasn't a weather-worker—the Arawen talent was darker and more morbid—but she loaned her strength to Griffyn through their clasped hands.

They still wore the clothing they'd escaped in—coarse cloth trousers and tunics. Griffyn and Ysabel also wore leather jerkins, with throwing daggers strapped to their arms and legs that made them look like they'd stepped out of the Middle Ages. From the little Addie knew, imprisonment at Oeth-Anoeth had been sort of like being trapped in medieval times. Ten generations of the Llyr and Arawen families, along with several others, had lived their lives in that fortress, dying out over the centuries until only these three individuals remained.

Freed from their prison, the survivors had flown from Wales to Greenland to this island—and then, at Kel's urgent summons, straight to New York City to rescue Addie.

Addie was, after all, the most important Kin girl on the planet, the sole remaining member of the Emrys family and the only person left to carry the Eighth Day Spell in her bloodline. If Addie died, the eighth day would cease to exist, along with thousands of members of the Kin race, all of whom existed solely within that day.

Addie's parents had been killed years ago, and she'd recently learned that her brother and sister were dead as well. In fact, according to her Dulac captors, her older sister, Evangeline—the smart one, the good one, their father's favorite—had died only five days ago while attempting to break the Eighth Day Spell in Mexico. Addie knew she should feel grief, pain—*something*—but it had been almost half her lifetime since she'd seen her sister. Addie didn't know how to grieve for her.

Instead she watched the growing storm.

Powerful magic came naturally to the Llyrs, even if Oeth-Anoeth had suppressed it all their lives. Addie had seen Bran wield lightning several times during their harrowing escape from New York in the early hours of this morning—at least during the parts when she wasn't covering her eyes in terror. But even that paled by comparison to what he was doing now. Thunderclouds grew into a city above the sea, with black skyscrapers towering heavenward and lightning arching like bridges between them. Rain plunged down in sheets. Addie's clothing clung to her skin.

Then Kel nudged her with an elbow and pointed at a rocky protrusion about a quarter mile offshore—a knobby twist of land not large enough to be called an island. In the rain and darkness, Addie barely made out the figure standing on rocks with black objects circling overhead. Addie's mouth fell open to exclaim that one of the Aeron girls must've gotten herself stranded offshore and needed rescuing—and then it dawned on her that the circling objects were crows.

Her warning cry withered on her tongue.

Bran Llyr barked out a final command and thrust his staff into the air. The monstrous storm moved southward, away from the island. He laughed with satisfaction, then turned to look at the rocky outcropping offshore.

Addie looked again too. The girl was gone.

"Did you see her, Madoc?" Bran demanded in an accent Addie vaguely identified as "British," but which she knew must be Welsh.

Madoc exhaled cigarette smoke. "I did. Closer this time than last."

"You've seen her before?" Kel asked incredulously.

"She was on the hillside above Oeth-Anoeth two days ago," said Condor Aeron, leader of his clan.

"And Ysabel saw her outside the Dulac building yesterday, while you were freeing Addie," Madoc added. The Arawen girl nodded in agreement.

The Girl of Crows was one of the three incarnations of the Morrigan, a supernatural force of chaos and destruction. The Girl was known to nudge events in the direction of chaotic conflict, while her Woman form prophesied death and the Crone changed the fates of individuals.

Addie shivered in her wet clothes. *That makes two of them I've seen now.*

"Where did you send the storm?" Kel asked Bran Llyr.

Bran waved a hand dismissively. "To that city—that nest of Transitioners. What was it called?"

"New York," said Addie, marveling that these ex-prisoners were so ignorant of the modern world they didn't even know the name of New York City.

Just then, she felt the skin on her arms and neck prickle. The would-be spy was at it again, scrying for her mere minutes after the last time. Oh, very clever—trying to catch her off guard. Too bad he didn't know who he was dealing with!

Whirling around, Addie faced the hangar where Madoc kept his personal plane. She pictured herself surrounded on all sides by featureless wooden planks like the painted white boards on this building, creating a fortress of them in her mind. Behind her, she heard Kel tell his father how she'd been repeatedly fighting off this scryer since midnight. Addie tried not to listen, focusing instead on her secret source of strength and her intent to block the spell.

Bran's voice, however, insisted on being heard. "Look at me, child." Addie glanced up, and Bran placed a rough hand on her forehead.

Blinding-white heat shot through her head, ripping a scream from her. Everything went black and spotty, colors winking in the darkness. When sight returned, she found herself lying on the tarmac. She gasped, over and over, trying not to vomit, and looked up with shock at Bran.

"There," the Llyr lord said with pride. "Let's see if the person on the other end of that spell appreciates my little gift."

2

IN A MOTEL ROOM outside New York City, Jax Aubrey watched his liege lady arrange a pan of water, a package of saffron, and torn pages of a letter on the table in front of her. If he was counting correctly, this would be Evangeline's seventh attempt today at casting a scrying spell for her younger sister. She'd made two tries shortly after reappearing last night at midnight and had taken only a few hours' break to sleep before starting again. For Jax, a week had passed since Addie Emrys had escaped from the Dulacs with the help of the evil Llyr clan, but for Evangeline and her sister, who lived eighth day to eighth day, it had been only yesterday.

"Is she hidden behind wards?" Jax asked.

"Today she is," Evangeline replied. "But for the first few hours after midnight last night she was actively blocking me."

"Doesn't she know it's you?"

"She has no way of knowing who it is," Evangeline replied grimly. "And she's got every reason to fight off someone spying on her." Jax nodded. Addie had been held for days in a Dulac basement prison. She probably thought they were the ones trying to locate her. "But blocking my spell will tire her," Evangeline added. "If I catch her outside the wards, I *will* break through. We need to know where the Llyrs took her after they got away from Sheila Morgan's clan this morning."

Jax wasn't so sure Evangeline would break through. Casting the spell was exhausting *her*, too. Her hands trembled as she pried apart the plastic tabs on the saffron container. "I think you should rest first, like you said you would," he told her. Evangeline had promised Riley she would sleep before trying again, but as soon as he and A.J. Crandall had gone out to the motel parking lot to change the fluids in Riley's motorcycle, she'd gotten up.

"I can't sleep, Jax. I have to know if she's okay. She's in as much danger from *our* side as she is from the Llyrs."

Jax understood Evangeline's desperation. They'd come close to rescuing her sister from the Dulacs last Grunsday, missing her by mere minutes. And in the early hours of *this* Grunsday, Addie had presumably been present during a skirmish that ended with a number of Transitioners from the Morgan clan dead and the renegade Kin escaping.

Adelina Emrys had gotten out of the frying pan and landed right in a very hot fire.

On the last eighth day, a couple of hours before midnight, the Llyrs and their unknown allies had left the Dulac building in Manhattan with Addie. Since they couldn't have gotten very far before their secret, isolated day ended, Sheila Morgan—head of the clan leading the search—assumed the Kin had a place to hide for the seven days they skipped over. The Morgans had spent a week scouting the area, and on Wednesday, multiple armed teams had positioned themselves to intercept the Kin wherever they reappeared.

On Wednesday evening, a few hours before the eighth day began, Riley had sent his vassal Arnold Crandall to the Morgan headquarters to serve as a courier of information between their clans, since telephones didn't work on the eighth day. Meanwhile, Riley had chosen this motel as a base. It was far enough from the action to keep Evangeline safe, but close enough that they could get into the city quickly if Addie's location was discovered—or if Evangeline saw her through the scrying spell.

However, Evangeline's scrying efforts had failed, and by dawn they'd received bad news from Mr. Crandall. An aircraft had been spotted taking off from a field south of the city, and two planes sent by the Morgans to intercept it had been knocked from the sky by lightning. Transitioner forces had acquired a description of the enemy plane and the heading it was on, although they suspected those headings were a feint in the wrong direction, because no one had seen the plane since.

"How does scrying work?" Jax asked as Evangeline sat down again in front of the pan of water. "Is it like looking through her eyes, or . . ."

"No. I should see Addie and her immediate surroundings."

"But so far you've seen . . ."

"Nothing when she's warded. Barriers when she's using a blocking spell." Evangeline rubbed her temples, like she was fighting off a headache, and took a deep breath.

"Is there any way I can help you?" Jax asked. "I know I can't cast spells . . ."

"Actually, you can." She looked up.

"Help you? Or cast a spell?"

"Both. Anyone with magical abilities can cast a spell."

Technically that was true. Jax had seen Lord Wylit cast a spell that nearly ended the world. But spells were Evangeline's *talent*—which meant she did it with more variety and more power than other people. "Then why does Riley say he can't do spells?" Jax asked.

"He *can*," Evangeline replied. "He helped me repair the Eighth Day Spell on the pyramid, didn't he?" She glanced toward the window facing the parking lot where Riley was working on his motorcycle with A.J., then whispered to Jax. "The voice of command makes him lazy."

Jax grinned. He loved poking fun at Riley, but it was rare for Evangeline to join in.

"I *am* fatigued," she admitted. "If you're willing, I could really use your strength."

"You have to ask?" He sat down beside her. "If I've

got this talent for information, let me use it."

They'd recently discovered that Jax was more than an inquisitor. He'd inherited his father's talent for compelling people to answer questions, but through a unique set of circumstances, he'd developed an additional ability to pull information out of thin air. This had earned him the right to claim *Aubrey*, the name his father had used as an alias, as a branch-off Transitioner bloodline.

"Your talent combines the normal inquisition magic with a sensitivity for information," Evangeline said. "It blends two categories of magic, which is pretty rare. With some training, you'd probably be good at scrying, but a crash course is all you need to throw your magic in with mine." She waved her hand at the items on the table. "Symbols are needed to invoke any spell. The pan of water reflects reality. The letter is in Addie's handwriting, so it's a connection to her. Saffron traditionally symbolizes clarity of vision." Evangeline tore a strip off Addie's letter and gently placed it in the water, where it floated.

"I've never seen you use any symbols when you hurl those invisible fireballs," Jax said. She'd thrown quite a number of those fighting a wyvern in the Dulac basement last Grunsday, which was only yesterday for her.

"For that one, I call on the energy of my own body. That's why I can't hold it long or do it very often without . . ."

"Getting weak and pale and tired?" Jax didn't mention the shadowy smudges under her eyes, but she gave him an insulted glare, so he said, "Symbols, got it. Plus, you mumble gibberish."

"I prefer Welsh, because that's the way my father taught me, but English works too. The words focus your concentration and magic." She held out the container of saffron. "Put a strand on your tongue, but don't swallow it. I'm going to cast the spell and draw on your strength to support me."

She took a strand of saffron for herself and held out her hand, which Jax clasped tightly. While Evangeline whispered her Welsh words, he leaned over the pan, willing Addie Emrys to appear in the water—preferably standing in front of a recognizable landmark.

Adelina Emrys, where are you?